THE DEAD NEVER FORGET

Books by Jack Lynch

The Dead Never Forget
The Missing and the Dead
Pieces of Death
Wake Up and Die
Speak for the Dead
Truth or Die
Yesterday is Dead
Die for Me

THE DEAD NEVER FORGET

A Bragg Thriller

JACK LYNCH

Previously published as *Bragg's Hunch*.

ISBN: 1941298303
ISBN-13: 9781941298305

Published by Brash Books, LLC
12120 State Line, #253
Leawood, Kansas 66209

www.brash-books.com

ONE

The answering service woke me a little after nine o'clock one Sunday morning to tell me a man who called himself Moon wanted to talk to me about a job. He'd said it was urgent and wanted to see me as soon as possible. I'm working toward the day when I'll be rich enough to turn down jobs that begin on a Sunday, but that day hasn't come yet. So I asked the answering service to phone him back and tell him I'd be in the office at 10:30 and then I took a shower.

The office is a sort of old-timey San Francisco suite of rooms I share with a couple of attorneys on the fifth floor of an old-timey sort of building on Market Street. The outer door of the reception room is of frosted glass, and when I went to answer the rapping on it at a little before eleven o'clock you would have thought maybe a hippopotamus had come calling, from the shadow it cast. When I opened the door it turned out I wasn't far wrong. He was a tall side of beef with slack jowls hanging on a face that would make dogs get up and leave the room. He had old knife scars along one side of his neck and trailing away from the opposite eye, and his nose had been shifted around some. He dressed colorfully in loose-fitting clothes. He wore a little white felt hat, white shoes, a pair of cream-colored flannel pants billowy enough to bring the Santa Maria to the New World, a pink shirt and a light blue sports jacket that made him look as if he played saxophone in an old dance band.

"Mr. Moon?"

"No mister about it. Just Moon. You're Bragg?"

"That's right. Come on in."

I ushered him into my office off to one side of the reception area. He made it look smaller than it really is just by standing partway between door and desk to stare around at the Remington prints, the tall case filled with books of the trade and the maps of here and there posted on the walls. He sat, finally, with one elbow on the edge of the desk, and leaned in my direction. The man had a presence about himself. For whatever reason he'd come, it wasn't because the other kids on the block were picking on him.

"Care for a cup of coffee?"

"You got some whiskey to put in it?"

"I could probably find some."

"Okay, then. I don't usually drink in the mornings, but I figure you're going to make some money off the boss, so I might as well take some of your whiskey."

I went out and poured a couple of mugs from the pot behind the receptionist's desk, then returned to fetch a bottle out of a cabinet. "It's your boss who wants to hire me?"

"Maybe. I been sort of screening the field for him this last week."

"What sort of help does your boss need?"

"He doesn't say. I guess it isn't anything physical, what with me already on the payroll and all."

He honked something I took to be a laugh. "Yeah. I guess you're right enough there. But how can you screen the field when you don't know what it is that needs doing?"

He leaned back and shrugged as I handed the mug full of coffee and bourbon to him. "I know I look like a pug, but I'm pretty good about people. The boss just said he wanted someone good at his stuff. Versatile."

He held the mug of warmth in both hands and lifted it to his mouth, as if his table training had been interrupted. He took a gulp, rolled it around in his mouth and swallowed with a nod of approval.

"I never knew private dicks specialized so much," he continued. "There's a guy here in town who does nothing but trip around the world tracing boats. Yachts. Things that been stolen, or just sailed off when a guy gets behind in his payments—all his payments. This guy goes out to nice places in the Pacific, or down to Baja. Finds the boats. Sees the world. Makes a nice living."

He took another slug of stuff and wiped his mouth with the back of one hand. "Your name's come up a couple times while I been poking around. Then I guess something new came up. The boss said we didn't have any more time to screw around. He wanted to get someone on things today. He said maybe we'll take a chance and go with you, only I should come see you first to make sure you ain't got three arms or something."

"Can you tell me who your boss is?"

"His name's Armando Barker. Heard of him?"

"Nope."

"He owns the Chop House on Grant, just up from Broadway."

I nodded. "I've eaten there. It's a good restaurant."

"Yeah. He has a couple other things going too. But what about you? How long you been in the business?"

"About eight years."

"Doing what?"

"Anything I figure I can handle. I've spent a lot of time going through court records and land deeds, running background checks, tracing people—a lot of that—trying to recover stolen property, guarding people and things, finding heirs. The list goes on."

"You ever been shot at?"

"Yes, I've been shot at. And hit. And beat up and threatened and sued and a lot of other things, and when those things happen my rates go up like a bad window shade. But the answer is still yes."

"Were you ever a regular cop?"

"No."

"How'd you get into the business?"

"Sort of through the side door. I used to be a reporter. Here and in Kansas City and Seattle before that. Then a lot of turmoil took place. I was fed up with the way the job was going and my marriage fell apart. I quit the paper and spent a while getting things out of my system. Took a job tending bar over in Sausalito. It shocked a lawyer friend of mine. He finally talked me into doing things on the side for him. Digging up background stuff for use in court. Finding witnesses. Things not all that different from being a reporter, only without a lot of people sitting back in the office waiting to second-guess me. I began working more for my lawyer friend and less at the bar. One thing led to another."

"Do all your own work?"

"Pretty much. I've got a loose arrangement with World Investigators. When they get a little overburdened locally I help out. In turn I can have their people find out things for me in most places in the Western world."

"Sounds okay, Bragg. Can you come along and meet the boss?"

"I guess so. But you don't have any idea what the trouble is?"

"No. But he isn't any cream puff himself. And whatever it is has been bothering him a lot lately, so if you take the job, you'll probably earn your money."

He said parking was bad up at the Barker place and suggested we both go in his car, a long, black Chrysler that was manufactured about the time the Chinese came across the Yalu River.

Barker lived in a stately old home on the northern slope of Pacific Heights. It's not a bad address in San Francisco. Moon clanged open a tall metal gate and went up a concrete walk flanked by scrubby lawn. We entered a dim, carpeted hallway and went down it to the main living quarters. I'm not an interior decorating bug, nor am I all caught up in San Francisco nostalgia, but what we stepped into was enough to make anybody wince. Somebody had taken out a wall or two and converted the back end of the place into something resembling a Las Vegas lounge without the gambling paraphernalia. It was split-level. The upper room had furniture made of leather hides stretched across chrome tubes, a bar to one side nearly as big as the one I used to work behind in Sausalito and a lot of paintings of nude girls on the walls. The lower level had more leather-cup furniture, a pool table, a pinball machine in one corner and more nude girl paintings on the walls. It also had a wide window overlooking the Marina and Golden Gate, floors graced with polar bear skins atop thick wall-to-wall carpeting and to one side, a girl surrounded by the morning newspaper.

"That's the boss, on the phone," Moon told me.

He was referring to a thickset man in his middle forties, talking on a phone behind the bar. His complexion was olive and his hair thinning, but it still fell in tight ringlets over his forehead. The hand that held the telephone receiver had a large diamond ring on its little finger. He spoke with a voice at low, loose ends with itself, as if he smoked too much, and had to keep clearing his throat.

"And there," said Moon, in a tone approaching reverence, "is Bobbie."

He pointed at the girl on the lower level with her long legs tucked up beneath her. She cocked her head and squinted in my direction. From where I stood I couldn't tell what gave Moon the big turn on. She had a cute enough face, more narrow than round, and might even have had a nose job. It looked delicate, with a slight bob at its end. She had a wide mouth that looked ready to break into a grin, and light hair clipped short. She got up and came toward us. She wore light blue bell-bottoms hitched low on her hips. She had long legs, this one, and the way she moved reminded me of a young colt. She was a little spare in the chest, but she had on a thin T-shirt and didn't wear a bra. What she had didn't hang, and the overall effect was kind of cute. The T-shirt didn't reach all the way down to where her pants started, so there was a flash of pale skin around her naval to correspond with the light coloring of her face. Maybe it was her fresh youth that gave Moon the ding-dongs. She came up the stairs slowly, smiling at me with a slight contraction of her brow, as if she should know me.

"Who's your friend, Moon?" she asked. Her voice had a brassy ring that seemed wrong for her.

"Somebody to see the boss," Moon said, his eyes lapping over her.

"Peter Bragg," I said. "You're Mr. Barker's daughter?"

She giggled and leaned back against the stair railing. "I'm more what you'd call a paid girlfriend."

She winked at me and I realized she wasn't as young as she appeared or sounded. "I took you for somebody not quite old enough for that yet."

"I'm old enough," she said flatly. "I give a terrific back rub too. Want one?"

"No thanks. Is Mr. Barker apt to be on the phone that long?"

"Sometimes he's on long enough so we'd have time to go upstairs and start a family."

Barker hung up and cleared his throat. "You the guy Moon brought?" he asked, coming from behind the bar and crossing to shake hands. He had a grip harder than he looked.

"That's right. The name's Bragg." I gave him one of my cards. The girl edged over trying to get a look.

"Go somewhere," Barker told her. He gestured Moon away with his head.

Bobbie made a little face at everybody and went down the stairs and back over to the morning *Chronicle*. Barker worked a control unit on the bar until vapid mood music came out of speakers hidden around the room. He gestured me to a chair and settled himself onto a sofa behind a marble coffee table. He picked up a humidor, took out a cigar and held the container in my direction.

"From Cuba," he told me. "Want one?"

"Thanks, no."

He lit up, having no truck with the finer points. He just stuck one end into the flame of a lighter and sucked until his head nearly disappeared in smoke, then put down the lighter, coughed a couple of times and knocked off any ash he might have had. "You know Frisco pretty well? The forces that make the town move?"

"I think so. I've lived here about fifteen years now. Several of those I spent at the *Chronicle*."

"Handy with your dukes, are you?"

I had to smile.

"What's funny?" He coughed and cleared his throat.

"Nothing much. It's been a while since I heard that expression is all. To answer your question, I've never been a professional fighter, but I haven't done too badly on the street."

"You can use a gun?"

"Sure."

"What kind do you carry?"

"When I carry one it's usually a .45 automatic."

"Kind of bulky, isn't it?"

"Kind of. But I figure if I have to stop somebody I don't want to stand around pulling the trigger all afternoon."

"They got lighter ones now. Them Magnums..."

"A friend gave me this one. It satisfies me. But I don't go out of my way looking for jobs where I have to carry it."

"How come?"

"I'm not that hotheaded now. When I'm working on something that calls for hanging a gun under my arm I find myself looking over my shoulder a lot. It isn't worth the bother, so maybe you'd better tell me what needs doing, and I can tell you whether I'm interested. Might save us both time."

"Don't get hot about it. I just wanted to know." He picked up the lighter and spent another few seconds laying down a gray screen. I heard the girl cough down on the lower level. She got up and did something to a box on the wall, and the smoke over us began drifting away.

Barker got up and crossed to behind the bar again. "Come on over, Bragg. I wanna show you something."

Behind the bar seemed to be where his office was. He poked around beneath the countertop and laid an envelope before me. "Somebody's trying to agitate me. This came in the mail about a week ago. Take a look."

I picked it up and turned it over. It was a stiff, white envelope of the sort graduation or wedding announcements come in. It had a San Francisco postmark and was addressed to Barker in block printing with a ballpoint pen. Inside was a sympathy card, the kind you send when there's been a death. There also was one of Barker's business cards, identifying him as proprietor of the Chop House on Grant. I held it up.

"This was included?"

"Yeah." He coughed a couple of times. "I thought it was some kind of dumb joke and tossed it into a waste can back here. Then a couple nights later I was leaving the restaurant after closing. I park in a private drive alongside the place. It dead-ends against a bank on Telegraph Hill. I was unlocking the car when somebody pumped six or seven shots in my direction. A couple slugs tore through the topcoat I was wearing. The others went zinging all over the place."

"Could you tell where the shooting came from?"

"Yeah. There's another street, about fifty, seventy-five feet up the embankment. The shooting came from somebody leaning over the railing up there. There's a streetlight you can usually see up there, but it was out. Course, I was too busy ducking and dodging to get much of a look."

"Was anybody with you?"

"No. I stayed late going over some invoices with the young lady who runs the place for me. She left about a half hour ahead of me. I closed up alone."

"Can you remember how the shots came? Random? In groups?"

He frowned. "Now that you mention it, I guess in groups. Two at a time, I think. It was during the second pair I started diving behind the car. Why? What does that mean?"

"It's more apt to be somebody with training that way. What did you do next?"

"I stayed pretty still for a couple minutes. When I didn't hear anything more I ran back inside the restaurant and got a gun I keep in the office. Then I went up Grant to the corner and circled around to where the shots had come from. Like I say, the streetlight was out. I couldn't find anything."

"What did you do then?"

"Got in my car and came home."

"You didn't call the police?"

"No."

"Any special reason not to?"

"I just don't like dealing with cops."

"I see. And you've been spending a week looking for somebody else to look into it."

"I hadn't made up my mind. I just had Moon go through the preliminaries, in case I decided to."

"And now you've decided."

He coughed and nodded at the same time. "Yeah." He grubbed around behind the bar some more, then handed me an envelope similar to the first. "This came yesterday."

I opened it. It was another bereavement card, accompanied this time by a photograph of the moon clipped out of a magazine. He cleared his throat. "I take that naturally to mean a threat to Moon."

"Have you told Moon about it?"

"Not yet. I hadn't figured out just how to move."

"I think if I were him I'd want to know."

"He can look out for himself. And I got my reasons to keep it quiet till I know what's going on. I didn't even tell him about the shooting."

"The girl?" I asked, glancing toward the lower section of the room.

"Knows nothing."

"What day of the week did you get the first card?"

"Same as this time," he told me, stuffing card and clipping back into the envelope. "Saturday."

"What exactly does Moon do for you?"

"He's sort of an all-round handyman. Bodyguard, companion, errand boy. We been together a lot of years. Anyhow, what do you make of it?"

"Sounds like a bad practical joke. As you say, Moon strikes a person as being able to shift for himself. Still, I think I'd tell him, if I were you. Maybe suggest he stay inside with a good book for a couple days."

Barker dismissed that with a wave of his hand. "I guess it wouldn't hurt to let him know, but he'll do what he wants. I give everybody the day off on Mondays. The restaurant's dark. People do what they want. Even Bobbie."

"I thought she was your girlfriend."

"She is, but she gets paid to be, so she gets a day off like everyone else."

"How do you feel about Moon? Think he's in danger?"

"I don't know. Like with me, last week, I don't think whoever held the gun was really trying to make a hit. I was wide open at first, and they shot a lot of times at me."

"Then why let it bother you?"

"Because if I really got some enemies out there—I mean somebody who really wants to hurt me some—I do have a weak spot. Me and Moon are rough sorts from way back, and I'm not worried about us. But there's a little girl, my stepdaughter. Beverly Jean. I promised her mother I'd take real good care of her. I got Beverly Jean stashed in a private boarding school up in San Rafael. If somebody's out to hurt me, and they find out about Beverly Jean, they'll be in one swell position to do it."

TWO

"Where's the little girl's mother?"

He was thoughtful for a while, with elbows on the bar and hands over his ears, remembering things.

"She died of cancer." He looked down at his hands and laid the cigar aside. "It wasn't fair. She was a young woman. Not a whole lot older than Bobbie over there."

He had to take time out for his thoughts. I half turned and looked down to where Bobbie now was going *click-click-thwuck* at the pool table. She knew how to shoot.

"Soon after that happened," Barker continued, "I moved to San Francisco here with Moon and Beverly Jean. Decided to go into sort of semiretirement. I got the Chop House, of course, and I got a piece of one of them topless clubs around the corner on Broadway. And I got a couple of massage parlors I try to keep halfway legit. Staff 'em with young girls who never have to worry about working up a sweat from all the clothes they're wearing, but I tell 'em if they do any whoring it has to be on their own time and they gotta know how to work a guy's muscles so they feel good. It's the same with the restaurant. I give the customers an honest shake. Same goes for the people I do business with. That's why I can't think of any reason for anyone to pull this sort of dumb stunt."

"Maybe it's not local action. What did you do before you came to San Francisco, and where did you do it?"

He hocked a couple of times and counted the black hairs on the back of his hands. "You wanna know a lot, don't you?"

"Sure. And if you don't want to talk about it, maybe I'm getting close to where your trouble is."

He looked up, his face ready for a little plea bargaining. "I'm not really ashamed of it. It's just that what's taken for regular in one town might sound a little under the table in the next."

"Sure. I've been to lots of towns myself. Don't be bashful."

"Did you ever hear of a town called Sand Valley? Not here in California. Over by the Sanduski Mountains."

I said I hadn't, but tried to remember what I heard one time about it.

"Not surprising," Barker told me. "It's just another semilegit gambling and whorehouse town. I was into some other things, but that's all in the past now. Nobody around here knows about it. Except Moon, of course."

"Sounds like the sort of town where you could leave some hard feelings behind."

"Maybe. But not rock-bottom hard. Just sort of." He tapped the grief cards on the bar top and filed them back below. "But I don't think it's tied to this business."

"Why not?"

"Because the sort of people I knew there don't operate that way. I mean they might try setting a torch to the Chop House in the middle of the night, but not this other. They don't have the imagination, for one thing."

I shrugged. "Okay, Mr. Barker, assuming you're right. What exactly would you be hiring me to do?"

"Two things. I want you to find out who's sending the cards. Second, I want to know if it poses any threat to my stepdaughter, Beverly Jean. And for now, I want you to concentrate on the here and now. San Francisco. See if there's someone who feels I'm crowding them, without me even knowing it."

"Would it have to be a business angle?"

"What else?"

"What sort of social life do you lead?"

"I don't have any. I mean I don't have what you'd call friends. Just acquaintances, and all them from my businesses."

"What about girls?"

"There's just Bobbie over there. And like I say, that's on sort of a business basis too. I prefer it that way."

"What about before Bobbie?"

"No one. She's the first one I took up with since Beverly Jean's mother died. I used to see a couple call girls, but that was strictly business."

I shook my head.

"What's wrong?"

"If you're telling me the truth, it seems the past, and Sand Valley, is just screaming to get your attention."

"Maybe. But I want the local angle checked first. Then we'll see what happens."

I figured it was a waste of time, but if that's what he wanted to pay for, that's what he'd get. We discussed my fee and he gave me the names and addresses of his businesses. I asked him to give me a note, introducing me to the people who worked for him. I also told him I wanted to visit his stepdaughter in San Rafael. Right then, if it could be arranged.

"How come?"

"Your major aim seems to be to defuse any threat that could be coming in her direction. I want to see how well cared for she is."

He rubbed his chin and cleared his throat.

"Defuse," he said, savoring the word as if he'd found it in a box of Cracker Jack. "I like that. Yeah. That's exactly what I want. But I got an accountant coming over here at one o'clock, and Moon scares the other kids up there. I'll have Bobbie take you. She gets on well with the kid. She oughta. She's goofy enough."

"I'd rather go up by myself."

"It wouldn't work. You gotta be with somebody they know the first time or they don't let you in." He turned and bellowed for Bobbie. She rejoined us, gave me another smile and rested her elbows on the bar.

"What's up, chief?"

"I want you to drive Mr. Bragg here up to San Rafael to meet Beverly Jean. Okay?"

"Sure."

"That's a good girl." One of his hands flashed across the bar and pinched one of the pleasant cups beneath her T-shirt. Pinched it hard.

"Jesus Christ, Armando! That hurt!"

It must have. Her lip quivered. The pain almost brought tears to her eyes. I felt a little uncomfortable.

"So what?" Barker told her. "You get paid plenty for it."

She turned and left the room quickly. It was none of my business, but I'm old fashioned enough so that I had to say something.

"Do you charm all the girls that way?"

"What's it to you?"

"Some people might take offense, is all. Like you said about differences between towns. The girls in Sand Valley might think that sort of stunt is a scream. Most of the girls in San Francisco wouldn't. I could think of a couple, if you did that to them, who might get a gun and wait for you some night outside the Chop House."

The challenge went out of his face. He just coughed and waved a hand. "Forget it. She's just a dumb little twitch who goes around asking for it anyway, the way she dresses and all. And like I said, there haven't been any other girls in San Francisco."

Bobbie came back wearing a tan car coat and black beret. She'd regained her composure. She kissed Barker on the cheek, and we went out to a Porsche parked in a driveway alongside the house.

"Want to drive?" she asked.

"No thanks. I'd probably drop the gear box or something."

We got in and she backed out. We drove on down to Lombard and turned left toward the bridge.

"Does he do much of that?"

"Of what?"

"Pinch you that way."

She wrinkled her nose. "What the hell. He's got some weird sides to him, same as all of us. And like he said, I'm well paid."

"I hope so. Do you spend much time with him, Bobbie?"

"Sure. Most every day. And evenings, when he isn't working at the restaurant." She dug into one coat pocket and brought out a stick of chewing gum. With the heels of her hands on the steering wheel, she deftly unwrapped it.

"What does he do, run the bar?"

"No, he's a cook. Once or twice a week he likes to spend time in the kitchen. It's sort of like therapy for him. Helps to chase the grunts away."

"He's moody?"

"Yeah."

"How come?"

We were on Doyle Drive approaching the bridge. She glanced at me, her jaw working on the chewing gum. "You ask a lot of questions for practically being a stranger."

"Does it seem that way? I'm just curious, is all."

"Is that it? What do you do for a living?"

"A little of this and that. Maybe I'll tell you later, if you're good."

"How good? You want to pinch the other one?"

I couldn't tell if she was serious or not, but I had to grin. "It's not exactly what I had in mind."

She gave me another fast glance and whipped around a Golden Gate Transit bus headed for Marin County. "I can't always tell with men. I guess I'm still sort of dumb in that department. Do I turn you off or something?"

"No. I just haven't given it any thought. But we're way off the track. You were going to tell me what makes Armando gloomy."

"I was?" She thought a moment. "Actually, I don't know. I think he's just bored, mostly."

"With four businesses to look after?"

"Three, really. He only has a part interest in the Palm Leaf Club. He doesn't really do all that much looking after any of them. He's pretty good at hiring smart cookies to run things for him. And he has an accountant to keep a sharp eye on the figures. So mostly he sits around being bored."

"Can't you brighten his hours?"

"Sure, for Christ's sake, what do you think I'm paid for? But he's a man of middle age and more. We can't spend all the time in the sack."

"So what else do you do?"

"We go to the races a lot. Hang around other dives in North Beach, and a jazz club over on Fillmore. It's almost like he's playing a role, instead of getting really interested in something to occupy his mind."

"I had sort of the same impression," I told her. "He and Moon both come on like a couple of old Chicago overcoats. They talk and carry on as if they stay up nights watching old gangster movies on TV to see how they should act."

She nodded. "You see the problem."

When we reached San Rafael she stayed on the freeway until we were past the center of town, then turned off and drove to the eastern outskirts and the Mission Academy for Girls. It was in a charming setting of redwood trees and greenery, but it also had a high stone wall around the place with barbed wire fencing atop that and regularly spaced signs warning that the wire was electrified. There was a metal drop bar across the entrance drive and beside that a little post house with a private guard inside. He recognized Bobbie and raised the barrier.

"What the hell sort of girls do they keep in this place?"

"All kinds—big, little, in between."

Once past the walls the place lost its custodial appearance. The grounds were well tended, a blend of wooded picnic areas, lawns, beds of fuchsia and bushes of bougainvillaea. We passed tennis courts and a swimming pool and clusters of gangling girls in their early teens. There were groups of visiting adults, some with wicker hampers, and the air sang with the squeals and shouts of kids having a good time.

A big, gray pile of old stones turned out to be the Administration Building. Inside I met a round-faced woman in her fifties named Marge who looked like everybody's mom. She took us out back past a play area with swings and slides and tether balls to a clearing with a couple of badminton nets. Beverly Jean turned out to be one of the onlookers on the sideline with a racket in one hand. She was a long, skinny kid in white shorts and blouse, with elfin features and black button eyes. When she saw Bobbie she came running over to us.

"Hi, Aunt Bobbie," she cried, giving me the once-over. "Where's Uncle Armando?"

"He said he'll be up to see you tomorrow, Beejay. He's tied up with business today, but he sent Mr. Bragg here to say hello for him."

"Oh?" She studied me some more, then extended one hand for me to shake. "How do you do, Mr. Bragg. I'm Beverly Jean Barker, age eleven going on twelve and I like it here very much, thank you."

"Happy to meet you, Beverly Jean. And I'm glad to hear you like it around here, but how come you told me all that?"

She put one hand on her hip. "It's just the next thing adults always ask. I figure we can get a jump on the conversation if I just go ahead and say it first."

Marge excused herself with a smile and returned to the main building. Bobbie turned to watch the badminton game.

"Would you like me to show you around the grounds, Mr. Bragg?"

"Maybe once around the Administration Building, anyway."

I told Bobbie to wait for us and we strolled off.

"I've never been in a place like this before, Beverly Jean. What's it like?"

"It's just fine. Now, at least."

"You didn't like it at first?"

"No. I missed my mother an awful lot. They told me she'd gone away. But after I'd been here a little while, Mrs. Garver—that's my special 'auntie' here—she explained that my mother had been very sick, and that it hurt her so that God had let her go join Him in Heaven, so that she wouldn't hurt anymore."

We walked in silence for a moment.

"I guess that made it better."

"Oh, yes," she told me. "Until then I thought she'd just gone off because she didn't like me, or something. I wish Uncle Armando had explained it to me in the beginning."

"Some things are awkward for a man to do."

"Anyway," she continued, "once I knew what really happened I was able to quit worrying about that, and now they just keep us so busy, and I have so many friends, and Uncle Armando comes to visit and is always taking me places—I can hardly catch my breath anymore."

She said it as if she wished her life would slow down a little. We made the loop of the building while the girl carried on a stream of chatter about her projects and her friends and the pet skunk they had in one of the outbuildings.

"Ever have anything to do with boys around here?"

"The older girls have exchange dances with the boys from Drexal. That's a private school up near Hamilton. And we all get together for picnics and things from time to time. It's such a bore."

"You don't like boys?"

"Not the ones my age. They're all so *young*."

We were back to the badminton game by now and it was Beverly Jean's turn to play. She offered me her hand again, thanked me for the walk and joined the game, while Bobbie and I returned to the Administration Building.

"Get what you wanted?" Bobbie asked.

"Some of it." Inside I asked Marge to take me to the ranking duty officer. She led us to an office down the hall that looked more like a sewing room and introduced us to a Mrs. Carrier, a spare, dark woman in her forties with a ready smile and the title of assistant superintendent. We went around in a sort of amicable but guarded Virginia reel, with her wanting to know my relationship to Beverly Jean and my trying to pump her about the Mission Academy for Girls. I told her I represented relatives of the girl who wanted to be assured that she was content and that her stepfather, Armando Barker, was doing right by the kid. I hoped, while I was telling her all this, that she didn't see the fleeting glance of wonder that Bobbie gave me.

Mrs. Carrier smiled, as if I were one of the slow kids.

"Anybody who spends the amount of money that Mr. Barker spends, to keep a child here, is doing 'all right' by her, Mr. Bragg."

"Costs a bunch, huh? How much?"

"We just had to raise the rates this term. Inflation, you know. The fee is now somewhat in excess of nine hundred dollars."

"And how long is the term?"

"Six months. We have a year-round, two-term program. But the nine hundred dollars isn't for the term. It's for one month."

I whistled. "At those prices the kids should get pocket money."

"They do."

I nodded. "Well, she seems happy enough. I'm curious about a few other things, though. Does she get off the grounds much, except for when Mr. Barker takes her?"

"Yes. Under supervision, the girls go in small groups to any number of places, depending upon their age level. It might be to the zoo in San Francisco, or an art museum, or the Exploratorium. And we have outings to Bodega Bay and camping trips to Yosemite and ski trips to Lake Tahoe. Sometimes they just take little trips to shop around downtown San Rafael or over in San Francisco. Our efforts, after all, are to expose them to as many experiences as possible, so that when they leave here they will be well-equipped to deal with the vagaries of life."

"How about the walls and electrified fence?"

"Many of the children are from broken homes, Mr. Bragg. Wealthy broken homes. There might be custody rows. One partner might want to spirit away the child. That sort of thing would be devastating to our reputation, so we are quite careful."

It all seemed sound enough. I thanked her for her help and Bobbie and I returned to the Porsche and headed homeward. I asked her if she'd mind dropping me off on Market Street.

"Where on Market?"

"Near the Emporium."

"What's there?"

"An office building."

She didn't speak again until we were on the Golden Gate Bridge. "Cop," she said finally.

"What?"

"I bet you're a cop."

"What makes you think so?"

"The way you ask things. Probably not a real cop, but a private one. How about it, Pete? If I look in the yellow pages when I get back home, would I find your name there?"

"Yeah. You're a lot smarter than you act."

That brought a grin to her face. "Woman's intuition." She turned her head away and spit the gum out the window. "But what's Armando need a private cop for? Something to do with Beverly Jean?"

"Not that I know of. I'm just checking into some things, is all."

"Like what?"

"Like you."

She gave me a wounded look. "You're kidding."

"You're right, I am. But how did you get tied up with Armando? I am curious about that. Seems to me you're young and fresh enough to do better."

"Aw, go on. I don't have all that much going for me. I'm a high school dropout. Ex-soldier's wife. Ex-hippie. Seems like I'm an ex-everything. Don't know enough to get a really good job. This pays okay. The hours are flexible. I'm just trying to get my head together. I don't know, maybe I'll go back to school someday."

"How long have you been with Armando?"

"Since the first of the year. Actually, I got a job at the Palm Leaf Club a little before Christmas. Topless go-go dancer. He took an interest. Asked me out to dinner a couple times, then asked if I'd be his paid companion. It sounded easier than dancing around all night with a bunch of tourists staring at my boobs, so I took him up on it."

"No regrets?"

"No. He doesn't have syphilis or anything, and he gargles with Listerine…" She shrugged. "What's a poor girl to do?"

"You live there with him?"

"Some of the time. It's no big sex trip so much. He just likes to be able to reach out in the night and touch somebody. Know how that is?"

"Yeah, I know."

"Are you married, Pete?"

"Nope. How do you get along with Moon?"

"Okay."

"He looks at you as if he'd like to carry you off somewhere."

"I know, but he never gets out of line."

"Do you spend much time with Armando when he's around other people?"

"Some. But it's mostly business acquaintances. The woman who runs his massage parlors or one of the restaurant suppliers. He doesn't have any real social life, aside from me and Moon."

"How does he get along with these business acquaintances?"

"Okay. I think he's a fair man. At least now."

"What does that mean?"

"I'm not sure," she said after a moment. "There's a town some place, called Sand City, or Sand something."

"Sand Valley?"

"That's it. I heard it mentioned in conversation between Armando and Moon once. I guess they used to live there. Anyhow, they were talking about somebody who lived there. I heard Moon say, 'Well, it's no more than he has coming.' "

"You didn't hear a name that went along with whoever they were talking about?"

"No."

"When was that?"

"Months ago. Just after I went to work for Armando."

That meant it was something that had happened at least four months earlier. It didn't seem likely that it would be connected with Armando's present problems. And then something completely different occurred to me. I asked Bobbie if she had dated other guys since taking up with Armando. She misinterpreted what I meant, giving me a sidelong glance and a smile to go with it.

"I haven't so far, but there's nothing in the contract that says I can't, on my own time, at least. What did you have in mind?"

"I didn't have anything in mind. I just wondered if you saw other fellows."

"No, but it's something to think about now that you mention it."

She swung onto Market and pulled over to the curb where I told her to. When I started to get out she put one hand on my knee.

"If there's anything more I can do, be sure to let me know, huh, Pete?"

"Sure. Thanks for the ride."

"In fact," she said, reaching in back for her purse, "I'll give you the address and phone number of where I live when I'm not with Armando. In case you want to call tomorrow." She scribbled on a piece of paper and gave it to me.

"Thanks. If I think of anything more to ask I'll give a call."

"Or whatever," she replied.

I got out of the car and she gunned the motor. I watched her roar down to the corner and turn. I went into the building shaking my head. Who the hell knew what went on in the minds of young girls these days?

THREE

I spent most of the rest of the afternoon on the telephone irritating cops and newspaper people and various other sources whose Sunday afternoon I interrupted to ask questions about the Chop House and Armando Barker and Moon and a couple of massage parlors—one, the Pressure Palace on Kearny, and the other, Adam's Rib near Union Square. I even asked some of these people what they knew about a town named Sand Valley, down by the Sanduskis.

The ones who knew anything about Armando Barker and his local enterprises had nothing bad to say. Barker wasn't a prominent community figure by any means, but nobody knew of anything that might turn into a grudge. Nor could they tell me much about Sand Valley. Whatever went on there seemed to go on in a quiet manner. There was one whisper about Moon. A fellow in the local U.S. attorney's office told me his real name was Rodney Theodore Jones, and a few years back Nevada authorities and FBI people had established that his car had been parked at a remote site where some bodies had been buried outside of Las Vegas. The bodies were of minor gangland figures from New Jersey. It wasn't established that Moon had anything to do with putting them there, just that his car probably had transported them. Moon had been able to show that any number of people could have used his car, so nothing came of it, although the investigators had felt that not only had Moon been the one to bury them, but that he'd also been the one to turn them from human beings into bodies. But it all was very old business, and didn't seem likely to have a bearing on the present.

That evening I went up to the Palm Leaf Club on Broadway and had a chat with Sam Whittle. Sam had run a series of small clubs through the years, with business ranging from not bad to awful, but he managed to stay afloat by one means or another, and one of the means had been to develop a capacity to charm money out of new bankrolls in town whenever he was on the shorts. That's how Armando had picked up a piece of the club. There is a type of guy who seems to feel if he has a piece of a dive like the Palm Leaf featuring thinly clad girls it was just a country spit from being proprietor of a Las Vegas showplace. Armando obviously was this sort, and Sam had built-in radar that could detect a penchant for sleaziness from clear across town. Sam said he was content with the partnership. Armando let him run the club pretty much the way he wanted, which is the way Sam liked to do things. Armando's only demands were that he not have to pay a cover charge when he came in to watch the girls dance, and that they not water down his drinks.

I strolled up Grant to the Chop House and sat around in the bar for a while listening to the help talk. Armando wasn't in the kitchen that night, and it turned out I'd just missed Connie Wells, the woman who managed the place for him. I tried phoning her at home but nobody answered. When I left the Chop House I took a look at the driveway alongside, where Armando said he'd been shot at. The light still was out on the street above. I had to agree with Armando, though. He would have been a pretty easy target if somebody had really wanted to shoot him.

I reached the Wells woman at her home the next morning. I told her I was hired by Armando for a special job and wanted to talk to her. She had a busy day scheduled, but agreed to meet me that evening for a drink at the Pimsler Hotel. Later I went around and talked to the woman Armando had running the massage parlors. She was a loud-talking lady of about fifty named Marcella Adkins who dyed her hair blonde and used language you're apt to hear when they play reveille over the barracks loudspeaker. I had to show her the note from Armando before she'd tell me anything, and even then she phoned him to make sure she was supposed to cooperate. She said she had done different things around town until she met Armando through a friend who ran a North Beach parking lot. The friend knew she was a good businesswoman and also knew Armando had cash to invest, so suggested they get together and see if they could work out something. It was Marcella's idea to open the massage parlors and Armando of course went for it. He provided the backing, paid her a salary and gave her a percentage of the profits. After laying down the ground rules he had told me about, he left her alone to run things and she seemed satisfied.

The Pimsler Hotel was one of San Francisco's newest. Jet age and trendy. It was near the foot of Market Street. From Treasure Island it looked like an Aztec temple; from Twin Peaks, a block of glass. The lobby was its major attraction. It was the core of the building and extended to the roof, shaped like a half cone, with the rooms built around it on ever smaller tiers as they rose. The floor of the lobby was imitation Italian terrazzo, polished to a high luster. In the center of this spacious area was a tall fountain that splashed water down over great plastic slabs with interior, colored lighting. Tape recordings of chirping birds came from discreetly placed speakers throughout the cavernous room, miniskirted room clerks tended the check-in desk in back, and to one side was a great bar called the Roman Lounge. It had been open for six weeks and the word was spreading that you didn't have to be from out of town to enjoy yourself there. It was a place you could bring your wife or girlfriend. Plenty of waterbeds were available beneath ceilings of mirrors. Already it had gotten four mentions in Herb Caen's column. It had a decent dining room and good drinks in the Roman Lounge that were served up by good-looking girls in skimpy outfits. The help enjoyed itself. Management had a smile on its face.

Connie Wells had told me what she'd be wearing so that I'd recognize her: a dark blue dress suit with high-necked white blouse. It was a simple outfit, and when you saw her you realized she didn't have to climb into anything fancy to attract attention. She was a tall, large-boned girl who had a great carriage, glossy chestnut hair and good-looking legs. Her eyes were smoky and her mouth generous. It occurred to me she'd seem much more the sort of woman to attract Armando than Bobbie was. Maybe the kid had something I'd missed. In the Roman Lounge I ordered some expensive Scotch and we made small talk about the hotel until the drinks came and we'd had a toasting sip. Her movements were measured, like a journey well thought out. It gave her an air of strength that measured up well to her size. I asked what she did for Armando.

One eyebrow rose slightly. "I sort of run the place, Mr. Bragg. Eighteen months ago I answered his advertisement for a cashier-bookkeeper and that's what I started as. But I learn quickly, and soon I found a lot of areas nobody could look after, and Armando didn't want to look after, so I did. I still work some as cashier, but I also hire and fire and oversee the people who work there and deal with the janitorial service and linen supplier and liquor salesmen and business agents for the union and representatives of the firm that we lease the building from. I even order most of the food now, which is the critical part of running a restaurant, but once Armando had the menu set up he taught me how to do that too."

I had ordered Scotch over ice and Connie stared at her nearly empty glass with a faint expression of surprise. "I guess I had a busy day."

"It happens to us all." I signaled for two more drinks.

"You never told me what it is that you're doing for Armando," she said.

"I'm a private investigator. He's had a problem come up and wants me to try solving it for him. I'm just talking to all the people he knows and deals with to try understanding his life a little better."

It didn't completely satisfy her, but she accepted it for the moment and raised the fresh glass of Scotch to her mouth.

"How is Armando to work for?"

"He treats me fine. I think he respects my abilities. He pays well. I'm better off than a lot of working girls."

"You're not married?"

"No."

She sipped at her drink and looked away, putting a little period to that line of query.

"Have you ever done any modeling, Miss Wells?"

"Whatever does that have to do with any problems Armando might be having?"

"I was just curious."

She stared at me another moment before replying. "Not around here."

"Somewhere else then?"

"When I was younger. But why are you curious?"

"You're a good-looking woman and you know how to use your body. Just seems more the sort of work you'd be into, instead of running a hash house."

"I don't think of it as a hash house, Mr. Bragg." She nearly drained her second drink and put down the glass rather firmly. "Modeling is a lot of hard work. And it's a brief career, unless you just want to drift on into laxatives and Preparation-H work."

Our cute waitress wearing a scalloped skirt short enough so you could see her underwear when she leaned over drifted past with a questioning glance toward Connie's glass. I signaled for one.

"Are you a local girl, Miss Wells?"

"No. I'm from Southern California, and that's all ancient history, Mr. Bragg, which I don't pursue with anybody. Mind?"

"I guess not. Seems there are a number of things you don't want to talk about."

"Perhaps. Maybe if you told me a little more about Armando's problem I'd be more cooperative." Her drink arrived. She took it with a nod and a smile to the waitress, lifted it in toast to me and drank.

"He's been getting threats in the mail. After he got the first one, about a week ago, somebody emptied a gun at him out in the driveway beside the restaurant."

She put down her drink. "You're joking."

"No. What makes you think so?"

"He would have told me."

"But he didn't. Now he's gotten another warning. A threat to his bodyguard, Moon."

She laughed outright. "That's ridiculous."

"Why?"

"Have you seen him? Armando used to have him around the Chop House as sort of a bouncer. I finally had to tell Armando the man was chasing away customers, just by standing around."

"We can all die, Miss Wells. Even the big and the mean."

"I'm sure, Mr. Bragg. But I think Moon has many more years of standing around and making people tremble left in him." She knocked back the drink and got to her feet. "I have to go to the john."

I got up and gestured to the area over near the desk. She picked up her handbag and strode across the lobby. Two elderly women a couple of tables away watched her with the jealousy of their years. One of them, with a tiny straw hat and skin that looked like flour paste, sucked a frozen daiquiri through a straw. Her friend had what looked like a glass of cherry pop. Maybe it was a Singapore sling. Everybody had a good time at the Pimsler.

I stared around at the waitresses when they leaned and wondered about Connie Wells. I wondered what she'd done in Southern California, and despite what she had said, I wondered why she was doing what she did for Armando. She was too beautiful for all that. I could understand if she'd been hustled one time too many and wanted to forget about her body, but that wasn't the case because she looked after her appearance. And I wondered why she drank as if they'd just opened the last bottle in town.

I was wondering these things when my eyes roved back toward the elderly woman with the pale face and silly hat and I saw her make a sharp little intake of breath and rise half out of her chair, staring upward. I turned in time to see a falling body drop from sight behind the plastic slab fountain and then heard a sound similar to a person whacking a large tube of salami onto the fake Italian terrazzo.

Screams filled the lobby. I got up and went around to see if anybody had been strolling where the body landed. Luckily, nobody had, not right there anyway. A middle-aged fat guy with a half-swallowed cigar stood a few paces away with the blood draining from his face, and a younger woman who must have seen it hit had fainted nearby. I took her under the arms and moved her around a corner of the fountain so that when she came to, the pulpy mess wouldn't be the first thing she'd see again.

People were beginning to gather. At a distance. There is a limit to how close normal curiosity will draw a person toward that sort of death. A few hotel employees went closer because they figured somebody had to. I pointed out the stricken young woman to a couple of them. Two clerks were standing near the body without really looking at it, discussing whether to call the police or a city ambulance.

"Police," I told them. "Look at the back of his neck."

They did, without much enthusiasm. One of them murmured, "Jesus," and the other went to make a phone call.

I knelt and confirmed two things about the shattered, battered, but colorfully dressed corpse. Somebody had jabbed an ice pick in the vicinity of his neck at an upward angle just below the hairline of what used to be his head. The other thing was that I recognized what was left of him. It was Moon.

FOUR

There were people in several of the overhead room corridors, staring over railings down into the lobby. I went back to the Lounge. Connie Wells hadn't returned yet, but the pale-faced woman who had seen the body fall was still there. I went over to her.

"Excuse me, but I noticed that you saw the falling body. Did you see which floor it fell from?"

She still was a little flustered, but she nodded quickly and scanned the upper floors then raised a veined hand and pointed. "Do you see that couple over on the right, toward the top? He's in a dark suit and she's wearing white."

"I see them."

"It was the floor just below there, and to the right a dozen steps or so. That couple was standing at the door to the room behind them, and appeared to be having some sort of argument. That's what I was watching when it happened. There was a little flurry there where I indicated on the floor beneath them, and then I saw the body come pitching over the railing."

"What sort of flurry?"

"I'm not sure. I was watching the couple above. But I had the impression there was another person there."

"A man or a woman?"

"I didn't notice. Then I was too busy watching the poor man fall. Is he dead?"

"Yes, he is. Maybe you'd be good enough to do me one more favor." I tagged a passing waitress and ordered a pair of drinks for the ladies. They beamed. “You might have noticed the tall young lady I was sitting with just over there.”

The observant one nodded.

“When she returns would you ask her to wait for me? I have an errand to run.”

She said that she would and I hustled across the lobby to one of the glass-enclosed elevators that serviced the floors above. The operator was an alert-looking young man with a blue uniform.

“What’s the fourth floor from the top?”

“Eleven.”

“Take me to twelve, please.”

The doors whooshed shut and we started up.

“Where are the stairs here?” I asked.

“At both ends of the corridors.”

That meant somebody could have stabbed and pushed Moon over the rail then made it to the stairs in half a dozen strides, gone up or down a floor or two then rung for an elevator or just joined the curious onlookers at the rail. At the twelfth floor I confirmed it was the one where the dark-suited man and white-gowned lady were, then asked the elevator man to take me back down one floor. He dropped me off and glided back toward the lobby. This corridor was empty except for a pair of black gentlemen at the far end. I looked around where I figured Moon must have been standing. There was nothing on the burgundy carpeting to show what might have happened. No stains, no scuff marks. The railing was unmarred. I rang at all the doors along there but nobody answered. It was the hour to dine. I went down to the far end, where the two men stared over the railing. They were dressed sharply, one in a powder blue suit, the other in tan. Both wore platform shoes.

“Hi.”

They looked at me coolly. One nodded.

“A witness thinks the body downstairs fell from this floor.”

It surprised them, which meant I could get in maybe three quick questions before they realized there was no call to tell me anything. A door behind them stood open and women's voices came from within.

"Were you in there when it happened?" I asked the one who had acknowledged my presence.

"Right."

"Door closed?"

"Yeah."

"See anybody else on this floor since you came out?"

"Just the white boy who brought up our drinks. He's the one told us something had happened."

"Where is he now?"

"Went back in the elevator there."

He indicated the one at this end of the corridor. The quiet one finally spoke.

"What is it with you, man? You police?"

"Just a concerned citizen. Thanks very much, gentlemen."

I rang for the nearby elevator. Down in the lobby a pair of patrolmen had arrived and were keeping back the crowd. I went to a pay phone near the desk and dialed Armando's home, but there was no answer. One of the police officers was on a phone at the desk. The other stood near the body. He was one of the new ones. Young, lean and watchful. I crossed to him.

"Somebody should talk to the pale little woman with the dark coat and nutty hat over there in the Lounge," I told him. "She says she saw something up on the eleventh floor just before the body came down."

"Thanks, we'll do that," he told me.

While he was staring across at the woman I bent low over the body once more for a closer look at the ice pick. The cop's hand quickly found its way to my elbow.

"You'll have to stand back, sir."

"Sorry." The closer look was worth the rebuke. The weapon sticking out of the back of Moon had been a promotional product. The lettering on it advertised a variety emporium in the town of Sand Valley.

Connie Wells had returned to our table. I went back to the Lounge.

"They told me what happened," she said, indicating the two elderly women. "Why did we have to pick this place to meet?"

"We wanted to capture the robust spirit of San Francisco."

I told her I had a few more questions to ask her, and offered to take her to another bar. One that didn't have high balconies around it. She said no, that the Scotch was affecting her badly. She preferred to go home.

She'd come in a cab, so I gave her a ride to her apartment off Bay Street, about three blocks from Fisherman's Wharf. It was a newish, three-story building. She said I could come in to ask my questions if I promised to make it fast.

The place was furnished neatly, but without much imagination. She put her coat in a closet, then sank onto a divan along one wall.

"What more do you need to know?"

"I want to hear about some of the things you didn't want to talk about earlier."

"Why?"

"Because of what happened back at the hotel."

"That man who committed suicide?"

"It wasn't suicide. It was murder. And the victim was Moon."

"Oh, my God," she said quietly. The more she thought about it the worse it became for her. "Oh, my God."

"I want to know more about you, Miss Wells. Where you're from. What you did before coming to San Francisco."

She got up to get a cigarette from a little teakwood box on a sideboard. She lit it and blew smoke toward the ceiling. "God, what a joke. It's as if somebody pulled a plug, and there's nothing I can do about it."

"I don't understand."

"No, you wouldn't." She turned and leaned back against the sideboard, watching me. "I haven't told people up here about my past. Why should I? A number of people would think it quite silly. You see, Mr. Bragg, I used to play the flute. I am twenty-seven years old, and for almost twenty of those years I played flute. In Los Angeles. I played in grade school and high school and junior college. I played in school bands and in trios and in ensembles and for television commercials and once in a Hollywood studio orchestra. But I never was quite good enough to play for the Los Angeles Symphony orchestra, and would you believe, Mr. Bragg, that all I ever really wanted to do was to play flute for the Los Angeles Symphony?"

She went back to the divan and took another long drag off the cigarette. "Then two years ago my father died. My mother had died some years earlier, but I wasn't as close to her as I was to my father. And after he died I learned his custom furniture business wasn't quite the success I'd been led to believe. In fact, it was almost bankrupt, so there was not even a modest estate left for me, the only child. At about that same time I entered a wretched six-month marriage. I suppose I was particularly vulnerable, after Father died. Anyway, my husband's name was Harvey Pastor. He has a small combo that plays clubs. In Southern California, mostly, but he does a fair amount of traveling. Among clubs and bedrooms as well, I belatedly discovered. He wasn't even decent enough to restrict it to when he was out on the road. He had three girlfriends that even I knew about during that six months."

"Were you civilized when you parted?"

"We didn't throw things at each other, if that's what you mean."

"So you keep in touch?"

"There's no reason to."

Her face had colored some. The subject was painful to her still.

"And so, one day, I just decided to say good-bye to all that. I moved up here and began reading the want ads, because I didn't want to get burned with men again, and it was pretty apparent

I would somehow have to take care of myself, and there was no way I'd do it by sitting around on street corners playing my damn flute.

"About ten days later Armando ran his ad for a cashier with some bookkeeping experience. I had taken bookkeeping courses in high school, because as part of the course you would get a little packet with a ledger and journal and make-believe invoices and balance sheets. It was fun. Like playing business. I remembered enough of it to handle what Armando needed at the beginning. The rest of the job was just being civil to people and looking attractive. Then, as I told you earlier, I took over more and more chores. Now he gives me a share of the profits in the form of part interest in the restaurant. It gives me a little feeling of security. Or rather it did."

She sat back down on the divan. The hand holding the cigarette was a little unsteady. "And now that's going to end also."

"I wouldn't say that."

"Maybe you wouldn't. But I'm not going to be a part of anything in which people are being murdered."

"I'm hired to stop it. And I charge enough so that if I can't stop it soon, Armando will fire me and hire somebody else. Mind if I use your phone?"

She gestured to a low stand in the corner. I dialed Armando's number again. Still no answer. Connie Wells meanwhile had gone out to the kitchen and returned with a small snifter of brandy. She sat warming it between her hands.

"How did you know it was murder?" she asked.

"Moon? He had an ice pick sticking out the back of him."

She looked as if she might be sick, and raised the brandy to her lips. "Who would do such a thing?"

"The forest holds many creatures. Just for the record, did you go anyplace else back at the hotel besides the ladies' room?"

"No. And I didn't run into anybody I know, either. But I most certainly did not stab anyone with an ice pick." She gave a fairly convincing shudder.

"What has Armando told you about himself?"

"Not much, really. I assumed he'd been in the restaurant business before. Maybe I should ask you. What sort of man is he?"

"He seems okay now, but he hasn't lived here for too long. About his earlier life, I can't say."

"Could I be in danger?"

"I doubt it. Unless you know a lot more than you're telling me."

"I don't."

"Ever heard of a place called Sand Valley?"

"No. I don't think so."

I nodded and got to my feet. "I guess that'll do it for now then. Thanks for your help."

She rose. "I'm sorry, I didn't even offer you a drink."

"That's okay. I try not to get fried while I'm working."

At the door she put one hand on my arm. "Do you have to go right now?"

"Why, Miss Wells. What's this, a pass?"

She smiled lamely. "Perhaps. I didn't mean to give the impression I'm off men entirely. I just don't want to have to depend on them. And let's face it. I've been badly frightened. If I hear any funny sounds I'm not apt to get any sleep."

She was standing closer to me than she had all evening. Despite the worry pinching the corners of her eyes, she was one tremendous looking woman.

"I have some Scotch," she told me. "We could talk some more. About other things."

"It's a temptation," I told her.

She closed the distance between us a bit more, until our bodies were touching in a couple of places. "I may as well come right out with it," she said. "I'm quite vulnerable when I've been frightened. What more can I say?"

"I think we both should say goodnight, Miss Wells."

"Connie, please. Why should we say that?"

"Because, Connie, I once knew a young fellow who was quite a ladies' man. He was a mail carrier. He told me the secret to his very active social life—active, yet uncomplicated—was that he never messed around with any of the women on his mail route. But every six months or so he'd try to change his route. And when he did, then he would go back to the women he'd struck up friendships with on his old route."

She took a step backward. "I don't know that I'd care to be known as part of somebody's old route."

"It's just an expression. Maybe when this is over with I'll drop in to see you at the Chop House some night."

"Please do."

I gave her one of my cards and told her if something went bump in the night she could call my answering service and I'd call her back. Then I removed her hand as gently as I could and left. That sort of offer comes my way so seldom I felt downright sanctimonious.

FIVE

I drove back down to the office and dialed Armando's number again. This time he answered. He said he'd spent the evening at a movie with Beverly Jean, then on his way home he had stopped in at Marin Joe's for a steak.

"Why, what's up?"

"Somebody got to Moon. He's been murdered."

He didn't say a word until nearly a minute went by. "I don't believe that."

"It happened. He fell eleven stories into the lobby of the Pimsler Hotel. There was an ice pick in the nape of his neck. He's dead twice over."

"How did you find out about it?"

"The place is a popular spot. I had met Connie Wells there for drinks and questions."

"You saw it happen?"

"Almost. I wasn't facing the right direction to see him fall. I went up for a close look afterward."

"Christ," he said quietly. "Old Moon. I never thought anything could hurt that lug."

"Did you tell him about the threat, like I suggested?"

"Yes. And he acted the way I figured he would. Patted my back and laughed."

"When you and Moon left Sand Valley, were you running from anybody?"

"Like who?"

"Like cops."

"Hell, no. Why?"

"Because when you talk to the police they'll be asking about Sand Valley. The ice pick came from a store there. Its advertising was on the handle."

He tried to hock and swear at the same time. The result was unintelligible.

"What have you learned so far?" he asked, after getting control of himself.

"Nothing to show your troubles are from around here."

"You still think it's old business from Sand Valley?"

"Yes. You're going to have to tell me about that sometime."

"But that doesn't make sense."

"Apparently it's not supposed to." There was no use bedeviling him further at this point, but a bad practical joke could hardly explain it any longer. Somebody was after him, but they didn't want to kill him outright. Maybe they wanted to worry him to death.

"When do I have to talk to the cops?"

"It depends. Did Moon carry anything on him that would link him to you or your address? A driver's license maybe?"

"Not that I know of. He had his own apartment down on Lombard Street."

"Then just play it like a good citizen. They probably won't trace him to you tonight. But it'll be in the *Chronicle* tomorrow morning. They like 1947 crime stories. After you see the paper, phone the police. The story will mention the ice pick probably, but not the connection with Sand Valley, so let that come as a surprise to you."

"Do I have to tell them about the cards in the mail?"

"I would. You might as well take advantage of their manpower. It doesn't cost you anything. Maybe they'll turn up something I missed. Another thing, after you've looked at the morning paper and before you phone the police, call the Mission Academy and tell them to restrict the girl to their campus for a few days, and be doubly careful of strangers."

"I'll call tonight."

"It would be better tomorrow. The police might check. I'd just as soon they didn't know I was working on this right now, as well."

"Okay. How did Connie take all this?"

"She's a little shaken, but I didn't tell her it was Moon until we'd left. Do you have any idea what Moon might have been doing at the Pimsler?"

"No. I'm surprised they let him in the front door, even."

He gave me Moon's address on Lombard and I told him I'd talk more with him in the morning. Before leaving I called the answering service to tell them I was on my way home. They said Bobbie had called several times. She hadn't left any message or number. I dug out the number she'd given me the day before and tried phoning her. There was no answer.

I drove on home, considered stopping by the No Name for a drink, but decided it would be better to do my drinking at home, where I wasn't apt to run into some old friends who might keep me up half the night.

I live on the bottom floor of an old two-story house with brown shingle siding on a hill about half the distance between the downtown section of Sausalito and the big indoor model of the San Francisco-Oakland Bay built and run by the Army Corps of Engineers. A dissolute young man named Pinky Shade, who works for an import firm in the city and spends a lot of time skiing during the snow season in the Sierra, lives upstairs. He's got the view of Angel Island and Belvedere and Richardson Bay. I have a view out of my front window of a neighbor's fence and rose bush, the roof of a one-time elementary school a block down and over and, on a clear day, the industrial section of Richmond. Out of the smaller, northern window I have a view of the carport, over which the landlady, Mrs. Parker, lives, and beside that a small utility and storeroom. There are windows on both sides of the utility room so that when they're clean I can see a small patch of Richardson Bay. Once every two or three weeks a fishing boat might be seen chugging through my patch of view. But my rent is several dollars less than Pinky Shade's, and I don't spend all that much time there anyhow.

I unlocked the door, took one step in and almost dropped to the floor. Only then I saw there was no need to. It was just Bobbie, curled up and dozing on the sofa bed under the window overlooking the carport. But it was unusual to find anybody there who hadn't been there when I left. Either Pinky Shade or Mrs. Parker would need some talking to. Across from Bobbie there was a picture on the small color television set, but the sound was turned down. I closed the door and flicked the switch that turned on the floor lamp at one end of the sofa. Bobbie made a grunt, then rose slowly with a sleepy smile and a big stretch. She wore blue jeans with flower patches at naughty places and an abbreviated yellow blouse that left her pale tummy bare again.

"Hi, sleuth."

"Hello, pest. Who let you in?"

"The nice landlady. I said we were supposed to meet here but that you must have gotten held up and I didn't want to wait out on the street in the dark by myself and everything. She seemed quite happy about it. Said she didn't think you had enough women friends."

"She wouldn't know. She can't see me when I come in, I keep my drapes pulled and you could fire off a cannon down here and she'd never hear it. The next question is, why? And don't tell me it's because I'm compulsively attractive or that you're drawn to father figures or anything like that because I'll know it's a crock. You can think up your answer while I go to the can."

To the left of the door as you enter is a kitchen, roomy enough for a fellow living by himself. It's separated from the living room, where Bobbie was, by a stomach-high counter that can serve as a breakfast bar, if you don't require too much room. The bedroom is off one side of the kitchen; the bath is off the other. I went into the bedroom and hung up my jacket and tie, looked around to see if she'd been going through things, and decided she hadn't. I crossed the kitchen and went into the bathroom, remembering just in time to pull shut the door behind me. I was getting careless in my solitude. When I came back out Bobbie was sitting at the small kitchen table drinking a bottle of Dos Equis. I noticed she'd found the chilled mug in the freezer as well.

"Got a good one ready?" I asked her, getting ice from the refrigerator and a bottle of bourbon from a cabinet beside the sink.

"I hope so. It's the truth."

"Let's hear it." I poured a drink and splashed some water over it and carried it into the next room and settled at one end of the sofa. She stayed at the kitchen table, but turned and gave me a funny stare.

"Actually I do think you're kind of cute. The way you're acting makes me think you might be a little chicken around girls. You must have been hurt pretty badly once."

I felt like a startled butterfly. And her so young. I flapped and fluttered to get away. "Quit stalling."

"I would have come to see you even if you were some woman Armando had hired. If we'd done the same things and had the same conversation we did yesterday."

"Why?"

"Because you're somebody to talk to." She stood up on her long, slim legs and walked past me into the adjoining room where I have a bookcase and desk in one corner, and a table where I could do more extensive dining if the occasion arose. She looked around for the overhead light switch, found it and turned it on, then went to my bookcase to see what was there.

"What's wrong with talking to Armando?"

"He's somebody to talk with, or listen to, not to talk to. He has me categorized. Dumb-little-topless-go-go-dancer thing."

"Why don't you try to show him some of your good stuff?"

"I did once, and he got mad. I was a threat to him that way." She turned off the light and came back in to sit on the other end of the sofa.

"I got the job dancing at the Palm Leaf Club right after I got to town. I wasn't there a week before Armando took a liking to me. So I haven't really had much of a chance to get to know anybody. And yesterday was just right. I mean, we didn't talk much, but you asked me a couple of things and I had the impression you were listening to me when I answered. I thought we could do some more of that."

I got up and went out to fix another drink. "When did you decide you wanted to talk some more?"

"Before I dropped you off at your office yesterday. What did you think I was doing, talking about having Mondays off and giving you my address and phone number and all? I thought the hint was broad enough to make an ape roar."

"It was," I said, rejoining her on the sofa. "I just couldn't accept it at face value. And I still can't. How did you find out where I live?"

"I'd spent most of the day hanging around the old farm, cleaning it and me and waiting to see if the phone would ring. You know, just like a dumb little teenager with a crush. 'Maybe he'll ask me to lunch somewhere.' Then after one o'clock had come and gone I let myself think, 'Maybe he'll ask me out for cocktails this afternoon, later, or even better…' "

She fluttered her eyelashes. "Dinner, maybe! It would of course be at some quiet little Italian place you knew about *not* in North Beach, with checkered tablecloths and candelight and red wine, run by somebody you called Mama Somebody, et cetera." She cocked her head. "What have you been doing all day?"

"Working."

"Until almost midnight?"

"Yes. But back to how you found out where I live."

"You wouldn't believe the romantic fantasy I lived. By seven-thirty this evening I was really irritated with you. Felt as if I'd been jilted. Yesterday, when I got back to Armando's place, I tried to gently pump him about you. I didn't get much, but he did mention that you used to be a bartender here in Sausalito. And although I am awfully dumb in some areas, I have been around the world a time or two and I know that in towns like this, bartenders in one place are apt to know bartenders in other places around town, and boy, they sure do here. I came over and the second place I stopped at, the fellow told me you used to work at the No Name, and at the No Name, everybody knew you. You must have been one helluva bartender."

"I was. But I'm going to have to go down there one of these days and have a chat with my former colleagues. Security is breaking down all along the line."

"What's the big deal? I noticed you don't have a number in the phone book, either. Which reminds me." She took pad and pencil from her purse and crossed to the phone on the breakfast bar. When she leaned over to copy the number, displaying the patches on the seat of her jeans, you could tell she wasn't as bony there as you might have expected.

"I should think you would have written down the number and prowled the bookcase and all that before I got home."

"Don't be silly. I was raised better than that."

"Well, don't hand out that number like chewing gum. I've had dealings with people who have later gone to prison or state mental hospitals, and sometimes they come back with a grudge. I don't mind encountering it at the office, but once I get home here I like to feel I can take off my shoes and relax."

"That makes sense," she agreed. "Can I have another beer?"

"I guess."

"I don't know why you have to be so stingy about it," she said, opening the refrigerator door. "It's about all you have in here besides the half gallon of gin. Don't you ever fix yourself a decent meal?"

"There's stuff for breakfast and to make sandwiches with. It's about all I mess around with here."

She took out another Dos Equis, uncapped it at the sink and came back to sit across from me on the sofa. We stared at each other a couple of minutes.

"What did you want to talk about?" I asked finally.

"Oh, Goddamn it, Pete, stop." She wasn't smiling this time. "Can't you just pretend I'm a girl you met and liked and asked back for a nightcap and a little conversation? You don't have to ask me to stay the night. I don't even know that I would if you asked. Can't we just talk, like yesterday?"

"Yesterday I was talking business. I don't know that we'd have all that much else to discuss, frankly. There's a lot of years between us."

"Not that many. Can't you tell me about your work?"

"There isn't that much to tell. Most of it is the same dreary legwork any cop does. You spend a lot of time on the phone and a lot of time walking around asking people questions. That's about all there is to it." And sometimes you forced yourself to take a close-up look at a body that had fallen eleven stories into the Pimsler Hotel lobby, but I wouldn't tell her about that part of it.

"Do you meet a lot of women who want to get laid?"

"Not as many as I did when I was a bartender. If you're in a line of work where you deal with the public, you're going to meet all sorts of people. Women and men both. Right now I'm beginning to wonder what sort of woman you are."

"A couple of minutes ago you gave the impression you thought I was still almost a kid."

"You are, almost. Were you just exaggerating when you told me you'd been around the world a couple of times?"

"Yes. I've only been to England and the Continent. Spain, France, Amsterdam and down to India once."

"How did you like it there?"

"Too many people."

"Still, you've been around. To more places than I have."

"Where have you been?"

"Korea."

"Oh. Not nice, huh?"

"Pretty bleak. Are your parents living?"

"No. Did you grow up around here?"

"I grew up in Seattle."

She brightened. "I was there last year. It's pretty. Mountains and water everywhere you look. And that funky downtown area they fixed up."

"Yesler Square, the original Skid Road. Yeah, it's okay when the sun is shining. But it's not England or Spain or Amsterdam. Neither was Korea. I always wanted to see London." I got up to pour another drink, feeling old.

"What's stopping you?" She crossed to lean on the breakfast bar, watching me. "You must make enough so you could get it all together, if you really wanted to do it."

"I really want to do it. But something always seems to come up."

"You could even take me along as your travel guide. I'm a happy companion. Would you think me awful if I turned in the rest of this beer for one of those things you're fixing?"

"No problem. There's also some Scotch, and the gin you saw."

"What you have is fine."

I fixed the drinks and we went in and sat again. She lifted her glass.

"To finding someone to talk to."

I lifted my own. "To pretty girls who come by in the night."

"Do you really think that I'm pretty?"

"Prettier than most. You have a very innocent, fresh quality about you, yet at the same time there's a cast to your eyes that suggests—I don't know, something beyond your obvious years. And you also have a nice, round bottom for such a trim figure."

"You think so?" She grinned. "Far out. I never thought about it, even."

"I know. You can tell that from the way you walk. You could do something with that. You could make heads turn when you walked down the street if you wanted."

"I don't, particularly. For a few good friends, maybe, if they wanted that sort of thing. But not everybody."

"You're a strange kid. How long were you married to the soldier?"

"Huh?" she asked, lifting her head. "Oh, that. That was a short, very dumb episode in my life. I was seventeen. Things were going badly around home. Billy was his name. He was in town on leave and sort of swept me off my feet. Asked me to go off with him. I did. He was on his way back out to Fort Ord. We stopped off in some little town in Nevada and got married. I spent the next three months waiting tables in Monterey and fighting with my husband. I finally packed up and went back home. End of the marriage bit.

"Where was home?"

"A town you've never heard of back in the Midwest."

"Try me."

"No. I consider it bad luck to even mention it."

"How were things when you went back home?"

"Better. My grades improved and finally I went away to college, in another, bigger town. I was there during some of that last big surge of antiwar demonstrations. We had National Guard on our campus too. Nobody got snuffed, but a lot of kids I knew were hurt and tossed in jail. That's when I dropped out for good. It was too heavy for me."

She drank quickly, the same as Connie Wells had. Maybe it was something about working for Armando Barker. She held out her glass. "Could I have another?"

"I guess so. Then I'll have to toss you out. It's nearly one o'clock and I have another busy day ahead of me." I went back to the kitchen, built her a fresh drink and topped off my own. While I was doing this she had followed me out and come up behind me to gently run one finger down the middle of my back.

"Was I really awful, coming here like this?"

"I guess not. From my standpoint you could have picked a better time, maybe. From your standpoint…"

She took her hand away and when I handed her the drink she rested one hip against the counter. "From my standpoint what?"

"It still doesn't make sense. Four months in San Francisco and even with your unusual job, to think you haven't met a lot of people more your own age you could go talk to when you felt like it. Or whatever."

She stared at me without her usually good-natured smile.

"I'm going to tell you just one more thing about my past," she said quietly. "There are few people who know about this. I am going to tell you, Peter Bragg, because maybe it will help you understand some things and not be so goddamn guarded with me, and maybe you'll treat me like you might any other girl."

"Is that so important to you?"

She straightened. "Yes," she said in a voice sharp enough to make Pinky Shade roll over in his bed upstairs. "I think it is." She took her drink back to the sofa. I followed, feeling a little more uncomfortable than a man in his own home should.

"You see," she began, "I am the product of one of those situations you might read about sometimes in a confession magazine, God forbid that you should read confession magazines. At your age, at least."

"Broken home stuff?"

"No, not broken home stuff. Gang rape stuff."

I took a careful breath.

"I wasn't a whole lot older than Beverly Jean is. Barely a teenager. But I looked older. And was dumb." She rolled her eyes. "Jesus, was I dumb. There was this loose, neighborhood gang of boys. I was used to seeing them on my way home from school. They never were any problem. Then a couple of older boys, brothers, moved into the area. They were from some city back East. They sort of took over the gang. I didn't know that. They had a couple of the younger kids, kids I was used to seeing, stop me one afternoon and ask if I'd like to see their clubhouse, in back of an old, vacated store. I told you. Dumb, right?"

I walked slowly over to the breakfast bar and stood with my back to her. I'd worked on a particularly cruel case of the sort she was describing. I had spent hours trying to coax the young victim to accept me. To talk to me. To tell me about the boys who had done it.

"Pete, look at me, please. I have to be sure you understand something."

I turned back. Her eyes were stinging her, but she kept her voice under control. "There were ten of them waiting for me. They put a gag over my mouth and the bigger boys held me down and tore off my clothes. It wasn't so bad with the kids I was used to. Some of the younger ones just watched. Some of them didn't even know what to do. The ones who did—it was over pretty quickly. But then, the two brothers sent all the rest of the boys outside. Those two knew what they were doing. The awful thing was I was afraid I wouldn't get out alive. I was afraid to try fighting them off, for fear they'd do even worse things to me."

She paused to drink some of the bourbon. I went back to the sofa and held her hand.

"It's what happened after, that explains now," she said quietly, a brief smile back on her face. "I've always felt lucky for the way they treated me at the hospital. But now I'm not so sure. One of their major concerns was that it not have the lasting effect of my wanting to avoid sex when I got older. There was a new, young psychiatrist there. They helped me through the initial trauma, and then they worked on this other thing. When I got older, it all seemed to have worked out fine. Except that something got lost in the translation. Can you get what I mean, Pete?"

I shook my head.

"It's not that I'm afraid to have sex with somebody. But all too often I've gotten into situations that are sort of iffy. Should I or shouldn't I, you know? And because of the swell job they did rehabilitating me at the hospital, I'm apt to opt in favor of the guy, just to prove I don't carry old scars around with me. And I keep getting a kick in the pants for my troubles. Not physically, but they'll do bad things to me emotionally. See what I mean now?

I shouldn't have anything to do with some people, but that little mechanism that would warn most girls of that got unhooked way back there when I was thirteen."

We sat and stared at each other some more.

"Maybe that attracts me to men who seem a little more mature than the ones my own age. Maybe it's why I took the job with Armando. He might pinch my boob, but he doesn't try to squash what is really me. He doesn't even know it's there."

I had run out of things to say. She drained her glass and got up. "I guess I'd better let you get your sleep."

"Suddenly I feel like a jerk."

She laughed. "I don't want you to. I just want…" She cocked her head again. "I just want you to be able to look at me and say to yourself, 'Hey, that's Bobbie. She likes me. I can handle that.' "

She kissed me briefly on the cheek and scooped up her bag. "Thanks for the drinks."

"Sure." I went over to turn on the outside light and open the door. She went out without another glance, across the small patio to the stairs leading up to the street, but then she paused. She stared up at the sky a moment, then turned and came slowly back to where I was standing in the doorway. She stopped a couple of feet in front of me and stood there holding the bag by its strap in both hands in front of her, letting it just dangle and giving her shoulders a slightly rounded, dejected look. She stared at me without expression. I was good for about five seconds of that, then I thought about what she said Mrs. Parker had said about my social life, and I thought about what Bobbie herself had said and I thought even briefly about Connie Wells and nobility and finally I thought to hell with it. Maybe they were right and I was wrong.

"You're apt to catch a cold out there in that skimpy top," I told her. "Maybe you'd better stay over."

She came in without a word. I closed the door quietly and turned off the outside light.

SIX

I had told Barker the *San Francisco Chronicle* liked 1947 crime stories. The next morning on page three there was a deep, three-column photo of the lofty Pimsler Hotel lobby. Their artist had painted in a broken line to show the approximate course that Moon's body took on its big drop from the eleventh floor. They called it a gang-style slaying because of the ice pick somebody had planted into him. Maybe they were right. The story said Moon had checked into the hotel early that evening. Police had no clues. They were investigating.

Bobbie had left my place sometime early in the morning. I dimly remembered hearing the shower going, and when I got up I saw that she had taken her life in her hands by stealing out to Mrs. Parker's small bed of flowers on our side of the fence and snipping off a single forget-me-not. It was in a liqueur glass of water in the middle of the kitchen table along with a page from her memo pad. She'd drawn a number of little exes on it, the way kids used to denote kisses, and signed her name in a slanted scrawl.

I drove over to Moon's apartment building on Lombard. It wasn't a place that had been built the week before last. The landlady had been around for several years herself. She was a frail, birdlike person with a perpetual cigarette in her mouth, curlers in her hair and breath that let the world know she didn't wait until late afternoon to celebrate the cocktail hour. Her name was Mrs. Kerry and she'd already talked to the police the night before, and the pencil press and a TV news team that morning. She figured there would be more TV crews by, and that's why she'd put her hair up in rollers. And what was it, she asked, that I wanted? I told her I worked for Moon's employer and was making my own investigation of the murder.

"Well, I'm glad he had the decency to die somewhere else," she declared with whiskey good cheer. "This isn't exactly the St. Francis Hotel I run here, but it's no flophouse either, and my heart doesn't need any murders happening on the premises."

"How was he as a tenant, Mrs. Kerry?"

"Just grand. He was gone most of the time. Except during the football season, when he'd sit up there in his room drinking beer and watching the Monday night game on TV and laughing like the dickens whenever somebody got blindsided."

"How about visitors? Did he ever have any?"

"Not that I know of. It even occurred to me that he might be some sort of traveling man. Like I said, except for during the football season on Monday nights, we never heard him. But I never asked him about it."

"Why not?"

"I don't like to pry. So long as the tenants lead a reasonable life, don't get so drunk that they throw up in the halls on their way in or bring home girls who'll moan loudly in the middle of the night waking everybody up, I figure they got a right to some privacy, same as me."

We carried on like that for a few more minutes. She even asked if I'd care for a mug of coffee with some whiskey in it. When I declined she looked at me as if there was something unwholesome about me.

I went on over to the office, exchanged pleasantries with the receptionist and went in and called Paul Kelly, the reporter who had gotten the byline on the *Chronicle* story. He'd been on the paper back when I was. We exchanged favors from time to time. I asked what he'd found out from the cops that hadn't been in his story that morning. He didn't have much to tell me. He said the closest thing to any eyewitness had been the little woman I'd pointed out to the patrolman. Nobody was around that part of the floor where Moon's room was when it happened. In his room they'd found a canvas overnight bag with shaving gear and a huge pair of purple pajamas. No sign of another person. Moon had made a reservation by telephone that morning. The reservation had been for two. The elevator operators couldn't remember anybody getting on or off that floor at the approximate time of his death. The police were trying to find out more about him. End of report.

He was the same old lovable Paul Kelly that he'd been when I worked there, holding out even on his friends.

"What about the printing on the handle of the ice pick?" I asked.

"How did you know about that?" he asked, after the briefest pause.

"A friend in the coroner's office told me."

"Oh. Yeah, I forgot, I guess. From Sand Valley."

"Ever been through there?"

"No, but I've got calls into some people who might be familiar with the place."

I thanked him and told him he was owed a couple of drinks the next time we bumped into each other. Then I called Barker to see how things had gone with the police. From his voice, more strangled than ever, it had not gone well. Either that or something else was wrong. He asked me to come by the house right away.

It took me about fifteen minutes to get my car back out of the parking garage over on Mission and drive out to where Barker lived. Bobbie answered my ring. She wore a smart, light blue dress and looked as if she'd had a good night's sleep. Her smile was brief and her voice low. It was part of the price you paid. You sleep together and from then on you're conspirators in another man's home.

"Something's really got him shook up. I'm glad you're here."

Her voice had that same funny ring to it that had been there the morning we met. I didn't like it as well as I had the night before. "Did he have a bad time with the cops?"

"I don't think so. Something else must have happened."

I started to go past her but she held my sleeve. "Pete?"

"Yeah?"

"Did you know about Moon last night?"

"Yes."

"Why didn't you say something?"

"I didn't figure that was what you'd come to talk about."

I went on down the hallway and into the game room. Bobbie followed. Barker was sitting glumly on a stool behind the bar clearing his throat. The telephone was near his elbow, as if he'd been making calls. He stood up when I entered and motioned Bobbie back out of the room.

"How was it with the police?"

"Okay for now. But that isn't what I wanted to see you about. This came in the morning mail."

He laid another stiff white envelope into my hand. I opened it. Another sympathy card. On the back side somebody had pasted a couple of names snipped from a telephone directory. *Beverly Jean.*

From the top of Lodi grade, the town of Sand Valley made the rough outline of an automatic pistol somebody had tossed onto the scrub desert floor. The barrel ran along the base of the Sanduski Mountains. That looked to be mostly residential, with grand old homes and lawns and a few swimming pools. The butt part was business. Several new buildings flanked a broad avenue. Off to the right the Grey River splashed down out of the Sanduskis and wandered out onto the basin floor. Older sheds, homes and miscellaneous buildings followed it like a stream of ejected shell casings from the town itself.

The new highway I was traveling bypassed the town by about a mile. Also out on the desert floor was what looked like a small airfield. That irritated me some. It wouldn't be large enough to accomodate the big jets, but it looked large enough to handle feeder line planes. It didn't, though. The closest field open to commercial craft was in the town of Spring Meadows, fifty miles back on the other side of Lodi grade. I'd gotten a charter flight to there from Phoenix, then had to make it the rest of the way by renting a car larger than I was used to driving.

The town looked sort of attractive, but the desert land that spread out from it didn't. Turkey vultures tilt-soared on the alert, scanning the sun-baked plain, their mean heads the color of blood. I continued down the grade at a conservative speed. Some of the big trucks I'd passed coming up the other side of the grade whined past like freed locomotives, their eighteen tires whistling. The new highway was a boon to cross-country truckers. It was an artery over the Continental Divide that allowed some of them to trim five to ten hours off a run between the coasts.

Down near the basin floor there were some billboards. One of them advertised the Sky Lodge in downtown Sand Valley. It promised "Sophisticated Action A-plenty!" A girl's pretty face winked out at you. Another board advertised Rancho Sanchez: "The Recreated Old West—Just Three Miles Straight Ahead." A third board seemed to beckon the fellows with rolled-up sleeves driving the big rigs. It showed a cute girl wearing next to nothing carrying a tray with a shot of whiskey and a mug of beer on it. The message read, "Ma Leary's—The Damndest Truck Stop Ever."

The truck stop wasn't far off the highway, and it was my destination, but I decided to take a look at the town first, before it got dark. There had been a lot of recent construction. Probably the result of the highway. There were several new buildings half a dozen stories high, built of light stone and dark glass.

People were walking the evening streets, giving the little town a sense of quiet bustle. There were smart, ground-level shops punctuated by airy restaurants. The broad, main arterial was Nevada Street. It led straight to the Sky Lodge, a recent building that rose a dozen stories to dominate the skyline, as if keeping watch over the whole town. It looked like one of the casino hotels at Lake Tahoe, fronted with smoky glass that rose to mezzanine level. A theater marquee out front advertised the appearance of an up-and-coming singing group that called itself the Yankee Slippers, playing the hotel's Monopoly Lounge. I felt drawn to the place, but circled around the block and headed back out of town toward Ma Leary's place. Armando Barker had told me he used to own it. He didn't tell me why it billed itself as the damndest truck stop ever.

SEVEN

The truck stop complex was off a secondary road that ran from town to out beyond the freeway. Beyond were Rancho Sanchez and the abandoned airfield. The Truck Stop sprawled over a plot of land near the river. There was a garage and other service facilities and what looked like a couple of warehouses of corrugated metal off to the left. I counted between thirty and forty big truck and trailer rigs parked in long rows fronting the service area. A hundred yards farther down river was a low, hacienda-style adobe building with a neon tube in the shape of a martini glass out front. Straw-colored lawn ringed the building, and in back of that, a long stand of big shade trees marched down to the water. It looked like a rambling picnic area, with a few cabins scattered through it. Near the entrance road was one other structure, a frame building resembling an army barracks.

I parked just beyond the patch of lawn. As I was getting out of the car a couple of good old, raw-boned boys came banging through the front door and moved off toward the barracks building in the dusk. One of them had the hiccups.

It turned out that about the most pretentious thing about the place was the straw lawn out front. You stepped into a long barroom with wooden floors, cuspidors and row upon row of slot machines, most of them chunking away under the steady arms and hopeful gazes of men in work clothes. The long bar across the room was claptrap old-fashioned, with all sorts of junk hanging from the ceiling and back wall—guns, elk heads, hats, helmets and old pictures, beer signs, a parrot in a cage and enough other stuff to keep a boy staring for hours. A wide archway led into a room filled with dice tables, roulette wheels and blackjack dealers. Most of the people working there were young women. Underwear and black hose seemed to be their uniform. I went over to sit at the bar. All four bartenders were women. To set them apart from the girls on the floor, they wore spangled shorts and halters. The girl working the section where I sat was wearing lavender. She was in her twenties, tall and a little bony, but cute, with blonde hair tied in a ponytail and her nose brushed with freckles.

She approached with a puzzled smile, eyeing my tie and sports jacket. "Need directions, sir?"

"Not at the moment. You do serve civilians, don't you?"

Her brow wrinkled even more. She didn't have a mean bone in her body nor a complicated thought in her head. "Oh, go on, sir, we're all civilians here."

"Sure. How about an Early Times in a tall glass with some water."

"Right you are."

She talked simple, but she had good moves behind the bar. She poured a good drink smoothly. She put it in front of me and took the dollar bill I'd put on the bar. When she returned from the cash register with a quarter in change, I put that coin and another like it in the bar gutter in front of her. It earned me a grin.

"Thanks, Lucky."

There was a jukebox near the front door with Kris Kristofferson singing one of his traveling dope songs. Among the junk on the back wall was a small sign listing room rates. An all-night single went for ten dollars. It said the rates for doubles were negotiable. An asterisk led you to a note on the bottom that suggested you inquire about Ma's dating service.

I called over the bartender and asked where the dining room was.

"There's a little eating area over the other side of the main casino, Lucky. Or I can call in your order and have it brought in here."

"That'll be fine. How about a cheeseburger, hold the relish, with some fries."

"That's simple enough, Lucky."

She ordered it on a house phone behind the bar. When she hung up I ordered another drink and told her my name was Pete.

"Mine's Harmony," she told me, stacking more ice in the glass. "I'll try to remember your name, but don't take it badly if I can't. We get so many fellas through here I just can't remember half of them. So I call most everyone Lucky. Of course you don't dress like most, so maybe I'll be able to remember yours…" She frowned with the Early Times bottle poised over the glass.

"Pete," I told her.

"Oh, yeah, Pete. Thanks."

She went about her work. My burger came and while I was eating it a curtain opened on to a stage in the next room. Guys on piano, drums and trumpet began playing "Blues in the Night," and a big, overdressed brunette came dancing out and began taking off her clothes.

I finished my food and swung around on my stool to watch the action. The machines were kept busy. There was a frequent clatter of coins into the payoff trays. A few of the players slowed enough to take quick glances at the stripper on stage in the next room. The others kept wrenching. A couple of fistsful of quarters cascaded into the tray of a nearby player. He was a short, wiry fellow in his thirties wearing blue work clothes and cowboy boots. He had a stubble of beard, a ragged grin and old fire in his eyes. He stuffed the coins into his pockets and lurched over a stool that had been vacated beside me.

"Whooee! Goddamn, ain't it swell, though. Get me a beer, Harmony!"

"Coming up, Lucky."

The man gave me a gapped-tooth greeting. “Howdy!”

“Hiya.”

“Ain’t it an everlovin’ bitch, though?”

“Appears that way.”

“You know it is,” he said, giving me a friendly poke on the arm. “The greatest damn runnin’ town in the whole Western world. My name’s Andy.”

He stuck out his hand and I shook it. “I’m Pete.”

“You’re not a trucker, Pete.”

“No, Andy, I’m just sort of passing through. You come here often?”

“You better believe it, ever’ fuckin’ chance I get. Gimme a run within three hundred miles of here and I’ll manage to get by for a day or so.”

“That long?”

“Shore. That’s why I won’t haul perishables no more. None of these boys will,” he said, encompassing the room with a wave of his hand. “I got me a Peterbilt California hauler that I sometimes pretend’s a moon rocket when I’m on a good flat stretch, and there’s only two places I’m ever lookin’ for, one of them bein’ end of the line and the other right here. I just bust my ass gettin’ cross-country, keeping an eye out for the law of course, then fakin’ breakdowns or whatever, so’s I can lay over here. Hell, it’s better’n Elko, Nevada.”

“How’s that?”

“Cuz the dispatcher back in Chicago knows about the whorehouses in Elko, that’s why, and ever’ time we’d phone in and say we was broke down there in Elko, he’d tell us to go break down somewhere else.” His eyes turned crafty and he leaned toward me and lowered his voice. “But the dispatcher don’t *know* about Sand Valley.”

His eyes hovered over the knot in my tie. “Say, you’re not a company spy, are you, Pete?”

“Nope. If I were, I’d dress like you guys.”

He grunted. "Good. More'n likely the boys would assassinate any company spies they found around here. Sand Valley's the best-kept secret on the road."

I wondered how that could be, and called Harmony back and asked her about the dating service.

"Well, there's nothing too formal about it," she told me, looking up at the wall clock. "But it's getting kind of late."

My own watch said it was a quarter to ten. "How do you mean, late?"

"I mean the busy spell has about peaked for this night. These boys are out and rolling at five in the morning. But if you're desperate, Lucky, I'll make an announcement over the P.A. system. Maybe one of the girls'll feel up to it. You can go for a short time in one of the guest rooms beyond the casino for probably ten or fifteen dollars. You negotiate the final price with the girl. Or an overnighter in one of the cabins goes for twenty-five. Or if you're staying in the barn, the bunk runs you five dollars and anything else you negotiate with the girl."

"What's the barn?"

"That two-story building across the way."

"The one that looks like a barracks?"

"That's it. It's semiprivate. No real rooms, but there are partitions. Little bunk stalls, sort of. It's where most of the boys bunk down. Actually, if you're staying there you can sometimes get a pretty good bargain from the girl. That's because they usually can do some additional freelancing over there after you fall asleep."

"Do you play?"

"Me? Shucks no, not anymore, Lucky. I'm an old horse of twenty-six. You want a younger filly."

"Not necessarily."

Her eyebrows rose. "No? You're sure a different one, I'll say that. Anyhow, now that I'm a bartender, I don't have to. That's because I'm usually tired enough at the end of my shift I just want to go home and stand at ease. I got a little place down river about a quarter mile. I can just sit outside and watch the old Grey ripple past under the moonlight and think about life and things. It's real peaceful."

She had picked up a dish towel and was shining glasses and putting them onto the back bar.

"Of course," she said, with a dimpled smile, "I am not exactly a virgin, if you know what I mean, Lucky."

"Pete."

"I'm sorry. Pete. Anyhow, I think man and woman ought to be able to enjoy each other's company. Which isn't the same as taking money for it."

"I should say not," I agreed, with my chin on one hand.

"So anyhow, since I'm currently between boyfriends, I have been known to invite a fella down after work for a couple laughs and things. That's when I'm not too tired. But I'm pretty tired tonight." She stopped rubbing the glass raw. "Sure you wouldn't rather spend time with one of the kids out there?"

"I'm sure. The girls I go with have to have more than just a pretty face. I like them grown up enough to be able to talk to them."

She resumed rubbing the glass with something between a beam and a blush. "Well, hey there. I guess you've been around some, huh, Pete?"

"I've been around."

"Well, if you're still around here tomorrow, I'll only be working a half shift. I'm off at six. Probably won't feel so tired and all then. If you're still around."

"I'll see. My plans are a little indefinite."

From where I sat it looked as if the stripper in the next room had gotten down to her birthday suit. She was engaged in an act of copulation with the side curtain. Despite that, the crowd was thinning out. Andy, on the stool next to mine, was near the unconscious point. His chin was slumped on his chest. He started to snore. It snapped him back awake and he left his beer and struggled over to the front door and out into the night.

"Where does the boss hang out?" I asked Harmony.

"Ma? She's got a place on the roof."

"A mutual friend asked me to stop by and say hello. That's really why I stopped in."

"I'll ring her for you." Harmony got on the house phone, and in a moment handed me the receiver across the bar. The woman's voice on the other end was no-nonsense, the way some businesswomen get. I told her quietly my name and that Armando wanted me to talk to her. She seemed dubious, but agreed to see me for a minute, and Harmony gave me directions back through the casino, down a hallway and up two flights of stairs.

A door at the top opened on to the gravel roof of the building. Nearby was a penthouse structure enclosed in glass with the drapes pulled shut. I knocked and was told to enter. I stepped into a carpeted office. Doors led off to other rooms. Ma herself got up from behind a large desk and came around to offer her hand. She was a tall, handsome woman in her forties with long black hair trailing down her back. She was dressed in some kind of Spanish gaucho outfit, all in black. Riding trousers, blouse, even a flat black hat with red dingleberries hanging from its brim. On the wall behind her desk was a long, coiled whip. She noticed my noticing.

"It's the costume I wear when I go down to close up the place," she said. "I snap the whip a lot and come on tough. Goose the fellows with the crop, sting some of the girls on the fanny. Everyone has a good time, but I get the boys bedded down that way so they'll get a good night's sleep."

"That's decent of you."

"Decent to myself is what it is. You can see what sort of operation it is. If any of the boys were to leave here in the morning still half drunk and wiped out their rig, how long do you think I'd stay in business?"

"You have a point."

"Sit down, Bragg." She went back to her desk. "So you're from Frisco. How's Armando?"

"Keeping busy. How long has it been since you've seen him?"

"Couple of years. That's when he left. How's the little girl?"

"Beverly Jean, you mean. She's fine. Growing up old for her age. By the time she's sixteen she'll be charting Armando's life for him."

It brought a smile to Ma's face. "That's good. Just what the old pecker needs. How about the gorilla, Moon? He still with Armando?"

"No. He didn't care for San Francisco and moved on."

"Doesn't surprise me. He was a rowdy even for these parts."

"Is this place all yours now?" I asked, glancing around at the flamingo prints on the wall. "Or does Armando still have a piece of it?"

Small hoods went down over her eyes. "I didn't quite understand, Bragg. What is your connection with Armando? You a friend? Hired help, or what?"

"A combination of hired help and what. I'm a private investigator. Armando hired me to find out some things."

"What things?"

"This and that. I know you're probably thinking I should have found out if Armando still has a piece of the place from him. As it turned out I left town under fast circumstances. We both decided it was important for me to get down here. If you want to check me out, phone Armando in San Francisco. You can even use my credit card for the call." I took out my wallet and she came over to the chair I was sitting in.

"Never mind the credit card. Let's see your license."

I showed her the photostat. She grunted and went back around to sit at the desk. "So things aren't so swell with Armando after all."

"He has his problems, same as everyone," I told her. "So what is it with the club here? Is Armando out altogether?"

"For all intents and purposes. We have an unwritten agreement. I still owe him a few thousand for the price we agreed on. He gets money every month."

"What if he should fall over dead tomorrow, what happens to his remaining interest?"

"I pay the balance into a trust fund for Beverly Jean."

"Just on the basis of a verbal promise?"

"That's right."

"The two of you must have been pretty good friends."

"Good business associates would be more like it. Bear in mind, Bragg, Armando with all his sound business sense couldn't have set up and run an outfit like this by himself. It needs the woman's touch. At least it needed more of a one than Armando had. So what I didn't have in capital to invest I made up for with time and energy far beyond what salary I drew."

"That does sound consistent with Armando's way of doing things. How many other operations like this are there around here?"

"This is the only truck stop."

"That's not what I meant. What sort of place is the Sky Lodge in town?"

"You'd have to ask there. I got my hands full running this place."

"Who owns the Sky Lodge?"

She hesitated a moment. "A man named Carl Slide."

"Is he local, or outsider?"

"He's from the area. Son of a prospector who never found much."

"How did he and Armando get along?"

Ma made a little face. She spread both hands atop her desk and got to her feet. "Mr. Bragg, I believe I'll give you a raincheck on any more questions. I believe I will call San Francisco and talk with Armando. Only first I have to go downstairs and close up. And with one thing and another, it'll be my bedtime when I finish talking to Armando, so why don't you just come back tomorrow. Say around noon, if you need to know anything more."

"I can understand your reluctance, Ma. But I'm not here on a whimsical matter. I charge too much money for that. It's serious.

There's murder in the air and events are moving swiftly. It's why I'm here. There might not be time for you to go close up, tuck in your girls, turn off the chandeliers and count the money or whatever you do, then call Armando, then sign off for eight or nine hours before I can talk to you again."

We stared at each other for a while.

"All right, I'll call Armando now. You can wait downstairs. Depending on what he tells me, maybe we can talk again after I close up."

"Appreciate it," I told her. I got up and crossed to the door. "But just in case one of us slips on a banana peel between now and then, was there bad blood between Armando and anyone in town at the time he left?"

"There are always people who can't get along with certain other people. But I don't think he had any troubles that would linger this long after."

"Of all the people you've ever known here, Ma, which one did Armando least get along with?"

"I guess anyone could tell you that. It would have been Carl Slide's brother, Burt. But that was long ago."

"Burt still around?"

"No."

"Would Carl be apt to carry a grudge over what happened between his brother and Armando?"

"I doubt it."

"How do you and Carl Slide get along?"

"We hardly ever see each other," she said, picking up the phone. "Now you get along. I'll see if we talk later."

EIGHT

It wasn't 10:30 yet, but downstairs looked like three in the morning most other places. A couple of diehards stood tugging at the slot machines, but the casino was closing down. Three drunks were arguing over their card game at a corner table and six or seven truckers were slumped along the bar assuring themselves of a night's sleep and a morning's headache. Harmony was giving last call. I went over and ordered another Early Times. She looked happy to see a sober face.

"How's it going, Luck..." She squinted. Her brain whizzed. Her ears wiggled.

"Pete!"

"Nice going, Harmony. You keep that up and we might have some big times ahead."

"Ah, go on with you."

She wrinkled her nose like a rabbit. She might have been single-minded as a brick pile, but she was cute. And I wouldn't have half minded spending some time with her. I overtipped her again and wandered into the casino, taking a stool at an empty blackjack table in one corner. There was a side to my nature I'd still never been able to come to grips with. It concerned girls. My relationships ran in streaks. Feast or famine. It was as if it didn't really matter so long as I kept my head down and went about my business. My glands didn't pump and stew the way they had when I was back in high school. On the other hand it wasn't as if they'd packed up and left town, either. About all it took was one episode, like with Bobbie the night before, and school started up once more. I didn't particularly like things that way, but that's how they were.

The card players settled their differences and left. I heard Harmony and the other girls singing goodnight to the boys leaving the barroom. The whole feel of the place changed, from friendly party tension and hilarity to the stale quiet of a big house after the guests have left. All dirty glasses and full ashtrays. I had to wonder why Ma didn't charge prices a little more realistic. She could pay off Armando and a couple of months later retire to the French Riviera, if she were of a mind to.

Occasional workers scurried through the casino. The girls out in the bar were cleaning up and talking in tired, low voices. Occasionally they'd call out to remind somebody it was closing time. Some guys just didn't like to admit the end to another evening.

I heard the loud bang of the front door and the mood of the place changed again. There was crashing and yelling. I could see a portion of the backbar mirror and got a glimpse of several guys who didn't look to be truck drivers. They did look as if they meant business.

Harmony screamed, "It's the Mafia!"

Somebody threw a bar stool into the mirror, shattering it. Harmony was on the house phone, but from the way she was punching buttons I could tell it wasn't working. There was the metal crash of slot machines being tipped over. It sounded as if people were using sledge hammers on them. Maybe it was the town cops, but I doubted it. There were some screams and slapping sounds. Ma hired mostly female help. It was a handicap in this sort of situation, whatever the situation was. A couple of guys in cooks' checked pants and white tops came bustling out from the kitchen and ran into the bar. A few seconds later they came bustling backward through the room again with fear on their faces. A couple of mugs who looked like Moon's younger brothers followed them at a quickstep, with drawn guns and wooden staves.

"Yeah, show us the kitchen, sweetheart," one of them said. It wasn't the town cops. It looked more like labor-organizing days back in Seattle.

I had a gun in a shoulder holster, but I was exactly one guy. I tipped over my drink, staining the green felt table top with bourbon and ice, then slumped over on my arms like a lot of guys I'd had to contend with at 2 a.m. closing time in Sausalito.

The hoods were ranging all through the place now. Somebody had spent a little while figuring out how to bust up the place most efficiently. In all, there must have been a dozen men in the party. I could hear them smashing the machines and bar stock in the next room, amid periodic screams from the girls. Once I heard a drunken voice raised in protest. It was followed by the thwack of fists or knuckles. It choked off the protest. I wondered if my passed out act would work or if I should find a table to climb under. They were moving through the casino. A couple of guys trotted through and I could hear them clumping up the back stairs. The fellows in the casino were busting up the gambling tables. Some attacked with axes. Others sloshed buckets of red and yellow paint onto things. One of the wrecking crews was working in my direction. I feigned a snore. They obliterated the tables on either side of me and the big dice table in front of me.

"What about him?" a voice asked.

Somebody else laughed. "Leave him the way he is. When the poor son-of-a-bitch wakes up and looks around he'll swear off drinking."

They roared at the swell idea and went off to wreak destruction elsewhere. I could feel dampening patches under my arms, and shifted my head slightly to peek over one sleeve. The two guys who had gone upstairs came back into the casino with Ma Leary. She must have resisted. One of them was dabbing a handkerchief to his bloody lip. Ma Leary had a red patch on her left cheekbone. They'd handcuffed her hands behind her. The other fellow escorting her was a rangy gent with a mottled face and pale complexion. He seemed to be running things. He called into the barroom.

"Lou, bring those people in here."

A short, stocky fellow in a dark suit herded in a dozen of Ma's staff and six or eight drunken truckers. One of Ma's people was an older fellow in a green eyeshade I'd seen directing the casino operations earlier. The rest were girls, the waitresses and bartenders and table operators. Some of the girls had their tops torn. One had been stripped altogether. Harmony looked all right, except she was missing a shoe, and as with the others, she'd been thoroughly terrorized. They seemed especially fearful of a young, soft-faced guy in a gray suit and wearing an old fedora that he might have picked up at a rummage sale. He had a little smile on his face. Every once in a while he'd reach out and pinch one of the girls someplace where it would hurt.

The tall guy with the mottled face ordered Lou to keep an eye on the hostages while they finished their work. "And see that Kenny keeps his hands off them," he ordered, referring to the boy in the gray suit. Mottle-face and his buddy went back upstairs while the others fanned out to finish their destruction of the casino, bar and kitchen.

The one called Kenny nudged his partner Lou and pointed up at the stage with a broad smile.

"Who plays piano?" he demanded. When nobody answered he hauled off and punched his fist into the mouth of the girl nearest him. It slammed her across a chair and onto the floor. Harmony made a little yelp and dropped down beside the girl to put her arms around her.

"I asked who plays the piano?" Kenny said again.

"I can play the piano," the guy in the eyeshade said.

Kenny shoved him toward the piano and told him to play. The fellow sat and played something.

"For Chrissake take it easy," Lou cautioned his partner.

"Ah, screw, I'm just having a little fun. I figure you ought to have a little fun, or why take the job?" He ordered several of the girls up onto the stage and told them to dance. They danced.

Mottle-face and his partner came back. The scene startled the apparent leader. "What the hell is this?" he demanded. "Cut the music, Pops. Lou, Kenny, let's go." He went over to Ma Leary.

"Maybe you ought to close down this operation," he said simply. "All of it." He turned and headed back out to the front with most of the others following.

Ma Leary was standing over Harmony and the girl with the busted mouth. The front of the girl's face was smeared with blood. She gurgled something about her teeth.

Lou and Kenny hadn't left yet. Then Ma did a foolish thing. With her hands still cuffed behind her back, she crossed to Kenny and spit in his face.

Kenny didn't like that. The initial shock left him motionless for a moment. His mouth hung open and he raised one hand to wipe at the spittle.

"Forget it, Soft Kenny," Lou urged him. "It's time to get out of here."

"No," said the younger man quietly. "Not after that." He pocketed his pistol and took out a package of cigarettes. His hands trembled as he removed a filter tip and lit it. Then he shoved Ma back against the front of the stage. He hooked his hands into the front of her black blouse and ripped down with such force it brought Ma to her knees. Kenny grabbed her by the throat and lifted her again. The wrench had torn open her blouse and broken her bra, exposing Ma's chest.

I figured I knew what Soft Kenny had in mind, and I slid off the stool like the last of the quiet Shoshones, crossing the room in a half crouch and reaching into my jacket to bring out my big, heavy, outdated, damn comforting .45 automatic. Kenny grabbed one of Ma's breasts with one hand and brought up his cigarette with the other.

I was closer to Lou than I was to Kenny. I came up beside the shorter man and stuck the muzzle of my pistol into his ear.

"Tell Kenny to let go of her. And drop your gun."

Lou's gun clattered to the floor, and Soft Kenny turned to blink dumbly at me.

"Drop the cigarette," I told him. "You're too young to smoke."

He dropped the cigarette. I moved around behind him and took his gun from his coat pocket. "Now scram. Both of you. You've done enough."

Kenny was getting his nerve back. Which meant he didn't have any more brains than Ma showed when she'd spit in his face.

He said, "Listen, dumbo…" while I was shifting my pistol to my left hand. I punched him hard on the Adam's apple before he could say anything more. It made a crunching noise. He pitched backward onto the floor, holding his throat and gagging.

"Get him out of here," I told Lou. "Your friend is crazy, you must know that. Making threats to him would be a waste of time. So beware. If you or any of your friends try to come back here tonight, you are the one I'm going to kill first."

Lou studied me a long moment, the way you do a face you want to remember. But he didn't say anything. He helped Kenny to his feet and out toward the front. I followed along behind, and peered outside from a crouched position. Nobody was around so I slipped outside into the darkness. Somebody had broken the neon sign. Several cars were headed out toward the road. Only one car remained, about twenty yards away. Lou was helping Kenny into the back seat. The driver was asking questions. Lou snarled something and climbed in back with Kenny. The car followed the others. I waited to see which way the caravan went when it got to the road. It turned toward town. I rose and put away my gun, then went back into what was left of the damndest truck stop ever.

NINE

The casino boss with the green eyeshade was working on Ma Leary's handcuffs with a pair of bolt cutters. A couple of girls were getting ready to take the girl Soft Kenny had punched to the hospital. Ma ordered the others to go and get a good night's sleep. They'd have a big cleanup job to do the next day. Harmony told me she was scared aplenty and wouldn't mind somebody walking her home. I told her I had more business to talk over with Ma.

The fellow with the bolt cutters finished his job and left with the others. Ma locked up with a remark about the horses already being down the road and into the next pasture, then I followed her up to her rooftop quarters.

Some drawers had been pulled out and their contents strewn around, but other than that the damage was minimal there. They hadn't even gone through the other rooms, which I saw now were a bedroom, bath and small kitchen. Ma went into the bedroom to change, and then into the kitchen to fix us both drinks. She gave me mine then went back to her desk. I lifted my glass in salute and took a sip.

"Those boys come through town often?"

"First time anything like that's ever happened."

"Seen any of them before?"

"Not a one of them. And I want to thank you for what you did down there, Bragg. I guess I was a little rash, spitting on that little animal the way I did."

"Wish I could have done more sooner. You should have a little protection around here."

"I will have, starting tomorrow. Anyhow, Bragg, whatever I have is on the house for as long as you're in town. Food, drinks or a place to stay. And there are several frightened young girls who'd be more than happy to give you anything else you might want."

"Thanks. Aren't you going to phone the law?"

Ma snorted. "Merle Coffey would tell me to go piss in the river. No, I'll find my own dudes to handle this."

"What's behind it? Those boys didn't look like the anti-saloon league."

"No, they didn't," she said flatly.

"You don't want to talk about it?"

"You're a bright man. No, I don't. Before they arrived I called Armando. He said I should cooperate with you. But whatever troubles he might be having aren't related to mine."

"How can you be sure? If Armando still has a piece of the place, and people come in busting up things, they bust up his share as well as your own."

"It doesn't work that way. Armando and I handle this just like a cash loan. It doesn't matter whether I have the cash invested here or in a thousand acres of desert outside of town. I just owe him X number of dollars and pay it off a bit at a time. Those dollars just happen to be invested in the Truck Stop here. Any troubles that come my way are mine alone."

"Okay, Ma, we'll let it go for now. But I still want to know about the troubles between Armando and this Burt Slide. What kind of troubles were they?"

"Girl troubles. Her name was Theresa. I don't know too much about it. My relationship with Armando was strictly business. But he and Burt both chased after her. Then she left here for a spell. Got married to some soldier boy who then got himself killed in Vietnam. Theresa came back to town with the soldier boy's baby. That's the little girl Armando adopted and is looked after now in

Frisco. But before he married Theresa and adopted the kid, he and Burt carried on just like old times again. It was all kind of sad and mixed up, because it turned out that Theresa had a cancer. Eighteen months later she was dead. That kind of took the passion out of any hard feelings anyone might have had."

She leaned back in her chair. "You know, Bragg, Armando told me he thought his troubles came from San Francisco. Why are you poking into things down here?"

"Because I don't agree with him. What was the last name of the dead woman, Beverly Jean's mother?"

"Morley? Moore? Something like that."

"Did she have any family here?"

"I don't know."

The evening was turning into a waste of time. I thanked Ma for the drink and got up to go.

"Where you off too?"

"Anywhere I think I might get the answers to some more questions."

"I wish you wouldn't," Ma told me. "You're just apt to stir up more trouble than's already going down."

"That sounds as if you don't want me doing my job."

"It's not that. But your timing is all wrong. You're apt to find trouble for the wrong reason."

"Then I'll just have to handle that along with whatever trouble I find for the right reason."

I drove back into town and passed four police cars parked alongside the road. I wondered what sort of crime they were keeping such a sharp eye out for. I was so curious about that, I drove around until I found the city hall and police department. It was a block off the main drag, a two-story brick building with a tall cupola. The asphalt parking lot alongside was a busy place. A couple dozen men in brown uniforms and blue helmets with plastic face shields were milling around swinging long batons. I didn't know cops felt they needed riot gear in towns the size of Sand Valley. I drove back over to Nevada Street and down to the Sky Lodge. I left my car with an attendant and went in to register for a room. The lobby seemed small for such a large building. Off to one side were three elevators and a stairway. Off to the other were some doors with black leather padding…

The fellow at the sign-in desk was tall, balding and a little effeminate. He pursed his lips and seemed to take offense that I hadn't made a reservation for such a late arrival.

"What's wrong?" I asked. "You all booked up?"

"No, sir, it's not that. It's just that we want to provide our guests with the every convenience, and that takes planning."

"I'm not all that hard to please. A room with a bed and a shower will do it for me."

"Did you want a water bed?"

"No, I'm figuring to go to sleep, not to sea."

"Mirrors?"

"How do you mean, partner?"

"I mean some of our clients like a reflection wall, or ceiling paneled with glass."

"I see. No, I'm not after that sort of activity at this particular time."

"Then I don't suppose you require the colored room lights with bedside rheostat."

"Hardly."

"Then TV. We have color sets in all the rooms, of course. But they come with or without our own closed-circuit adult movie channel. That's an additional seven dollars."

"Then let's forget about it."

The clerk smiled tentatively and gave me a card to fill out. "My, we're just after a room as plain as bones, aren't we?"

"I'm a simple sort of guy."

A fellow and girl came through the leather-padded doors. Beyond was music, laughter and the sound of gambling.

"What's in there?" I asked. "Place where a fellow can get a drink?"

"It's the Monopoly Lounge, sir. A private club." His eyebrows summoned a uniformed young man who now stood at attention beside my bag. "Club membership is open to our guests."

"How much?"

"One dollar."

"Swear me in and have the boy take up my bag."

The clerk gave me a room key, a membership card to the club and pressed a buzzer that unlocked the leather-padded doors.

It was obvious that the customers in the Monopoly Lounge didn't have to get up as early in the morning as the blue collar sorts at Ma Leary's. The place was lively. It was a big room with rich carpets, soft lights and a lot of girls hanging around. They didn't dress as sparingly as the girls at Ma's, but they appeared to be sisters of the trade. At the deep end of the room was a stage where the Yankee Slippers were putting on their show. The bar was in a low-ceilinged alcove to one side. I made my way through the rows of slots and past the tables. There were girls dealing blackjack, but men ran the roulette wheels and dice tables. In the bar, a swarthy gent in red cummerbund was down at the far end pouring drinks for girls in evening gowns who came and went from the casino floor. A girl poured drinks for the few customers seated at the bar itself. She was a tall, formidable-looking creature who seemed to be of black and Indian mixture. Her dark hair was piled atop her head, making her look about seven feet tall. She wore red pants and a white jersey top.

"Hi, baby," she greeted me. "I'm Simbrari."

She stood undulating in a gentle way. "What can I bring you?"

"My throat would go dry trying to say it all. So I'll settle for a tall Early Times and water."

She dazzled me with a smile and poured the drink.

"Is Slide around this time of night?"

"Really couldn't say, baby. You a friend of his?"

"Friend of a friend."

When she went to the cash register I noticed her press a button alongside it. A moment later I had company. A pair of girls in evening gowns drifted into the alcove and headed for me. One was tall and angular, with short dark hair and carefully painted rosebud mouth. The other was fleshier, with long, honey-colored hair. She had a pale blue gown with a deep neckline to show off with.

"Hi," said the tall brunette. "I'm Wendy."

"And I'm June," said the chesty blonde.

"We're your companions for the evening," said Wendy, pressing a cool hand across the back of my neck.

"Because the Monopoly Lounge just insists that everybody enjoy themselves," said June, leaning over and spilling half out of her clothes. "Have you been here before?"

"No, I'm new in town. Name is Pete."

"Well, Pete," said blonde June, taking one of my hands in both of her own, "the way it works is, we all get acquainted, and then you can have either one of us…"

"Or both," said Wendy with a wink.

"To bring you luck out at the tables…" said June.

"Or have a few drinks…" said Wendy.

"Or just *anything*," breathed June.

"Here?" I asked.

"In your room, silly," said June.

"You girls are so lovely I don't know that I could afford either one of you, let alone the pair."

"You shouldn't worry about money at a time like this," Wendy said. "You'll just have the time of your life."

"And you can use a charge card," June said.

"What do they put you girls down as?"

June giggled. "Merchandise."

"Or if you're on a company expense account," said tall Wendy, "we can show up on your room bill. For a short visit we're laundry and dry cleaning."

"For longer visits," said June, "with the three of us, we can be major auto tune-ups in the garage downstairs. And boy, will you ever feel tuned up."

"It won't be the three of us," I told them. "I'm not that young anymore."

"Well then," said June, "if you take me, I'm the shy type. I like to pretend it's the very first time, like a little girl, a little bit frightened."

"I, on the other hand," said Wendy, sitting on the stool beside me and running one hand up and down my leg, "am definitely the bold type. I'm an explorer. Even with my tongue."

With that she used it to briefly explore one of my ears, so that I couldn't hear out of it for a moment, while June was speaking with Simbrari behind the bar.

"How about it, Pete?" Wendy said softly. "I know a couple of secrets to make you feel young again."

June squealed. "Oh, listen, you two. Simbrari just told me there's an opening for the three of us in the Leopard Room, if we hurry."

Wendy stood and tugged my hand. "Oh, wow. Come on, Pete, you don't want to miss this. And it doesn't cost anything, either."

"What is it?"

June took my other hand and the three of us crossed the lounge.

"Wait until you see," said June. "I dare say it's quite unlike anything you've ever seen."

"Unless," said Wendy, "you were in Havana before those terrible communists took over. It'll put you in the mood."

"I'll say," said June. "You might want the both of us yet, Pete."

We left the casino and crossed to the elevators. They were self-service. "Look, girls, I'm not sure about all this. All I really wanted was a quiet drink or two."

"We'll have drinks brought up once we're seated," Wendy told me. "It's right up here on the mezzanine."

We left the elevator and went down the hall. The three of us paused at a door and June rapped. The door opened slightly. It was very dim inside, but I heard low music.

"Lead the way, Pete," Wendy told me with a little shove.

I stepped into the room but the girls didn't follow. Somebody slammed the door shut behind me while a gloved hand tried to knock one ear through my head. In the next few seconds I felt strong guys grab my arms and pin them behind me. My .45 was ripped out from under my jacket, somebody tried to knee me in the groin and about a hundred guys seemed to be trying to punch me silly. And then I was pitching toward the floor.

TEN

I wasn't out for long. They didn't want to give me that much escape. Somebody was throwing cold water in my face. I was seated in a chair with my hands locked behind me in cuffs. It was in an office with a small bathroom off it. A guy went back to get more water. Three guys I recognized from the raiding party at Ma Leary's were standing around rubbing at where my head had hurt their hands. They'd pretty much left my face alone, except for my ear and where somebody popped my cheek and scraped the inside of my mouth over some teeth. I could taste blood and my ears were singing.

One of the bruisers was the mottle-faced guy who had seemed to be in charge back at Ma's. He knelt down and looked at me closely. "Yeah. It must be the guy Lou told us about."

"Too bad Kenny couldn't have been here," said somebody else.

"Yeah," Mottle-face repeated. "He'd like to have ripped your balls off, pal."

He slapped me along the side of my head again. When the blur went away I saw a desk across the room. Behind it was a man in his fifties with carefully combed gray hair. He wore a dark suit and cuddled a Siamese blue point. Both he and the cat were staring at me with no special expression. Then he introduced himself.

"I'm Carl Slide."

I couldn't talk yet. They'd punched me pretty good in the stomach and it still hurt me to breathe.

"I know who you are and what you do for a living," he continued, holding up my wallet. "I want to know who you're working for. What you're doing in Sand Valley. And these guys haven't anything better to do the rest of the whole night than slam you around if you don't feel like telling me."

I took a raspy breath. "Arlington Trench." It came out a little slurred.

"What?"

"The guy I'm working for." I took a couple more shallow breaths. "Arlington Trench. He's a swimming pool contractor in San Rafael. That's near San Francisco."

"What are you doing for him?"

"Trying to trace a guy who skipped town owing him some money."

"How much money?"

"Eighty thousand dollars."

"What the hell kind of swimming pool does this Trench build?"

"It was more than one. The guy who skipped was a housing developer. Trench put in several at a tract cluster in Sonoma County. That's north of San Rafael."

"What's the name of the missing developer?"

"Virgil Graham. At least that's the name he used in Sonoma. He's supposed to have relatives here."

"Have you talked to the local police?"

"No. I just got into town."

"What were you doing out at Ma Leary's?"

"I was thirsty. It was the first open place I saw on my way in."

"Why did you crunch Kenny's windpipe?"

"He'd already smashed in the face of one of Ma's girls. He was about to stick a burning cigarette on one of Ma's sensitive places." I nodded in the direction of Mottle-face. "That was all after this guy here told Lou to keep Kenny from handling the help."

Slide frowned at Mottle-face. The tall gunman raised his palms.

"I didn't know what sort of beef it was," I continued. "But Kenny seemed a little out of control. So I stopped him."

Slide stared at me for a long moment, then bought it. "Okay. Do you have any complaints about the way you were treated here?"

"Of course not."

Slide nodded to Mottle-face, who came over and unlocked the handcuffs.

"Get going," Slide told me, shoving my wallet across the desk.

I opened it and counted the money.

"Don't you trust me?" Slide asked. The cat squawked at being shifted around.

"I want my pistol, or I might have a complaint about the way I was treated here."

Slide snorted. "It wouldn't matter much whether you did or not." But he took out my .45, removed the magazine and shoved it across the desk. I tucked it back under my shoulder and left.

Up in my room I found my bag had been opened and gone through. I closed it up and took the elevator back to the lobby. There I told the clerk to give me back my dollar for membership in the Monopoly Lounge, because I hadn't found it satisfactory. He gave it back. I went out and got my car and drove over to the next block and parked it. From under the front seat I took out a spare magazine for the .45, locked the car and walked back to the Sky Lodge. There was a loading dock around back next to the parking lot. I went in and worked my way through the kitchen and service area until I found a stairway that led up to the mezzanine. I walked around until I found Slide's office and knocked softly. It opened and I went in with my gun out. Mottle-face was the only one still there with Slide. I told him to take a hike and locked the door behind him. Then I told Slide to move out from behind the desk and to sit in the chair I'd been in and put down the fucking cat and keep his hands in his lap.

He did all that, then told me grimly, "You're a dead man."

I settled on the edge of his desk. "Not yet."

The cat came over and jumped up on the desk to nuzzle me. It was a fickle cat.

"Why did you come back?"

"I have a job to do. Because of Soft Kenny and my beating, I can't do it subtly any longer. There isn't any swimming pool contractor named Arlington Trench."

"I might have known."

"How did you connect me with the Truck Stop?"

"Lou described you. Frenchy on the desk spotted you. We have a TV monitor in the bar. We all agreed you fitted the description." He made a gesture with one hand. "Maybe we should have asked some questions before jumping on you that way."

"That's not why I'm here. Why the rally with all the boys out at Ma Leary's?"

"Ask her."

"I did. She doesn't want to talk about it."

"I figure you to be working for her."

"No. I'm working for Armando Barker."

"The one's the same as the other."

"Not the way they tell it. And if I were working for Ma, Soft Kenny would have a bullet in his belly."

He thought about that for a moment. "Then there's no need for you to learn why the boys busted up her joint."

"I'm not sure. Anyhow, I like to get the feel of a new town I'm working. I'm beginning to get a pretty good idea about this one, but I'd like you to tell me some more about it."

"Ma's is a sleazy operation. It could give the town a bad name."

"Illegal gambling and whoring? I don't see that it's much different from what you have going on downstairs."

"It's more than that. We're trying to make this a nice tourist town. Get a little spillover from Vegas. We keep it clean. No mob elements."

"Who were those guys who tore apart Ma's place and beat up on me, the Welcome Wagon?"

"That's different. They're just temporary manpower working day rates. They won't be around long."

"How long?"

"However long it takes."

"What takes?"

"Closing up the truck operation."

"What have you got against truckers? They like a good time the same as anyone else."

"That's not what I'm worried about."

"What are you worried about, Mr. Slide?"

"Things that would give the town a bad name. Look, Bragg, you're sitting here in my office with a gun on me, but we both know it's just a temporary situation. You're in my town. Unless you know some way to make yourself invisible my boys would eventually find you, and at that time, so far as the rest of the world is concerned, you would indeed become invisible."

"Knowing that, if you're not cooperative, there's no reason for me not to put a bullet through your head before I leave here."

"You wouldn't be apt to do that, or you wouldn't have that photostat of a license in your pocket."

"That's only partly true."

"Can I sit back at my desk now?"

"No. What is it that worries you? You never told me."

"And I don't think I will. Get it from Ma Leary or Armando."

"I don't think Armando knows or cares, except however it might affect his own privacy. That of course is why I'm here. Somebody's been affecting his privacy in San Francisco."

"I never get up that way."

"Somebody from around here does."

"So ask around." He tilted his head in a speculative fashion. "Maybe he really is in the dark about things. Maybe instead of getting tough with me you should get tough with his partners."

"He doesn't have any. He gave Ma Leary a cash loan so she could buy the Truck Stop. But on paper the joint belongs to Ma."

He shook his head. "She owes him money. He could still shoulder his way back into town if he wanted. And I'm not so sure that isn't what he's planning."

"What makes you think that?"

"You being here."

"That's not why I'm here."

"So you said. So whether you are or not, if Armando doesn't know what's going on over at Ma's and out at the airport, he should. If he knows and doesn't care, then it shouldn't be any concern of his or yours what steps the responsible elements around town take to clean it out."

"Responsible?"

"Exactly. Now that's it, pal, scram." He got up and went around to sit at his desk. "That's a lot more than your big gun should have bought you. But if you're at all leveling with me, it might be to my interest that Armando finds out how things are."

"How did you and Armando get on when he was around town?"

"We had a cool and distant relationship. We tried not to get into each other's way."

"Did it work out that way?"

"Usually. Anyhow, that's all past history."

"I understand Armando and your brother had differences over a girl."

Slide's face turned wooden. "Yes, they did. But both Burt and the girl are dead now, and I don't like to think about it. There's the door, over there behind you."

The cat stood on the desk and stretched, arching its back. They both were tired of me.

I checked into a motel where the Grey River came out of the Sanduskis, near the town bend where the business section gave way to residential. It was the convenient sort of location where you might drop out-of-town relatives and friends you didn't want staying at your own place. The comfortably plump fellow with pipe and slippers at the registration desk didn't particularly like the beat up look to my face.

"I tripped and fell down," I told him.

He grunted. I paid for a night, got a waxed carton bucket of ice and carried my suitcase to the upper unit I'd requested. I didn't like people walking overhead in the morning. The unit was comfortable. I got comfortable, cleaned up my face and got the traveling bottle out of my bag. I made an honest drink and stretched out on the bed to think about things. Then I decided that was a waste of time. I didn't know enough to think about things yet. I looked at my watch. It was nearly one. But I'd been on Mountain Time since crossing the Nevada border. It was midnight back in San Francisco. Bobbie had asked me to call her when I settled in for the night. She said she would make whatever excuse was necessary to be at her own apartment instead of at Armando's. I gently touched my throbbing ear. I would have to use the other one for the phone, but it would be nice to hear a friendly voice. I used my credit card and she answered immediately.

"Hi. Pete Bragg here."

"Oh, wow. I'd about given up on you."

"How come?"

"It's late there. I looked you up on a map. Saw that it was an hour later there."

"What did you look me up on the map for?"

"I like to keep track of my friends. You're about the only friend that I have right now. So I want to keep extra good track of you. Okay?"

"Okay." I smiled to myself and had some of my drink. I was as vulnerable to this sort of stuff as the next slob. I just tried not to show it.

"How are things going?" she asked.

"It's an active little town. Been here the one evening and already seen one roadhouse torn apart by a gang of toughs, and been worked over some myself."

"Worked over?"

"Beat up. I got some bruises around where you were tracing your finger last night."

"Oh, Pete, that's awful."

"It could be worse. What's happening up there?"

"Not much. Armando talked to the police some more. And he spent a long time on the phone with Beverly Jean. But I didn't have to make any excuses to come home. He complained of a headache himself. I've been here since nine. Been thinking. Quite a bit."

"What about?"

"Things. You and me. I'll tell you when you get back. When do you think that will be?"

"It's hard to tell. This town's a lot more complicated than you'd think. It might take a couple days to sort it out. But you've made me curious. This thinking you said you were doing. About you and me. What's that all about?"

"Oh, boy-girl stuff. Dumb things like that. I'd rather be able to reach out and touch you when I talk about it. You don't think you could get back tomorrow, huh?"

"Afraid not. But about this boy-girl stuff. I enjoyed last night, Bobbie. I mean, really enjoyed it. But I've lived alone for a lot of years now. Kind of like it that way. A guy gets into a comfortable routine."

"I know, Pete. I could tell. But I'm not asking you to marry me or let me move in, dope."

"What are you asking?"

"I don't know. But I think I'm going to quit my job with Armando soon. I mean, I won't just run out on him when he's in the middle of some big crisis. But later."

The whiskey was beginning to make me feel better. It and the girl's voice over the phone talking about nutty things was beginning to make the hurt go away.

"Pete, you there?"

"Yes, Bobbie. I'm here. Just relaxing. Enjoying myself, listening to you talk nonsense kid stuff."

"It's not nonsense. But you are enjoying it? Honest?"

"I'm enjoying it. Honest."

"Good. I don't know what sort of life you've been living—personal life, I mean, but I think you need a little sunlight in it."

"What makes you think that?"

"Just the way you are. The way you were last night. I think you need somebody like me around once in a while."

I rolled it over in my mind, and thought about the tug I'd felt toward Harmony on the spur of the moment.

"You could be right."

ELEVEN

An eight-year-old fire engine with freckles and a high-pitched siren woke me up early the next morning making runs along the balcony outside my room. There was a small café attached to the motel. After breakfast I drove back down to city hall. I went up to the police offices on the second floor, showed my credentials and asked to see the chief. I was ushered into his corner office a few moments later.

Chief Merle Coffey looked like an out-of-shape cowboy. He was in his late forties, with sharp features that his sitting behind a desk so much had rounded off for him. Droopy eyelids presided over a brown, seamed face that had spent a lot of time in the desert outdoors. But that was behind him now. His khaki uniform shirt was open at the throat. He wore a T-shirt beneath that, and chest hair the color of steel wool climbed over its edge. The morning heat was beginning to shimmer on the foothills of the Sanduski mountains, framed in a big window behind his desk, but there was no shimmering heat inside the office. A heavy-duty air conditioner took up the lower section of a window on the other wall and pumped cold air into the room. It was a place where a fellow's uniform and underarms stayed dry.

"What can I help you with, Bragg?"

His voice was flat with a slight twang, as if he'd come out from Indiana to make his fortune.

"I'm working for a fellow named Armando Barker. He lives in San Francisco now, but came from here. Maybe you knew him."

"Oh, yes, I knew Mr. Barker."

"Were you chief of police here then?"

"I was appointed while he was still here, yes. Does your investigation involve me?"

"No. It's just that whenever my work takes me to a small town I like to become acquainted with the local law. Let them know I'm here and working."

"Uh-huh. Well, I think you'll find it a nice, peaceable little town."

"It's an unusual town, certainly."

He sat silent and immobile.

"I was on my way into town last night when I stopped by Ma Leary's Truck Stop."

"Mr. Barker used to own the Truck Stop."

"I know. There was a little ruckus there, along about eleven o'clock. A bunch of hard guys stormed through and pretty well tore apart the place. A little after that, when I drove into town here, I saw a small army of what appeared to be police officers in riot gear down below. They appeared to be waiting around for something to happen. After that I paid a visit to the Sky Lodge. Believe it or not, I saw a bunch of the same men who'd been tearing up Ma Leary's place earlier. And I got it on good authority that they were hired muscle from out of town."

He sat staring at me for long enough so that when he finally cleared his throat I almost jumped.

"Mr. Bragg, are you here to file some sort of complaint on Ma Leary's behalf?"

"Nope. I don't work for Ma Leary. I was just comparing what I'd seen last night with your own assessment that this is a peaceable little town."

"It is, so far as I'm concerned. We received no complaint of any disturbances out at the Truck Stop last night, Mr. Bragg. I check the night log every morning, first thing. In fact, last night was pretty quiet. I can let you look at the log, if you'd like."

"That's not necessary."

"As for the boys outside here last evening, they were our auxiliary police. This is turning into a tourist town, Mr. Bragg. We hope to make it even a bigger one. That means crowd control on holidays and certain other occasions. So we need a large auxiliary force, and I'm not willing to just slap a badge on a man's chest and call him a police officer. No, sir. You just happened to come by on one of their training nights. I guess last night they were drilling riot dispersal. We have a lot of those federal LEAA funds to fight crime, you know, and in a nice little town like this it's hard trying to figure what to spend it all on. Last year we bought a bunch of riot-control equipment. This year I don't know what to get. Maybe a tank with a water cannon. Oughta be fun to train with."

He got up and lumbered over to stare out the window, with thumbs hitched in his pants pockets. "I know nothing about strangers in town being at the Sky Lodge, but as I say it is a tourist town and we have a lot of strangers going through all the time. A lot of them like to stay at the Sky Lodge." He turned back to stare at me. "I have an old-fashioned view about law enforcement, Mr. Bragg. I believe in underpolicing, if anything. I don't go out of my way showing a lot of muscle. We got a town where people can have a good time, free of outside mob influence. We got a town where the citizens are secure in their homes and on the streets. No burglaries. No muggings. And as I say, we received no complaint last night from the Truck Stop. We never receive complaints from the Truck Stop. If we did we would respond. If we received too many complaints, of course, we might start looking on that operation as a public nuisance."

"I see. Chief, I'm going to come right out and ask, how come state law enforcement people haven't come down on this little town for all the whores and gambling hereabouts?"

"We have cordial relations with people in the state capitol. These things you mention are often more some people's moral feelings than anything else. There are places all over this country where people gamble and exchange money for companionship. You must know that, Mr. Bragg. The people of this town have obviously determined that it adds to the flavor they want this town to have. I just try to see that the girls are honest, and that the gamblers are honest and that the cops stay honest too."

"Honest in what way?"

"Not on the take from any elements, local or outside either one. We had a fellow we suspected of just that a few years back, so we tied the can to him."

"Okay, Chief, you run a tight ship. Maybe you can tell me how Armando Barker left town."

"By automobile, I suppose," he said with a little smile.

"I meant did he leave any hard feelings behind? With Carl Slide, for instance, or you, or anyone else in town?"

"Not that I know of."

"Are there any other places like the Truck Stop or the Sky Lodge that you underpolice around here?"

"Nope."

"How do Slide and Ma Leary get along?"

"I haven't heard any complaints from one about the other."

"So the official police position is that everything in town is just swell."

"Sure. Just the way we like it around here."

He was reminding me I wasn't from around there. I thanked him and drove over to a municipal parking lot on Nevada Street. The sidewalks were bustling. In the daylight I could see there were a lot of attractions. They had a historical museum full of old mining gear and displays of local lore and legend. A stable off Nevada Street offered rides in buckboards and a restored stagecoach. The bus station had tours out to the Rancho Sanchez. And the Rancho, according to the advertising boards, offered gun collections, rodeo exhibitions, old-time dance halls and a recreated range war featuring opposing gangs of cowboys, a band of real Apaches and units of the U.S. Cavalry. Sounded like fun for the whole family.

I went into the Sand Valley Home Bank, a trim, brick building next door to the branch of a brokerage firm. I told a gimlet-eyed woman that I was from out of town, was thinking of starting up a business in Sand Valley and wanted to speak to one of the firm's officers about the lay of the land. A few minutes later I was ushered into a glass-enclosed office and introduced to a vice president named Howard Morton. Morton was of medium height with a slight build. He'd lost most of his hair, had a nice suntan, wore rimless glasses and wouldn't have offended anybody with his handshake. I told him I was a printer of posters and other specialty items distributed nationwide by direct mail. I said it was the sort of business a man could run from anywhere, and my doctor had told me I'd probably add several years to my life by moving to a dry desert climate. Morton sat there nodding his head as if it was the sort of thing that brought a lot of people to Sand Valley. We chatted for twenty minutes, and at the end of that time I wished maybe I was what I'd told him I was. The way Morton described it, you couldn't find a better combination of reasonable commercial properties and favorable tax situation.

Then I asked him about the whores and gambling.

"I don't think they'll interfere with your poster business, Mr. Bragg."

"Maybe not. But sometimes those activities attract elements that could make my doctor change his mind."

He chuckled at my little joke. "You needn't worry, Mr. Bragg. One thing we in Sand Valley pride ourselves on is that we keep the bad elements out. These are just homegrown activities."

"Do all the homegrown folks get along with one another?"

"I don't understand."

"I hear a fellow named Slide owns the Sky Lodge and a woman calling herself Ma Leary owns the Truck Stop. Is one of them apt to get jealous of the other's activity?"

"It wouldn't seem likely. They really attract two different kinds of crowd. And then there is the Rancho Sanchez, just outside of town. That attracts a third kind of crowd. Whole families of people."

"I was wondering about that operation. Who owns it?"

"A medium-sized conglomerate headquartered in Los Angeles. Western Seas, Inc. It was a small piledrive and dredge outfit started by some ex-Seabee right after World War II. Now it's into everything from fast-food stands to plastics and entertainment complexes like the Rancho Sanchez. They were very astute to build the Rancho here. It's a natural stopping place for folks traveling the shortcut route over the Rockies."

"What happened to the ex-Seabee?"

"I understand he goes into the office a time or two each year. The rest of the time he's hunting in Africa or flitting around Europe. He certainly will never have to look at another piledriver the rest of his life. Anyway, do you see my point? We have all sorts of people making money in different ways here in Sand Valley, because we have all sorts of different people coming down that lovely new highway."

"It makes sense. One more thing, Mr. Morton. On my way into town I noticed a small airstrip outside of town. Any chance of getting some sort of air service in here, you think?"

"Not in the foreseeable future, I'm afraid. It's privately owned."

"That's too bad. I have to do some traveling in my business. It'd be a lot easier if I didn't have to drive over to Spring Meadows all the time."

"I know. There used to be a nonscheduled air operation out there, but it went out of business about eight years ago. The town fathers made queries to see if they could interest another carrier in operating from here, but they didn't find anyone. Then they put the field up for sale, hoping the Western Seas people might buy it as a part of their Rancho Sanchez operation. But the Western people didn't bite, either. Then about a year ago a fellow came through town, made an offer, and the city sold it."

"What does the fellow use it for?"

"Don't ask me. He flies airplanes in and out."

"What's his name?"

"Saunders, I believe. You could find out at city hall."

"What did he pay for it?"

"I think ten thousand dollars. It isn't very big, really. It has the runway and a couple of old hangars. That's about all."

"Has the city ever thought about buying it back?"

"As a matter of fact, yes, once the tourist business started getting heavy. But this Saunders wanted something in the neighborhood of a million dollars for it. He plainly doesn't intend to sell."

I thanked Morton and went out to walk along the street some more. It was some town, no question about it. I was beginning to suspect there was more quiet wheeling and dealing going on than even banker Morton knew about. I passed a drugstore with newspaper racks out front. There were papers from Los Angeles, Phoenix, Denver and Salt Lake City. They also had an eight-page weekly newspaper called the *Sand Valley Piper.* It carried a lot of advertisements, vital statistics, columns written by correspondents in places called Wind Canyon and Salt Bluff, innocuous town gossip and an editorial about the mess in Washington. The editorial was signed by one Roland Carrington, who identified himself as editor and publisher. Inside the drugstore I asked for directions to the *Piper* office. The clerk told me it was three blocks over, where the town started to dissolve into sage and sand, the only concrete-block building in town that was painted pink.

Carrington turned out to be a stout old fellow with a cold cigar in his mouth. He was working an adding machine at a scarred desk just inside the front door. There was the rumble of a flatbed press behind a door leading to the printshop. I introduced myself as a former newsman from San Francisco who had always wondered if there was any money in weekly newspapers. I also congratulated him on his Washington editorial.

He grinned, leaned across the desk to shake hands and said people called him Doc. He also said the only reason he ran the editorial was because one of his travel ads fell out at the last minute.

"I batted it out one afternoon when I was sitting around with nothing much to do but feel righteous. Washington is far enough away so I figured it wouldn't hurt to get some of the steam out of my system and still not offend anyone. I also wrote it cleverly enough so that it was timeless. Been sitting back there in type since the last administration was in office. All ready to be slapped in when some emergency comes up leaving a hole. Now I got to sit down and do another one."

"Do your editorials always involve problems so far away?"

"You're damn right. That, my boy, is your first lesson in how to make money in weekly newspapering. You cannot afford to tweak the people who fill your pages with all those lovely advertisements. There aren't that many people who spend money on ads in a little town like this. It's plain economics. I used to live and work in Los Angeles. Spent a while writing editorials there as well. Wrote some stuff you could be proud of, and it didn't matter whether it concerned local people or not. If you hurt Bill's feelings and he yanked an ad, your salesmen could always go sell one to George. And pretty soon Bill would be back because he needed you. In Sand Valley—hell, any little town—it's different."

"Sand Valley seems different from most."

Carrington took the cigar out of his mouth and grinned up at me. "Noticed that, did you? We're trying to create the robust sort of atmosphere they have up around Virginia City, in Nevada."

"I'd say you're even a little more robust than Virginia City. I stopped by the Truck Stop on my way into town last night. I thought that operation was pretty robust until a gang of guys came through at about closing time and tore up the place."

Carrington leaned forward. "That so? I'll be damned. Doesn't surprise me all that much, though."

"Why not?"

Carrington screwed up his face and scratched under one armpit. “There seems to be some conflicting currents here in town. I try to keep my nose out of things, like a good weekly publisher should, but a fellow hears stories.”

“What sort of stories?”

“Oh, folks at one end of town not getting along with folks at the other end.”

“You mean Carl Slide and Ma Leary.”

“Yes. But they’re both advertisers. God knows they don’t have to be. The people who go to either one of their places aren’t much apt to pick up a copy of the *Piper.* So I try to remain an impartial observer.”

“Meaning not observing anything.”

“That’s right, son, and what’s your interest in all this?”

“Like I said…”

“I heard what you said, but you’ve been pumping me pretty good. What do you do now that you’re not newspapering?”

I gave him a card. He studied it and nodded.

“I see. Now I really gotta be careful. What’s your business here?”

“My client keeps getting threats in the mail to do with the people close to him. One of them proved genuine; a man was killed. The weapon came from here. I’m trying to find out why.”

“That all you have to go on?”

“Just about. That’s why I shotgun my questions. I don’t know where the threat comes from. Hopefully I’ll stumble across something. The problem is, I’m stumbling across too much down here. In fact a man can hardly take an uncluttered step around here.”

“How do you mean?”

“Places like the Truck Stop and Sky Lodge.”

Carrington scratched a match and sucked a little life into his cigar. He sat back and stared at the ceiling. “You would think a community of civilized people could carry it off, wouldn’t you?”

"Carry what off?"

"A little gambling. Girls. Things like that, so long as it doesn't offend the local residents. It's really a nice little town, Mr. Bragg. We don't have any of the problems a lot of towns do, let alone all the terrible stuff happening in the big cities."

"Everybody keeps saying that. Merle Coffey even boasts about firing a dishonest cop a while back. But at least an old newspaperman from Los Angeles must be aware of the risk you run when you start looking the other way about things. Things tend to drift and become other things. The guys who ripped apart the Truck Stop last night were from out of town. It hardly matters whether they were hired by somebody from around here or out of town. And I don't think it's the end of it. From what Ma told me afterwards, I don't think the prudent traveler should be booked into the Sky Lodge right now."

Carrington chewed his cigar. "I'd sure hate to see something like that get started. The shame of it is, it hasn't anything to do with the rest of us."

"It's your town."

"I know, but…" He thought some more then threw up his hands. "Ah, hell, if it happens, it happens. And don't think I kid myself about being a newspaperman any longer, Bragg. I'm a space salesman for a little weekly shopper. It's funny, though, that you should mention the fellow that Coffey fired. I was thinking about him when I wrote my Washington piece. If I were still a newspaperman, or had been back then, it's an episode I might have looked into."

"How come?"

"Because despite what Coffey will tell you, the fellow he fired might well have been the most honest cop this town had. John Caine was his name."

"What excuse did they use to get rid of him?"

"There were rumors of a bank account he had that was a whole lot bigger than a man on his salary could be expected to have. But all I heard were rumors, and it's been a long time since I followed up a rumor."

"Did Caine seem like the sort of cop who might go bad?"

"No, he didn't. He was a third generation native of the area. Loved Sand Valley. Didn't want it to change, I think."

"You're almost telling me something."

"When Slide and the fellow who owned the Truck Stop before Ma Leary started to expand their operations, so to speak, I don't think Caine liked it. I don't know just what all he was looking into, but you might say he was starting to fight city hall."

"So they fired him."

"Yes, sir. For a while it didn't seem as if it were going to make much difference. He kept poking around, and I think he was in touch with somebody in the state attorney general's office. Then all of a sudden he just dropped it."

"Do you think he was threatened?"

"I have no idea. But John Caine wasn't the sort to be threatened very easily, I can tell you that. His wife was dead. His kid had left home. No, it was more as if he just got tired, like we all do sometimes. He started hitting the bottle pretty hard."

"Where could I find this Caine?"

"In the cemetery."

"Natural causes?"

"If you can call it natural for a fellow to stick the barrel of his service revolver inside his mouth and pull the trigger."

"When did that happen?"

"Christmas season before last."

"You mentioned a fellow who owned the Truck Stop before Ma Leary."

"Yes, let's see now. His name was Barker. He left here a couple of years ago."

"What was he like?"

"I never got to know him much. I'd only bought the paper a short time before he left town."

"Does his name ever come up?"

"Not that I ever hear. But then…"

"I know. Hear no evil, speak no evil."

"You're catching on fast, son. You might make a good weekly newspaperman some day."

TWELVE

One time, early in my own newspaper career up in Seattle, there had been a mass slaying in the middle of the night of a family of seven. I was one of the people working on the story. I learned in the course of my asking around that there was a remote cousin of the slain family who lived up in Bellingham, near the Canadian border. That was before the freeway was built, and I never got around to going up to interview her. It was a long, irritating drive on a two-lane road in those days, and I figured she probably couldn't have added much color to the gory stuff we already had. For purposes of the story right then I was right. It turned out she was a plain, mousy-looking girl who wasn't very glib or bright. In the long run, though, it turned out I was very wrong indeed, because she was the one who envied her relatives and had hired the dude who pulled the trigger and snuffed the family of seven. It was a lesson my city editor back then was to make sure I never forgot. I call it my plain girl rule. That's why, when my major job was to protect a little girl up near San Francisco, I took a drive out of town to look at the airfield that had come up in a couple of conversations.

I took the road out past the Truck Stop and Rancho Sanchez. A fence ran along the road near the airfield, and there was an open gate leading down to the hangars, but I didn't drive in. Somebody else was already there. I parked alongside the road and got out my binoculars from the trunk of the car. A camper truck was parked alongside one of the buildings. Two men lounged against it as if they were waiting for somebody. They appeared to be in their twenties. One wore old army fatigues. The other had on an Australian bush hat with the brim tied up on one side. He was bare chested and had some creature's missing ivory tooth on a leather thong around his neck. Out beyond the runway itself, in the land of desert, were a bunch of guys on horseback dressed like Custer's Cavalry. They seemed to be getting ready to go charging into the Rancho Sanchez.

I decided that was a good idea. I got back into the car and drove to the Rancho Sanchez parking lot. I paid a five dollar admission and hiked on through the replica of an old frontier town among a couple hundred other tourists. At the end of the town, near the desert's edge and not too far from the airfield, was a riding stable. There was some curious activity going on that made me pause near the corner of a building where I wouldn't easily be seen.

A gang of guys dressed in new Levis and blue workshirts and cowboy hats were talking about renting some horses. They looked familiar despite the costumes. They all wore holstered pistols. Some of them thumbed their noses at authenticity, in the event they were trying to recreate history, by wearing shoulder holsters. They were some of the same people who had torn up the Truck Stop the night before. One of them was telling the guy in charge of the stable that they weren't all that used to riding, and they wanted some gentle mounts. The guy said he would do the best he could and whistled some helpers together. They began bringing out the horses and showing the other fellows which side to climb up on and things. I skulked on past and took a hike out into the desert.

About two hundred yards out of town I skirted a party of fellows made up to look like Indians. They appeared to be part of the show put on by the Rancho Sanchez. They were squatted down in a little arroyo drinking cans of beer from an ice chest while their horses looked on.

I nodded and wished them a good morning. One of them saluted me with his beer and said, "How."

I intended to hike up the airstrip until I got near the hangar which was between me and the camper truck with the young loungers. I would then cut over to behind the hangar and see what there was to see. It didn't work out that way.

I was halfway up one side of the runway when a twin engine Beechcraft glided past me and landed gently on the strip. It taxied down about a hundred yards, then wheeled around and came back in my direction. It wheeled around once again and came alongside me. The side hatch was open and a young Latin-looking fellow wearing a tie-dye tank top was squatting there pointing a shotgun with a short barrel and a large bore at my stomach. He said one word.

"Jog."

I jogged, and the plane kept abreast of me clear up to the camper truck with the pair of loungers who quit lounging and brought out handguns. I was gasping, but they didn't pay much attention to that. The one with the ivory tooth around his neck motioned toward the side of the vehicle.

"Assume the position," he told me.

I spread my legs and leaned easily with my hands apart against the side of the camper.

"That's not good enough," he told me.

Maybe he was an ex-cop. At least he followed the procedure. He jerked me back from the vehicle then pushed my shoulders forward, so that leaning with my hands against the camper again I felt very off balance. He handed off his gun to the guy in fatigues and now thrust one leg between my own and patted me down. He was very thorough. He took the .45 out of my shoulder holster and my wallet, then went back until he'd found the .38 revolver in the belt holster near the small of my back. The only purpose in carrying firearms seemed to be to give other people something to take away from me.

"You *must* be an ex-cop," I told him.

"You better believe it, sweetheart." He stepped back. "Okay, you can relax, but don't plan on going anywhere."

I turned around. He was going through my wallet. "He's a PI from Frisco," he shouted to the others.

"Please," I told him, "San Francisco."

"Shut up, sweetheart," Ivory Tooth told me. Then to the others he said, "He came armed like he knew his business."

There were three of them who had been in the plane. The Latin youth who'd covered me from the hatch, the pilot, who was a medium-built man approaching thirty and wearing a white Stetson, and a lean girl with dark hair wearing tight Levis down below and only a leather vest hanging loosely open up above. But she also carried a small automatic pistol in a holster at her suntanned waist, so I didn't do too much staring. Besides, I wanted to keep track of the little wisps of dust being kicked up by the posse or whatever a few hundred yards beyond the runway.

The pilot took charge. "Terry," he told the girl, "you cover the dude."

She took out her pistol and pointed it in the direction of my crotch.

"Hicks," he said to the lounger in army fatigues, "you and Turner unload the plane." He glanced around at the Latin crew member. "Sam, you help them, then gas the plane."

The pilot was going through my wallet, studying the license photostat, the gun toting permit, counting the money and inspecting my social security number. The tanned girl held her gun on me steadily, sober-faced and quiet. I smiled at her. With her free hand she gave me the finger.

Turner, the ex-cop, and Sam were inside the plane, tossing out gunnysacks filled with vegetable matter. Hicks was picking them up and throwing them inside the camper. The vegetable matter smelled like a lot of relaxation.

"Is marijuana all you guys deal in?" I asked. "With that much iron everyone's carrying I figured it must have been heroin or escaped convicts."

The pilot was still going through my wallet. I think he was reading my discharge papers now. Without looking up he told me, "You're an interesting dude. If you keep real still, now, you might live one more day."

"Maybe, maybe not. But either way, it won't be because of anything you or the tanned kid here do to me."

He looked up with a little smile. "Why would that be, Mr. Bragg?"

"Because I'm going to give you some information that might save all six of your asses just in the nick of time."

"I'm curious."

"You should be. From asking around town I've received the impression there's a link of some sort between you and Ma Leary's Truck Stop down the road. I of course couldn't begin to guess what that might be." He didn't say anything. I went on. "If that's true, you'll be interested to learn the place was busted up last night and some of the girl workers there were mistreated by a raiding party of imported gunmen."

"How good is your information?"

"Firsthand. Several of the gunsels were hanging around Carl Slide's casino later on. They banged up my ribs and things some when I went calling."

"Show me."

I opened the sports coat and pulled out my shirt, unbuttoned it and showed him the bruises. He nodded and I tucked my shirt back in.

"Your story is barely interesting. I'd rather hear more about you. Who you're working for. What you're doing out here."

"Better let me finish the other story first. The imported guns are still around town. Or just outside it, rather. On my way through frontier land down yonder I saw six or eight of them renting horses at the riding stable. They were outfitted like cowboys, only they carried shoulder holsters and things."

He finally reacted, along with a couple of the others. They craned their heads toward the fake Western town.

"That was several minutes ago," I continued, enjoying myself. "Since then they have come riding out and made a big loop around the field. They're trying to ride their horses on tiptoes up behind the hangars here, but they don't really ride very well, and right now they're only approaching the upper end of the runway."

There was a lot of swiveling around and a couple of swear words. The pilot tossed me my wallet and called to the others.

"Sam, get the Jeep. You other guys go with him. Drive down the front here out of sight from the horsemen until I do my thing. Terry, you just keep the guy right here until I get back."

He climbed back into the plane and closed the hatch. The engines kicked over. He wheeled the plane around and taxied down the runway, away from the oncoming horsemen. The others got into a Jeep Sam drove out of the hangar and went down around a corner of the next building. The Beechcraft was airborne by the time it got up the runway to where we were.

"Well, there they all go," I said brightly to the girl, edging a bit closer and trying to gauge how good she was with the gun.

"Don't try it, asshole," she told me frankly, now clasping the weapon in a two-handed grip. "Move back."

She was pretty good with the gun.

"The ex-cop, Turner, must have taught you how to use that," I told her.

"You better believe it."

She even used the same words he did. Only she spoke with a flat, plains voice, or one suggesting a border state.

"Are you his girl?"

"No, I'm Joe's girl. He's the pilot, Joe Saunders." She smiled, and a couple of dimples appeared. "We call him the Colonel."

"I suppose we do at that. Why don't we walk out on the runway so we can watch the fun?"

"Okay, but don't try anything smart."

We went out to where we could see the bobbing horsemen. The sound of the plane taking off had made them anxious. They wanted to arrive before the camper left, and they were trying to ride their horses at something a little more brisk than a walk, but there wasn't a rider among them. They were doing a lot of banging up and down on their saddles. There was going to be a lot of soreness tonight, where their legs joined together. Saunders was going to make things even sorer for them. He had climbed high beyond them, then circled back and now was looming larger and larger down out of the sky. The horsemen were nearly to the first hangar when Saunders pulled out of his dive, about two feet over everybody's heads. The horses hadn't expected that any more than their riders had. They leaped about six feet into the air and came down without their passengers, then broke into a gallop down the strip toward home. One, with wild eyes, seemed hell-bent on trampling the girl and myself. Maybe Terry didn't feel threatened by private cops, but the badly scared horse pounding in our direction was another matter. She froze.

"Come on!" I yelled. I grabbed her by the wrist and jerked her out of the way. As the horse galloped past she forgot about the gun, until I wrenched it away from her. Even then she was too frightened to do anything about it.

"Buck up, Terry, girl, it's all over with now. You're safe."

I put her pistol into my jacket pocket and led her back to the hangar. The out-of-town cowboys were still rolling around on the concrete, clutching various parts of their hurt bodies. The Jeep was parked nearby and Turner, Hicks and Sam were tossing handguns into it. They finally got the fellows on their feet and had them limping toward us with their hands on their heads. Saunders was landing the plane again. I hooked a finger inside the waist of Terry's Levis and tugged her inside the hangar.

"Sorry, kid, but I have to use you for a minute to see that I'm treated right."

She tensed, realizing for the first time that I'd taken away her little automatic. "Goddamn. Joe and Turner aren't going to like this."

"Joe and Turner weren't nearly run over by a wild horse."

"Maybe you could explain that to them, mister."

"Depends on how you behave."

The sore riders and their herders arrived about the same time Saunders shut down the plane again and climbed out. The would-be raiding party was ordered to lean against the front of the hangar.

"All right, tourists," Saunders called. "Take off your pants."

"Hey, what kind of crap is this?" one of them asked.

Hicks kicked him where he'd been bouncing in the saddle. The man began groping at his belt buckle.

"Tie them up," Saunders ordered. He took what appeared to be a five-gallon can of gasoline from the Jeep. As the gunmen stepped out of their pants, Saunders scooped them up and made a pile of them to one side. He doused the clothes with gasoline and threw a lighted match onto them. There was a loud *poof.*

"But my wallet!" protested one of the bare-legged men.

"One more word," said Saunders, pointing a finger at him, "and your underpants join the blaze."

Turner and Hicks finished tying up everybody.

"Okay," said Saunders, "now line up behind one another real buddy-buddy like. Close."

They did as they were told, and Saunders took a coil of rope out of the Jeep. He tied one end around the cord binding the hands of the man at the front of the line, passed the rope beneath the crotch of the second man and then around his bound hands, then beneath the crotch of the third man and so on. When he was through they resembled a shaky centipede. He pointed toward the road and told them to take a hike. They did, grumpy but thankful.

Turner, Hicks and Sam went back to unloading the marijuana, while Saunders began looking around for Terry and me. I stepped into view with the girl in front of me.

"That was nicely done," I told him.

"Oh, no," Saunders moaned. "What the hell is this?" Everybody stopped working and looked over in my direction.

"Where's your gun?" Saunders asked the girl.

I held her in front of me with my left hand on her bare tummy and rested my right hand holding her little automatic pistol on her shoulder. "I got the gun."

"You dumb bitch," Saunders said quietly.

"I have you to thank for it, Joe," I told him. "When you stampeded the horses, one of them came our way. It damn near killed us. It brushed the girl here, sending both her and the gun flying. I got to it before she did."

The other three weren't moving, not knowing what to do.

"So what now?" Saunders asked.

"So how about everybody giving back everybody else's small arms and you and I having a chat about things in a civil manner? After all, I didn't have to tell you about the raid on the Truck Stop. I didn't have to tell you about those guys trying to sneak up on you. So it happens that you import grass. Big deal. I suspected that much when I first heard about the very private airport. It's not my concern, unless somehow it's involved with a recent death in San Francisco, and the threat of another. This other being a little girl."

Saunders looked concerned. "Christ, no. I don't know anything about that."

He turned toward his crew with a questioning look.

Hicks, in the fatigues, shrugged. "You know what they say in the Army, Joe. Either trust 'em or snuff 'em."

"And like I said," Turner added, "he acts like a pro."

They were the two who seemed to count. Sam just stood there scratching his stomach.

"Okay," said Saunders.

Turner brought over my tools. He showed me that the .38 was loaded and slid the magazine into the .45. I released the girl and handed back her automatic.

"Come on into the office," Saunders told me. He led me into the hangar and over to one corner with a card table and telephone, a couple of chairs, a trash bucket and a refrigerator. "Want a beer?"

"Sure."

He pointed me into a chair and took a couple of Budweisers from the refrigerator, opened them and passed me one. "What did you want from me?"

"Some help in understanding the town. I think the problems here are the source of my client's problems in San Francisco."

"I told you, I don't know anything about that."

"Still, you are a part of this amazing town's operation. I heard different people around bemoaning the fact you bought up their airport."

Saunders grinned and lifted a pair of scuffed cowboy boots onto the top of the card table. "Yeah, I guess that sort of irritated everybody. But nobody else wanted it. And it's handy to have your own strip where you can bring in cargo during daylight hours if necessary, like it was this time. Legally it would be very difficult to impede my operation, unless the local law wanted to cooperate with outside authorities, and ol' Merle just works his ass off to keep outsiders away from his domain."

"But just now there were some guys trying to impede your operation. They weren't law, but they were serious."

He dismissed it with a wave of his hand. "They were just lucky. This isn't a scheduled cargo line I run. Somebody could have had the field under surveillance, and seen Turner and Hicks waiting. Maybe some truckers talked. It doesn't matter. It wouldn't have done anybody any good without the imported gunmen hanging around town to take action on it."

"You don't think they'll stay around?"

"I don't think I'm going to be staying around. But no, they won't either, come to think about it."

"You're sure?"

"Yup. You said they hit Ma's place last night. And I know Ma, or at least some of the guys who wheel and deal through there, won't sit still for it. It must have been Carl Slide's work." He shook his head with a snort. "What a loser. But no matter. He'll learn."

"Are you partners with Ma?"

"No. Oh, I sort of lay a little money her way—a little, hell, it's a lot—so I can operate through her concession is all, the same as the others."

"I'm beginning to understand. The truckers of course. They're a nationwide distribution network practically at the back door to your own private airfield. You truck the stuff over to Ma's and the cargo goes off from there. Do all the guys who stop there carry the stuff?"

"No, only some of them. Some more of them carry other things. A number of them don't carry anything except legitimate cargo. But everybody who is working a sideline pays Ma Leary a nice concession fee for use of the maintenance sheds out back."

"It must be an easy living for her."

"I'd say so. You don't think she gets rich with the cheap drinks and practically giving away the pussy, do you?"

"I had wondered about that. What's the other stuff transported out of there?"

He tilted his beer bottle and studied me for a moment, then lowered it with a shrug and a slight belch. "What the hell, it's not my racket. It's like a big wholesale interchange of stolen merchandise. Big ticket numbers. Color TVs, microwave ovens, motorcycles. A guy in L.A. can buy a hot TV from Toledo at a reasonable price. Guys in Toledo can buy stolen Hondas from Seattle. A Denver housewife on her birthday gets a new microwave oven from Kansas

City that her old man bought in a bar on his way home from work. Stuff coming from areas having antiburglary drives where you have your items branded is still no problem, it being so far away, and the guys buying at those bargain prices know what the score is. They're not about to check it out at the local police station."

"A nice setup."

"Right. I was tumbled to it by an old Air Force buddy now working for a long-haul line. It was the answer to a dope mover's dream. It takes care of the riskiest part of the operation. Finding the stuff and making buys and picking it up in remote areas down South is no problem. Flying across the border isn't much of a problem. But touchdown and getting rid of the stuff is chancy. With my own airport and the truckers, it no longer is. I make a lot of money. I'm happy in my work. I have no reason to threaten anybody in San Francisco. I live around there myself. Why make waves?"

"Before Ma Leary took over the Truck Stop it was owned by a man named Armando Barker. Ever hear of him?"

"From my Air Force buddy is all. He said Barker was the one who started letting the truckers exchange the hot merchandise out back. But it was on a very small scale and he kept it low-key. Ma's the one who let things sort of expand."

"That was two years ago. Why should Slide have waited this long to make a move against the operation?"

Saunders grinned loosely. "I'm afraid I have to take credit for that."

"Why?"

"Because he feels I represent the biggest threat to him. He thinks a big dope hauling operation is most apt to draw state and federal attention to little ol' Sand Valley. He's too dumb to see it just ain't so. If I had just one receiver for all this cargo it would be one thing. But within three hours of getting this stuff to Ma's place, it'll be in a dozen different rigs moving in four different directions. He doesn't see that, so he's dumb enough to hire outside guys to try throwing a scare into me and Ma. Well, now, do you think the guys running a million-dollar fence ring are going to stand still for that sort of thing? They'll probably hang him from a lamp post before tonight. But it's nothing I have to worry about. The guys in the stolen goods business will handle it."

Tucker came to the hangar door. "We're ready, Colonel."

"Right," Saunders told him. "You and Hicks button up things and stay with the plane. We should be back inside an hour." He finished his beer and got up. "Gotta roll."

I finished mine and threw the bottle into the trash bucket "Why do you suppose he does it?"

"What?"

"Slide. What is it you suppose he's doing that makes him afraid of outside law coming in and nosing around?"

"Beats me, pal. But it must be something pretty big. It sure isn't the penny-ante gambling and girls operation he has. He's an ambitious man, I've heard. He's got a hard-on to get a piece of the action in Vegas. I heard he tried to buy into a place once but didn't have enough cash. Another time something else went wrong. So far as I know, he's still trying. But what else he has going on here, I have no idea."

Saunders, Sam and the girl dropped me off back at the Rancho Sanchez parking lot, but instead of getting my car I went back into the mock frontier town looking for a site that would offer good surveillance of the nearby airfield. It wasn't hard to find—the only four-story building there. It had an old-time dance hall on the ground floor, rooms for overnight guests on the second and third, and a dining room and the Gold Stirrup Room on top. A playbill out front said the Stirrup Room offered the melodic rhythms of the Harvey Pastor Sextet from Los Angeles.

That would be Connie Wells's ex-husband. This old world just seemed to grow smaller every day.

I took an elevator up to the Gold Stirrup Room. The bar was open, but there wasn't anybody around the piano. Windows on one side of the room looked out over the main street of the frontier town. Windows on the other side looked out over the desert and the Colonel's airport. It would have been easy to spot Hicks and Turner waiting there by the hangar, if you'd been looking for them.

I ordered a beer and sipped it while making friends with the paunchy bartender who was peeling lemons and cutting the rinds into narrow strips. He said Harvey Pastor didn't come to work until the cocktail hour. However, it turned out that he had been into the bar earlier that morning.

"Sitting about where you are," the bartender said. "Checking his ascot in the backbar mirror and waiting for some dame to come by and pick him up." He laughed, and looked up from his lemon peels. "Said he was going to tune her piano for her."

"That's funny?"

He shrugged and went back to the rinds. "Well, you know. It doesn't matter what he'd say. He's quite a chaser, if you know what I mean."

"Did you see the woman he left with?"

"Yes. She was a good-looking girl. Young. Nice tan."

"Did you know her?"

"I've seen her in here from time to time. So I guess she's a local girl. It's kind of surprising, really. Old Harvey usually hits on the tourist broads."

There was a stand card atop the piano advertising the sextet. It had a head shot of Harvey. In the photo he appeared to be about thirty, with a round face, glasses, kinky blond hair close to his scalp and a capped-tooth grin. I didn't think I'd trust him with tuning my piano.

THIRTEEN

The guys who'd lost their pants must have gotten a ride back into town. I didn't pass them on the road. In Sand Valley itself, the bustling spirit seemed to have died out. There weren't many people out and around. It looked as if they practiced the quaint custom of siesta. Businesses and shops along Nevada Street in the block just before the Sky Lodge were all closed up tight. There were only a couple of cars parked along the street. Mine made three. A worried-looking little fellow with a thin mustache and sweat on his forehead was locking the front door of a jewelry and gift shop. I crossed over to him.

"Hi, there."

He hadn't seen me approach. When he came back down onto the sidewalk and turned around I smiled. "Sorry. Did I startle you?"

"What the hell do you think?"

"Guess so. How come everybody down at this end of town is closed up?"

"I don't know about everybody else," he said, "but about twenty minutes ago two of the biggest, meanest-looking oxen I have ever seen walked into my store with some wooden staves and told me to be locked up and gone within ten minutes or they'd be back and break everything in sight, including my arms and legs. Well, I didn't make it within ten minutes, but when they came back and saw I was working as hard as I could to get the expensive stuff back into the safe, they gave me a little extension. They said not to let them catch me here again when they came back, though, and that's who I thought it was when you said hello to me, and my God, you bet it startled me and now I'm leaving."

"You're just going to let a couple of strange goons scare you off like that?"

"You bet I am. If you were as puny as I am, mister, you'd do the same. You have to be ready to roll with the punches in this town, and that's what I'm doing. Rolling. Good-bye."

"But why don't you call the cops?" I yelled after him.

"You call them," he cried over his shoulder.

I walked up the street until I came to a phone booth. I dialed the police number, told the man on duty who I was and asked to speak with Merle Coffey.

"He isn't in right now. I'm Sergeant Stoddard. Can I help you?"

"I'd rather speak to the chief. Know when he'll be back?"

"No, I don't. Look, Bragg, I'm in charge around here right now. Do you have a complaint?"

"Not really, why do you ask?"

"Because you're about the tenth person who's called for the chief in the past fifteen minutes. They all sounded just like you. All questions and no answers."

"Sorry, Sergeant, but I think it'd be worth your while to try getting in touch with the chief, wherever he is."

"I've been trying to, but nobody answers the phone out there."

"Out where?"

"The Truck Stop. Ma Leary called and asked for the chief and Lieutenant Trapp to pay a visit. She said it was urgent. We'd heard there was some kind of trouble out there last night, so the chief decided...Hey, what the—excuse me a minute, Bragg."

He put down the receiver. A moment later I heard him raise a window and begin to shout. It was something about a truck blocking the driveway. Then it sounded as if he'd gone into a nearby room and was doing more shouting.

I hung up and started back down the street in the direction of the Sky Lodge. I was about fifty paces from the corner when

I heard the deep-throated roar of a truck tractor. I turned and watched a large moving van thunder up the middle of the street. Its side hatch was open, and when it went past I saw the insides were filled with men, not household goods. At first I thought it was going to drive straight into the Sky Lodge, but it swung to the right, into a cross street, wiping out a mailbox and street light on the corner. I heard the sharp gasp of air brakes, then a chunk of gears and the renewed roar of its diesel engine. This time when the backing truck came into view it was headed for the Sky Lodge. Its big, boxy rear rammed into the glassed-in lobby, and kept moving until only the cab of the vehicle was still outside the building. It must have busted through the leather-padded doors leading into the casino. A lot of lusty yelling was going on, accompanied by the sharp bangs of small-arms' fire.

I ran across the street and into the doorway of a closed liquor store. Great shards of glass covered the intersection. From my vantage point I could see that the smash-in had transformed the front of the Lodge into something resembling a very ragged sidewalk café. The entire glass front had collapsed, leaving only steel support beams. Guys packing guns and swinging staves—as if trying to impersonate the men who busted up Ma Leary's the night before—were going up in elevators and pounding up the stairs. They seemed to be evicting what guests were in their rooms that time of day. People were being forced out into the street. There was nothing gentle about this. Some of the guests must have resisted. They came into the sunlight bruised and stunned.

The din and punishment continued from inside the Sky Lodge. But the people Slide had hired must have suspected something of that sort could happen, and had plans for counterattack. I could hear the slamming of car doors around both corners of the cross street. There were other autos now being parked in the next intersection down Nevada Street. They formed a barrier of steel, and men were setting up positions behind them.

The people up and down the near cross street were beginning to shoot at the cab of the truck. The guests from the Sky Lodge scattered. A headlight on the truck exploded. Slugs ricocheted off the hood and fenders, and several pocked the large windshield. Somebody inside the casino blew a whistle. The guys with staves began coming down from the upper floors. There was more gunfire inside the casino and from the back of the truck, apparently aimed at the people on the cross street. A moment later the big diesel engine roared again. The moving van drove out of the gaping sore it had punched into the Sky Lodge and turned in my direction. I thought for a moment I was dead. It swung in a wide arc. One huge tire bounced over the curb. I pressed myself flat against the doorway as the truck's side mirror ripped off the overhead canvas awning. The van straightened and rolled on up Nevada, picking up speed and heading for the auto-blocked intersection. It must have been doing nearly 40 miles an hour when it slammed into the side of a blocking auto. It was like a locomotive hitting a fifty-gallon drum. Guys at the barricade fled. The truck just kept on going, punching the smashed car ahead of it. At about the middle of the following block the auto became wedged under the front wheels of the truck. There was a horrendous scraping noise. The truck slowed, and then stopped. Men came boiling out the side hatches and back. This time they left their staves behind and took to the street with just their guns. The blocking force at the intersection scrambled back around to the other side of their cars and everybody got down to a serious gunfight. I wondered where the cops were, because not all of the civilians were gone from that stretch of Nevada Street where the truck had stopped. There was a lot of scurrying around going on. Autos were leaving the cross street in front of the Sky Lodge, Some roared up Nevada to reinforce the gang at the next intersection. Others were taking off on the cross street, probably to try flanking the truck. I ran across the street to take a look inside.

The casino looked as if somebody had swung a gigantic spiked ball through the place. There were huddled groups of customers and people who had worked for the casino. All of them had been knocked about some on the head and face. There was a lot of blood and torn flesh. One of the hostesses had a shattered jaw. She stared wild-eyed at her face in the backbar mirror, then fainted.

I started to leave when I saw a man's foot sticking out from around a corner of the bar. I went down there to see if he needed help. It was too late. He must have been the service bartender. He was lying on his back, with a short-barreled shotgun on the carpet a few feet from his outstretched hand. He stared at the ceiling through eyes that couldn't see. There were two bullet holes in his forehead.

Some of the bystanders stared at me dumbly, but most just stood around aimlessly. They were in profound shock. They didn't seem injured anywhere except around the head and face. Some of them had been hit so hard that facial bones had broken, so they couldn't support muscle and tissue the way they were meant to. Some of them looked like exhibits in a sideshow. I couldn't take any more of it. I got out of there just before getting sick to my stomach.

I went back up the street to my car and drove over to the next street that paralleled Nevada. About four blocks up was another parked truck and more gunfire. That meant the battle was spreading, which meant more bystanders would be hurt. At the intersection a block this side of the new fighting, there did finally appear a small knot of khaki-uniformed police officers. Coffey was with them. I drove up and shouted to him. He was a shaken man. I asked him a straightforward question.

"Do you have a plan?"

"Not one I can implement at the moment. They were real smart. Called me and my assistant out to the Truck Stop. Then there was a flurry of calls for help from different parts of town, away from the center of things. When my men responded and left their cars to investigate, several of the units were disabled. I didn't get word of what was happening until my one active patrol vehicle drove out to warn us. They even blocked the driveway at city hall so we couldn't get more units out on the street. I just can't do much of anything until I have more force, except to block the roads at either end of town. That I have done."

"Would it help if I loaned you my car?"

"Not without a radio, thanks. Besides, I need the manpower more than anything, and I guess you wouldn't want me to swear you into the force."

"No. I still have my own job to do."

"You came from the direction of Sky Lodge. Did you see that?"

"Yes, and it's bad. They worked the place over violently. One of the bartenders was shot dead. There may be more. And there are bystanders over on Nevada Street near the fighting."

"I know. I put in a call to the hospital for an ambulance. I'm hoping to arrange a truce so we can escort those people out. But until then, or when I get more of my men back together, I'm just one frustrated man."

"I know the feeling. I think I'll go on over to Nevada and see if I can help out the folks some."

Coffey wheeled around. "Michaels! Go along with Bragg here. He's going to try aiding some of the civilians. See if you can help."

He'd called to a thin, blond man whose jaws were working quick time on a wad of chewing gum. He was in civilian clothes.

"My one plainclothes man," Coffey told me. "I don't dare send in a uniform until I can send in one helluva lot of them."

"Right. Thanks for Michaels." The young officer got in beside me and we took off.

"This is bound to get hairy," I told him. "With the odds what they are, we'll have to be more sneaky than brash."

He just nodded, leaning forward in the seat with his eyes straining ahead and his jaws working a mile a minute.

I parked on the cross street just short of the gun battle. Michaels and I edged up to the corner and crouched where we could get a look at things. They all were about where they'd been when the battle started. The guys working for Slide were entrenched behind the cars in the intersection and the truckers were firing away from behind their rig halfway down the block. There were two pockets of bystanders who'd been trapped in that block when the fighting started. One group huddled across the street, three doors down from the intersection, in front of a locked-up savings and loan office. The others were trapped in a doorway on our side of the street almost even with the stalled truck. There was enough shooting going on to endanger them all. The din of cracking guns was beginning to give me an earache.

Michaels and I began a chancy leapfrog game, taking turns moving from one doorway to the next down the street. At his suggestion, we moved with our hands open and extended in an attempt to show we weren't a threat to anybody. There was some pinging and smashing of glass around us but we managed to reach the pocket of bystanders on our side of the street. There were four of them—two middle-aged woman, an upright elderly gentleman and the bank vice president I'd spoken to about setting up a poster business, Howard Morton. Morton had been hit. He was lying on the pavement, unconscious. The women had tried to stem the flow of blood from his left arm. It had been smashed pretty badly.

"Somebody's using big slugs," said Michaels, snapping away on his chewing gum.

"Yeah," I agreed. "He needs medical help. If we can get him on down around the corner I can go get my car and get him to the hospital."

"But we could all get killed trying to get him down to the corner," said the officer. He got to his feet and peered into the darkened café we were huddled in front of. "There's an alley that runs down this block. Maybe the joint has a back entrance."

He drew his service revolver and smashed the glass door near the doorknob, bringing a gasp from one of the women. It was heartening to see some of the old virtues still present in Sand Valley. They'd been trapped there in the doorway with bullets whizzing past and an unconscious wounded man at their feet, but they wouldn't even think of breaking into a business that might afford them some protection.

Michaels reached inside and unlocked the door. We carried Morton to the kitchen behind the front counter and shooed the others in there with him. Behind the kitchen was a storage area and refrigeration unit, and a door that led out to a loading dock.

"Okay, get your car," said Michaels. "Can you and the others load him in?"

"Sure, but where are you going?"

"To try and get those other people off the street."

"I'll have one of these others get my car and cover whatever you do."

Michaels didn't wait to argue about it. He went into the front of the café and eased back out onto the street.

The elderly man in the kitchen said he'd get my car for me. I gave him the keys and told him where to find it. He slipped out the back and stepped briskly up the alley. I went back to the front doorway.

Michaels had gotten farther down the street and crossed over to the other side. He must have shouted something to the truckers when he circled around behind them. They were letting him back past them on the far side. He ducked from doorway to doorway. He was still short of the trapped bystanders when one of the gunmen behind the cars up at the intersection took an interest in him. It was a fellow behind a new Buick with the nose pointed toward my side of the street. Everytime Michaels tried to make those last few steps the guy would raise up and shoot over the hood. The young officer made three attempts, then looked across to where I was. He was so angry he spit out his gum. I got out my

.45, braced myself and waved Michaels on. I fired the first time as Michaels started forward. The gunman at the corner rose up just in time for my slug to explode new Buick metal and paint in his face. He even dropped his gun before diving back down behind the car. I fired all seven shots. Michaels made it easily to the trapped people and smashed the glass in the door to the savings and loan office, setting off an outside burglar alarm near the roof of the two-story building. He herded the people inside and followed them. The din of the ringing bell acted as a nervous trigger to the warring factions on the street. Everyone began shooting. I moved back into the café.

The older man came down the alley in my car. He helped me load Morton into the back and gave me directions to the hospital. I urged him and the ladies to remain inside the café kitchen until the police came for them, not knowing when the battle might move into the back alley. I started out for the hospital. A couple of blocks from the main battle site I spotted more opposing teams of guys battling at another intersection just in time to avoid driving into the middle of it. I backed around and got turned away from it just as the ambulance Merle Coffey had summoned came rolling unsuspectingly into the intersection from the opposite direction. All four of its tires were promptly shot up and the driver ducked down out of sight. The wagon banged over the curb onto the sidewalk and came to a stop. I turned at the next corner and started a more roundabout trip to the hospital.

FOURTEEN

Sand Valley Hospital seemed like another world. Calm and clean, it was a two-story building a couple of miles outside of town with shade trees and green lawn to keep the desert at bay. A sweeping drive led up to the emergency entrance. I parked and went in to ask for some help from the nurse on duty at a desk. In about a minute a pair of attendants in white smocks came out to the car with a gurney to collect banker Morton.

I followed them back inside. They wheeled Morton into an emergency receiving area while I gave the nurse some basic information. She was an older woman with graying hair and an efficient manner. The nameplate on her desk said that she was Mrs. Foster, R.N. A tall man of about thirty came out and introduced himself as Doctor Stambaugh, the resident physician in charge. I told him what had happened. He listened to my story with folded arms and a trenched brow.

"That does sound serious," Stambaugh said. "I was in conference when the message came in from Chief Coffey. We sent an ambulance into town."

"Do you have another?"

"Yes."

"You'd better send it, and tell the driver to stay alert. The first one just got the hell shot out of it. How's Morton?"

"He's in pretty poor shape right now. He's lost a lot of blood, and there's extensive bone damage. Luckily we don't have too many gunshot cases here."

"You're apt to have several before this day is out. When was your last one?"

His trenches deepened. "A year ago last January. Actually it wasn't really a medical case, as you think of those things. It was a suicide. I've specialized in pathology. I did the autopsy."

"Was it a man named John Caine?"

He studied me closely. "That's right."

"And there was no question that the wound was self-inflicted?"

"None whatsoever."

"Something else. There's a man in town named Carl Slide. He owns the Sky Lodge. Know him?"

"I know him by sight. Not to say hello to."

"I hear he had a brother named Burt who died some while back. I was wondering what he died of."

"That must have been before my time."

The attendants came out of the emergency area with Morton on a different conveyance, this one with overhead rails from which they'd hung bottles of fluids being tubed into his good arm. Stambaugh joined them at the elevator. I turned back and saw that the nurse was staring at me. She lowered her eyes and became busy in some sort of log. I crossed back over to her.

"Excuse me, Mrs. Foster, but did you overhear me and the doctor talking?"

"I don't have cotton in my ears, young man."

I took out one of my business cards and gave it to her. "I have a client in San Francisco. The client, a man who worked for him, and a little girl the client is looking after, have all received death threats. The man who worked for my client is already dead. Murdered. I'm trying to save the lives of the other two."

She pushed her glasses up on her forehead. "That's quite a story. What are you doing down here?"

"There's a connection between here and there. I just haven't found out yet what it might be. Were you here two or three years ago?"

"Yes and no. I was living a few miles outside of town, but I wasn't working here at the hospital just then."

"Can you think of somebody who was? Maybe a native of hereabouts?"

She thought a moment, tapping the card against her teeth, then her face brightened and she consulted a clipboard.

"Do you like girls, Mr. Bragg?"

"You bet your boots, but that isn't really what I'm here for just now."

"I know. But interesting men help relieve the tedium in a little town like this. I'm just doing a friend a favor. She isn't due in until late this afternoon. I'll see if she's home."

Mrs. Foster dialed a number and a moment later was talking to somebody she called Cathy. She described me as an exciting character from San Francisco who needed some information that Cathy might be able to give me. And she, Mrs. Foster, felt that Cathy should try to help me because I'd probably saved banker Morton's life.

"Besides," she continued, staring me straight in the eye, "he looks to be a cut or two above the run-of-the-mill male we're apt to find in Sand Valley or the surrounding boonies.

"What dear? Just a minute, I'll ask." She held the receiver aside. "Are you married, Mr. Bragg?"

"No."

"He says no," she told the telephone. "I know they all say that, but it wouldn't hurt to speak to him, dear. Right."

She hung up.

"I'm glad you don't live in my own town, Mrs. Foster."

"Why is that?"

"I'm afraid you'd upend my personal life. What is it with this girl, ugly as a bag of mud and looking for a husband?"

"Not at all. It's just a little joke she and I have. What with her being single and all. Besides, she can probably give you the information you want. Now just go on out this road for about a half mile until you come to Hollings Street. Turn up the hill there and in about a mile you'll reach a yellow and white mailbox alongside the road with the name Carson on it. That's her."

"I'm much obliged."

"Just act like a gentleman. And see that no harm comes to that little girl in San Francisco."

"I'll do my best."

Ten minutes later I was at the mailbox and turned up a gravel driveway. It terminated at a carport formed by an overhead deck fronting the house. I parked beside a red Ford and climbed concrete stairs leading up and around the house to a lawn in back. Through an open window I heard somebody playing "Deep in the Heart of Texas" on a piano. I hadn't heard that tune since the last time there was formal fighting in Europe. I rang a doorbell. Either nurse Cathy Carson was older than Mrs. Foster had led me to believe or she had the radio on a station that played old time melodies.

The girl who opened the door wasn't all that old. She was a curious mixture. Somewhat on the small side, with a slender build. She had a face built for mischief and hair trimmed short, black as new tar. But it was the cast of her eyes that would keep you guessing about things. They were dark and knowledgeable, as if they'd lived other lives. She wore a pair of shorts cut out of old blue jeans. Her legs were brown as berries. She had on a man's blue shirt that she wore untucked. There were enough things about her to make a man stumble.

"You're staring," she told me. "Mr. Bragg, is it?"

"That's right. Mr. Bragg, and I am staring. I guess I owe Mrs. Foster an apology."

She glanced once over her shoulder then came outside and quietly pulled the door shut behind her as a male voice began singing.

"*The stars at night, are big and bright…*"

I couldn't hear whether he clapped his hands. The girl led me across to some canvas lawn chairs. "We can talk over here. Unfortunately, I have company. Why do you owe Mrs. Foster an apology?"

"I half expected you to be the town's old maid, with stringy hair and a figure like a drainpipe. Instead, you turn out to be the sort of girl a guy would like to tuck into his duffle bag and take home with him. What are you doing in a burg like this?"

"Working. The same as I would anywhere else. When I feel like playing I can always go to a bigger town or city. Which I do fairly regularly. But I like to come back here. It's more restful."

"It sure seems to agree with you. How about the next time you feel like playing you come up to San Francisco?"

She had a nice smile and she showed it to me. "You're the third or fourth man I've met from San Francisco, Mr. Bragg, and you've all been terrible flirts. What makes you that way? All that drinking you do up there?"

"I'm not flirting, I'm serious. I think you'd stand the town on its ear, and I'd like to watch."

"Mrs. Foster said you were an exciting character. What's exciting about you?"

"She probably meant the work I do," I told her, getting out another one of my cards and handing it to her. "She probably figures it's a glamorous profession."

"Isn't it?"

"It's mostly a lot of hard work."

"That never hurt anybody. Besides, you need that to keep you out of trouble."

"What sort of trouble?"

"Girls, what else? You've got crinkly good looks, Mr. Bragg. I know girls who would roll over like puppy dogs so you could scratch their tum-tums if you came their way."

"Now who's flirting?"

"I am. Want to make something of it?"

I glanced toward the house where the guy was singing his heart out and playing the piano. "I'd love to if the circumstances were right."

She tucked her brown legs beneath her with a grin. "Why Mr. Bragg, I don't believe I've ever had anybody get jealous so quickly in my life. It's a nice compliment. Going to be in town for long?"

"Probably not. And I'll probably never come by this way again, so you'll just have to come up to San Francisco some time so we can flirt in earnest."

"I might, some day. I'd like to stay at the Pimsler Hotel. I saw a picture of its lobby in *Sunset Magazine*. It looks charming."

"It's not always that charming. I've got a comfortable apartment across the Golden Gate Bridge, in Sausalito. You could stay there and save all that hotel money."

"Then you really are single."

"I really am."

"That means a bachelor's apartment with all the dust and crud that accumulates in those places."

"I have a cleaning lady who comes once a month to stack and buff things."

"I think I'd rather stay at the Pimsler."

"Suit yourself."

"Now you'd better tell me what you're doing here. I should be getting back to my company."

There was a rattle of gunfire from down in town.

"Whatever is that?" she asked.

"Gunshots. You probably would have heard it sooner if it weren't for all that piano music and hollering inside."

"Who's doing the shooting?"

"Couple of gangs of outsiders. One bunch is working for Carl Slide. Know him?"

"I know of him."

"He wants to close down Ma Leary's Truck Stop. Some of the hoods working out at that end of town don't like the idea. Do you know the sort of operations Slide and Ma Leary run?"

"Not too much. Crap games and painted ladies, isn't it?"

"There's more to it than that. There's a big stolen goods exchange and a dope importing ring operating out of the Truck Stop, and God knows what all going on at Slide's place. You have a town cop who doesn't believe in looking too closely at either operation, and a general town population that doesn't seem to give a damn. I can't figure it out, myself."

"I wouldn't know about those things. I'm not a patron of either the Truck Stop or the Sky Lodge. I deal in neither dope nor stolen goods nor anything else. Like most of the people who live here I just happen to like the way the sun sets behind the mountains in the distance and the way the desert looks in the middle of winter and a lot of other hometown things. But I don't suppose that's what you came to ask."

"No, it isn't. I'm interested in Carl Slide's younger brother, Burt. I understand he died a couple of years ago. Would you know what he died of?"

"Yes, he was shot. It was downtown, outside of St. Agatha's Catholic Church." She concentrated for a moment. "I think it was some sort of argument over a girl."

Across the front lawn the door to her house opened and a familiar looking, round little fellow wearing glasses and losing his hair stepped outside. "Telephone, Cathy."

The girl excused herself and went inside. The round guy squinted in my direction for a moment and went in after her. A scrub jay in the oak tree near where we sat shook out its feathers and chatted for a moment. He didn't have anything to tell me I didn't already know. Harvey Pastor had grown balder since they took the picture that appeared on the stand card atop the piano at Rancho Sanchez. I guess it needn't have surprised me too much that he was there. Cathy said she didn't patronize the Truck Stop or Sky Lodge, so she probably relaxed over a drink from time to time out at the Rancho. Harvey was a chaser, and the girl didn't appear to be dumbstruck in the presence of men, so it probably figured they would become acquainted. It was a perfectly logical coincidence. I just wish it hadn't happened.

She came back outside but didn't sit down again. "I'm awfully sorry, Mr. Peter Bragg from San Francisco, but this will have to wait. The hospital phoned again. A lot of hurt people are being brought in. They want me there in a hurry."

"My luck," I said rising. "Do you know who shot Burt?"

"Some man. I can't think of his name."

"You said it was over a girl. Was her name Theresa Moore?"

"Yes," she said slowly. "That's right, it was."

"Does she have any family living around here?"

"No, she wasn't a local girl. I mean she wasn't raised here. But she lived here for a number of years, then went away."

"Why did she go away?"

"I'm not absolutely sure. There was talk of a husband in Vietnam."

"You don't sound convinced."

"Actually, I'm not. This is still a fairly straitlaced town Mr. Bragg, despite the boldness some of us might display for crinkly looking strangers passing through. Anyway, Theresa Moore came back to town with a baby girl. And this talk of a husband in the Army nobody ever saw—it's the sort of story a girl might tell when she went away to have a baby. There was speculation it might have been Burt's child."

I sat down again. "Burt Slide was thought to be the father of Theresa Moore's little girl?"

"By some, at least. There was gossip about it at the time Burt was killed."

"What happened to the man who shot him?"

"I don't really know. He wasn't arrested. Witnesses said Burt shot first."

"Were you working at the hospital back then?"

"Yes. I was on duty when they brought him in."

"Did you ever get a chance to talk with him? Or overhear conversation he might have had with anybody else?"

"He didn't have any. He was unconscious when they brought him in. He died an hour later."

"Did an ambulance bring him in? Or his brother, maybe?"

"No, it was a police officer. A former policeman, actually." She raised a hand to the side of her head and thought about it. "John Caine was his name. I was more shocked at his appearance than I was at Burt Slide's."

"Why was that?"

"He was—he'd been drinking. It wasn't even ten-thirty on a Sunday morning, and he was—well, drunk. I hadn't seen him in almost a year, and his whole appearance was different. I didn't even recognize him at first. His face was puffy and half dead looking. I don't know if you've ever known any really heavy drinkers."

"I have. How come Caine is the one who brought Burt Slide to the hospital?"

"He was at the church when the shooting occurred. He just thought faster than anybody else, I guess, despite his condition. Packed Burt into his car and drove him out." She shook her head briefly, as if to clear it of the memory. "But I've really got to get going now. I'll be either here or at the hospital if you want to talk later."

"I'd like that. Not just to talk about old bodies and things, either. Is the piano player going to be hanging around much longer?"

She smiled again, making me feel genuinely happy I'd come to Sand Valley, beatings, threats and all. "No, in fact maybe you could do me a big favor."

"What's that?"

"Give the funny little man a ride back into town. I got a little drunk myself last night at a place where he entertains. We got to talking and I told him I had this piano that was horribly out of tune. He said he could fix it for me. I offered to fix breakfast for him in exchange."

She looked at me with one of those looks women give you when they're not going to tell you a great deal more.

"Did he tune your piano?"

"Yes, but you showed up before I had time to give him breakfast. I have to send him away hungry. That's why it would be nice if you gave him a ride."

"Okay. Tell him I'll meet him down at the car."

FIFTEEN

From his grumpy mood in the car, Harvey Pastor wasn't very happy about losing out on breakfast and heaven knew what else by a combination of circumstances that included myself. It had taken him a while to get down to the car, which suggested he'd tried to talk Cathy out of rushing in to work. He couldn't be openly hostile to me because I was saving him the price of a cab, but he didn't have to love me like a brother, either. He asked me finally what I did for a living. I told him I was a detail man for one of the drug houses. I asked what he did and he told me.

"Sounds a lot more interesting than my line," I said. "Do you meet a lot of girls in your job?"

It helped lift him out of his funk. He laughed and clasped his hands behind his head. "Yes, quite a few. How about yourself?"

"It's not bad in the cities. But it's tough in smaller places where people know one another. Girls in small towns are still small-town girls."

"I know what you mean, brother. That's why I usually try to hit on the tourist dames in areas like this. They're out looking for a good time to begin with. A dash of adventure And they're not apt to get phone calls asking them to go into work early."

"Yeah, it's tough. Do you know many people in town?"

"Naw. This place is eerie. First night here, the day before my gig started out at Rancho Sanchez, I went into town, to the Sky Lodge. Been there?"

"Just briefly."

"That's the best way. I thought the place was sensational at first. Then I discovered all the girls were whoring for the house. That's when they gave me the bill for three hundred dollars. I damn near choked. Started to make a beef about it. One of the girls I'd been with told the guy I was arguing with that I was a piano player from out at the Rancho Sanchez. I expected it to get me a discount or something. Instead, all the guy said was if I didn't pay up he'd have somebody break all my fingers. Thank Christ for Master Charge. But that's the last the Sky Lodge will see of this big spender."

"Where you headed for now?"

"Back to the Rancho, I guess, but you can drop me off anywhere I can catch a bus or something."

"That's all right. I'm headed that way myself. Ever get up to San Francisco?"

"Haven't for a couple of years or so. I have an ex-wife living there now."

"Been married, huh?"

"Thrice. They're a weakness. I've finally gotten smart, and decided to quit marrying them. I just fall in love and let it go at that."

"Ever get the urge to see the ex-wives?"

"Of course. I'm great friends with all of them. It's better this way. When we were married, they all wanted me to themselves."

"Some girls are like that. What does the one in San Francisco do?"

"She runs some sort of restaurant. Seems happy enough."

"You keep in touch, huh?"

"Sure thing. We exchange cards at Christmas and on birthdays and things. I phone once in a while. I never know when I might get up her way again."

We talked some more but I didn't learn much else. I managed to dance the conversation around to the airport near the Rancho, but he said he'd never noticed it. I dropped him off in the parking lot.

From the road I saw that Turner and Hicks still were waiting over by the plane. Something must have delayed the Colonel. I drove on out to the Truck Stop. Somebody had been doing some road work out there. About halfway from the county road into the Truck Stop, near an old shed, somebody had created a number of ruts and furrows that would have your head banging against the car roof if you didn't slow down to about three miles an hour. I was jouncing through this stretch when a guy stepped out from behind the shed and aimed a rifle at my head. He was a big man, wearing coveralls.

"Why don't you stop a minute, bud?"

It sounded like a good idea to me, if that's what he wanted. I braked and carefully removed my wallet to show him some ID. "I did Ma a favor last night. Do you have some way to check?"

"Yeah." He handed the ID to somebody inside the shed. The somebody had a walkie-talkie type of radio and used it. A minute later the other guy lowered his rifle and gave me back my ID.

"Just be sure you go to Ma's place. Nowhere else."

I gave him a salute and bounced on down the road. When it smoothed out I didn't speed up all that much. There was a lot of activity going on over by the maintenance station and sheds near the river. Trucks were backed up at a loading dock and a lot of stuff was being carted out of the buildings. It looked as if they were expecting air raids. Colonel Saunders's camper was parked over in front of the Truck Stop. It was jacked up with both right wheels missing. The Colonel's girlfriend, Terry, was squatted down beside it, resting her chin on her hands.

"Hi, deadeye, what's going on?"

She waved a hand in the general direction of the maintenance station. "Sam is over there fixing some shot-out tires."

"What happened?"

"The Colonel spotted the ruts back on the road on the way in. It worried him, so he swung off the road and tried going around an old shed there when a man stepped out and began shooting at the tires. After he got three of them Joe decided to stop."

"Where's the Colonel now?"

"Inside, talking to Ma Leary. If you see him, ask him to forget about the camper and see if we can't buy something else and boogie on out of here. I'm ready to leave this place."

"I'll tell him." I went on inside. The girls had nearly finished straightening the mess from the night before, but there wasn't much hilarity in the air. The gambling room was deserted. Waitresses sat around in thin underwear and long faces. A pair of truckers at the bar tossed back shots of whiskey, swallowed their beers and headed for the door, giving me mean looks on their way out.

Harmony was over behind the bar in yellow shorts and top. She seemed to be in a thoughtful frame of mind until she saw me.

"Hey there, Pete, how are you?" she grinned.

"Mostly flattered that you didn't call me Lucky."

"Shucks, after what you did last night? How could I forget? Besides, we got a date for this evening, right?"

She was worried about it, as if she'd been stood up a lot during her life.

"I'd like to, Harmony, but the way this town is right now, it's hard to tell what I'll be doing by this evening. Where's Ma?"

"Up in her office. Want some Early Times?"

"Not now." I went through the casino area. It had the empty feeling of a place that's lost its license. I went upstairs and across the roof. The drapes were open and Ma waved me in. She was sitting behind her desk talking on the phone. She didn't have on the dingleberry hat and whip outfit today. She was all business, in a tailored, lightweight suit. Colonel Joe Saunders was seated across from her. He lifted a couple of fingers in greeting.

"Saw your girl downstairs," I told him. "Sounds as if you ran into some bad luck."

He shook his head briefly. "It's tough, man. I'm beginning to sense bad vibes about this part of the country."

"How's that?"

He nodded toward Ma Leary. "She's getting reports from around town. It's bad, man."

"Your girl suggested you try to buy another car and abandon the camper. Says she'd sort of like to leave the area."

"I wouldn't mind that myself, but the guy who's supposed to pay me for the load of grass is in shooting up the town. I'm not leaving before I get paid."

Ma Leary hung up the phone. "Hello, Pete."

"Hi. How's tricks?"

"Whatever it is you're talking about, they aren't good. There's a lot of badness going on."

"I know, I've seen some of it. You have a lot of animals coming through here dressed up like truck drivers."

She spun her chair half around to stare out the windows. "So?"

"So I imagine that by about now Carl Slide is livid. He has pride, money and connections. He'll be coming back to get you, Ma, you must know that."

"It's not my fault the boys got mad at how I was treated last night. Besides, how did I know what these gorillas would do?"

"Come off it, Ma. I've heard about the operation you have going on out in the sheds. Those aren't a lot of happy-go-lucky knights of the open road. You've got a bunch of crooks operating out of here."

"But I haven't got any control over them. I don't watch what they might be doing out there. And they pay me well for my lack of interest."

"But Slide won't look at it that way. You're the captain, just like aboard ship. You're the one who's responsible, even for what goes on below decks."

She sat and thought for a moment. "What does Slide want?"

"He wants the shed operation closed down. And he wants the Colonel here to find another airfield."

She did some more thinking. “What if all that happened? Would he leave me alone then?”

Saunders scraped his cowboy boots and sat up a little straighter. “Hey, wait a minute, Ma.”

“You stay out of this, fly boy. I have every cent I own invested in this place. It can’t just take off and land somewhere else, the way your business can. Besides, there’s the girls to worry about.”

Saunders muttered an impolite word.

“What do you think, Pete? Would that satisfy Slide?”

“I’m not sure. It might be too late for that now. That’s what he told me last night, before his casino and all the people inside it got torn up. It wasn’t a very pretty sight.”

She tapped a knuckle on her desk top. “How’s your job for Armando going?”

“Just so-so. The things that go on in Sand Valley could cause all sorts of murder and mayhem. I just haven’t got it sorted out yet.”

“Then how about taking a couple hours off to do a little job for me?”

“What kind of job?”

“Go negotiate with Carl Slide for me. See if we can’t stop the fighting before the whole town comes down around our ears. It could put us both out of business. Tell him I’m willing to close down the stolen goods exchange.”

“What about the Colonel here?”

“I’m not willing to go that far. Not yet anyhow.”

Saunders relaxed back in his chair. I looked across at him.

“You must pay her pretty well.”

He made a little face and fanned one hand in the air as if he’d singed his fingers.

“Okay, Ma,” I told her, getting up. “I wanted to have another talk with him anyhow. Do you have any idea what he’s really afraid of?”

“What do you mean?”

"I've gotten the impression he has a sideline going that he doesn't want the rest of the world to learn about."

"I don't know anything about him, beyond his having the same kind of joint that I have here. A little tonier is all."

"I've also learned his brother didn't die of natural causes. Who shot him?"

"Moon did, if you have to know."

I whistled. "How did it happen?"

"I wasn't there, so all my information was second or third-hand. I heard that Burt came toward a scattering of people just leaving church. He had a gun and started shooting. Moon carried a gun too. So he dropped Burt. It was pretty clear-cut."

"I wish you'd told me that last night."

"Last night I had other things on my mind. By the way, how much do you charge?"

"Depends on how much trouble I have getting to see Carl Slide. We'll talk about it later."

Downstairs somebody had put some money into the jukebox. Kris Kristofferson was singing about death again, making everybody feel real good. I waved at Harmony and headed for the front door. She came out from behind the bar and followed me to the car.

"Pete?"

I turned. "What is it, pretty?"

She lowered her eyes and sniffed.

"What's wrong, Harmony? I have an errand to run."

She tugged at my jacket lapels and pressed her face against my shirt. "Don't go, Pete. I'm scared. I'm afraid they'll come back and hurt me. Let's just go on down to my place. I'll take the rest of the day off."

Over her shoulder I noticed the Colonel's girl, Terry, watching us. She had a little smile on her face.

I patted Harmony's behind. "Later, maybe. I have work to do now. Honest. But don't you worry. There are guys around here who know what they're doing. They're very particular who they let in here just now. You'll be okay."

Harmony stepped back and looked up at me with another sniff. She didn't say anything, but her face told me I'd let her down. She turned and went back inside. Terry still watched me with that little smile.

I drove back to the edge of town and phoned Slide's office, explaining that I was on a truce mission. I figured he might have been enraged enough either to refuse to see me or to shoot me on sight. Also, there was no sense in driving through the combat area if there wasn't anybody to talk to once I got there. His voice sounded a little tight, like he was having a problem controlling it, but he agreed to see me. He said he hadn't been at the Sky Lodge when the place was invaded, but he was there now. I drove around the town to park behind the building and went in through the loading dock. The place had a stilled air to it. What staff I saw were still numbed by the ferocity of the raid, and were standing around in groups reliving it all. I didn't have any trouble making my way through to the front and up to Slide's office. A bodyguard was posted outside. He checked with Slide and ushered me in. Slide had been conferring with two more of his hired guns. They left the room and Slide, with elbows on his desk and hands holding the sides of his head, listened to Ma's proposition. He was outwardly calm, but his face had lost some of its color. When I finished talking he leaned back in his chair.

"My personal feelings aside," he began quietly, "about what those apes did to all the innocent people who were working the lounge downstairs when they came through here, my hands are tied. The temporary help I brought in have taken things into their own hands. Some of them were here when the truckers came through. One of them will never see again. A couple of others had bones broken. One of my bartenders downstairs was murdered. We were expecting some attempt at retaliation, but nothing quite like that. It prompted the fellows I brought in to go a little crazy.

They are out to hunt down and kill as many of that raiding party as they can find. They have—again, on their own—phoned other people in other towns. Those additional people are on their way here right now. So the answer is no, Bragg. My boys are going to have their revenge. Nothing I could do will stop them."

"I guess you must have promised them pretty good wages to come in and work for you."

"I promised them pretty good wages."

"Have they been paid?"

"A third of what we agreed on."

"You could call them off under threat of not paying them the rest of it."

"And they could maybe stuff me into the trunk of my own automobile and shoot several hundred rounds of ammunition into it. I am not a foolish man. I am at this moment a sad man. Sad that things got out of hand. But you don't know what went on downstairs."

"For whatever it's worth, I do know. I watched from just across the street. I went through the lounge afterward. I can guess at your feelings. But that's beside the point. If they're not stopped—all of them—they are going to destroy this town. Is that what you want?"

"No, Bragg. And for that I am saddest of all." He wagged his head. "But it's too late. It's just too late."

"Maybe not. And somebody has to make the first move to save it. That's what Ma did by sending me over here."

He stared at me with tight lips, then got to his feet. "Her truckers made enough first moves to last a lifetime. Let me show you something else they did."

He crossed to the closed door to his small bathroom and swung it open. The blue point Siamese cat had been pinned to it by a cargo hook that someone had driven through its neck. There still was a spatter of blood on the bathroom floor that had drained from the cat. Slide closed the door and returned to his desk.

"Now I'll tell you a couple of things with my personal feelings not aside. First, you can tell Ma Leary that I hold her, and Armando Barker before her, personally responsible for what is going on in this town right now. It is going to cause me a great inconvenience. It is going to cause me more inconvenience than she can even imagine. And she does have a limited imagination. Running a cheap whorehouse for working stiffs pushes her to the limit. So I want her out of this town. You can tell her for me she will either leave this town or I will have her killed. Within the next twenty-four hours. Tell her I am not kidding about that.

"Second, is about you, Bragg. I still am not satisfied that you are here for the reason you say you are. But it no longer matters. This town is now coming apart. I am going to be a very busy man trying to salvage what I can. I do not want any other little worries nagging at me. Worries like you. So I want you out of town within one hour. Or I will have you killed. A lot of the guns I hired have seen you. In one hour it is open season on Mr. Peter Bragg. Now beat it."

I'd been hired to get his answer, not exchange threats. When I got to the door his voice stopped me one more time.

"And Bragg. In the event you were telling the truth, and your concern is for the little girl, you don't belong around here anyhow. God knows I have no beef with children, so I might as well tell you. If you want to help her, you belong back in San Francisco."

"How would you know that?"

"Just coincidence. Lou and Soft Kenny were here in the office when the call came in for them."

"What call?"

"I don't know who it was. But it was from San Francisco. It was about a job. I overheard Lou on the phone explain how they already were working. For me. But then they talked price and I guess it was a pretty good offer. Lou said they'd be in San Francisco by this evening."

"Offer to do what?" I asked quietly.

"Lou wouldn't tell me much about it. Didn't mention any names. But he did say they were going to snatch some kid."

"How do you know it's the same girl I'm concerned about?"

"Because Lou did tell me, when he was apologizing about their ducking out on me for the new job, that they'd still be doing me a favor at the same time. He said their new job would be like delivering a kick in the balls to Armando Barker. Wishful thinking will get you nowhere, Bragg. It's the same girl, all right."

SIXTEEN

I had to make an important phone call, but I didn't want to do it from Slide's place. I drove back down Nevada Street, looking for a phone booth that hadn't been shot up or run over. Except for the car that the truck had smashed, now shoved over to one side of the street, the next intersection and street beyond were empty. Somehow the two forces had disengaged. Maybe everybody had to go over to the bullet factory to stock up again. Two more intersections ahead I saw a funny sight. A truck roared through along the cross street. A couple of seconds later a pair of cars raced through, apparently in pursuit of the truck. A few seconds more and another truck barreled through after the cars, and I heard gunfire fading in the distance. It was like a floating shooting gallery around town.

I found an intact phone booth outside the drugstore. I parked and used my credit card to phone Armando Barker. It took him a while to answer.

"Yeah?"

"Peter Bragg here."

"How are things going?"

"Good and bad. Things will never be the same in Sand Valley, but that isn't what I called about, and I'm in a hurry. I want you to go fetch Beverly Jean and go some place. Quietly. Take a week off and enjoy the sights of one of the outer Hawaiian Islands or something. Some place very remote. But fast."

He hocked and coughed for a while. A truck tractor without a trailer came up the street. The guys inside were looking for trouble. I thought for a minute they'd leave me alone. Then the guy sitting beside the driver leaned out with a handgun. I ducked low in the booth while the guy shot up the glass panels overhead.

"What the hell is that?" Barker asked.

I brushed bits of glass from my hair and around my collar while the tractor picked up speed and continued on down Nevada. "The gun salesman's been through town and everybody's out practicing," I told him. "How soon can you get packed and pick up the girl and get out of town?"

"I can't. I got a trick knee that goes out on me from time to time. This is one of the times. I'm hobbling around here on crutches. Why, what's up?"

"There are a couple of hired guns coming your way. They've been working for Carl Slide, doing some dirty business down here, but he says they just took another job, up in San Francisco. And from what Slide told me, it sounds as if it involves you and the girl. These are very bad guys. If you can't do it yourself, send somebody you can trust. Have them check into a motel somewhere outside of town. Keep in touch by phone."

"How about Connie? The girl who runs the restaurant for me. She's a good head."

I agreed that she seemed to be a good head, but there were things about Connie Wells that I didn't like. Either she lied when she told me she had no contact with Harvey Pastor, or he lied when he told me differently. Maybe it was just a coincidence that out of the hundreds of piano players in the western United States, it turned out to be Harvey Pastor who was working in Sand Valley right then. Maybe Harvey lied out of sheer boastfulness. Maybe Connie lied because she wanted to see more of me and didn't want me thinking she had anything to do with her ex-husband. It was altogether too many maybes.

"I don't want you to send Connie. Don't even tell her about it. I don't want to spend the time explaining it right now, but there's stuff in her background that needs more looking into. How about sending Bobbie? She and the girl seem to get along okay."

"Are you kidding me? Trust Beverly Jean to Bobbie? I mean Bobbie's a nice kid, but she wouldn't know the time of day if she worked in a clock shop."

"She might have some qualities you overlooked. But have it your way. If you don't want to send her, get somebody else. How about that Adkins woman, or one of her girls at the massage parlors?"

"I wouldn't feel right about that, either." He thought about it some and cleared his throat a dozen times. "Tell me honest, Bragg. You really think Bobbie's got something cooking upstairs?"

"Sure I do."

"Okay, I guess it'll have to be her. Anyways, how smart do you have to be in order to check into a motel?"

"Is she there?"

"No, I sent her out to the liquor store. This knee hurts like hell when it's acting up. Can't do much for myself."

"That's tough. Anyhow, have Bobbie get the girl out of the Academy right away and go into hiding. Call ahead and have them pack a bag for her. The guys on their way up are named Lou and Kenny. Lou's about your age and size, only he doesn't have curls on his forehead. The one they call Soft Kenny is something else. He's in his twenties, slender, has a fair complexion, about five feet ten. He's got a screw loose and likes to hurt people. Can Bobbie use a gun?"

"I don't know."

"Ask her. If she can't, give her one, and a couple of lessons to go with it."

"You make it sound like maybe this is the sort of thing I hired you to do."

"Not quite. I still think that Sand Valley is where I'll learn who's behind it all. And if I don't learn that, there'll always be guys like Lou and Soft Kenny heading for San Francisco."

He accepted that and promised to do what I'd asked. I hung up and stepped out of the booth to shake the rest of the glass off me and my clothes. I also tried to decide what I should do next. It really wasn't my job to spend any more time trying to save the citizens of Sand Valley from the heathens. It was to find out who was complicating Armando Barker's life. On the other hand, Armando was a fellow who could look out for himself, and I had a lot of faith in Bobbie's being able to look after the little girl. While the citizens of Sand Valley appeared to need all the help they could get.

Another ambulance sirened past. In the end, it's usually something like the sound of an ambulance that makes up my mind for me. I'd try doing the citizens one more good turn. I went over to the car and drove to city hall.

They had used a fire engine to shove aside the truck that had bottled up the driveway into the police parking lot. A pair of officers wearing helmets and carrying rifles came down the front stairs. They told me Chief Coffey was back up in his office. I found him alone, standing and staring out the window with his hands clasped behind his back.

"How are things, Chief?"

He didn't turn from the window, but just took a breath a little deeper than normal. "We're doing all right for the moment. I have men with rifles up on roofs around the business district to guard against looting. I have men at barricades on streets leading into the residential section to keep out whoever doesn't belong there. The local radio and TV stations are warning everyone to stay home. I'm hoping things'll settle down as the day goes on. Maybe everyone will get tired of shooting at one another and go on back to wherever they came from. I've been trying to get calls through to Carl Slide and Ma Leary to see if we can't work out something."

"Nothing will work out," I told him. "I just came from Carl Slide. Ma Leary sent me to see if I could arrange a truce. Slide says he's lost control of the men he brought in. I doubt if Ma would have much better luck trying to pull back some of the fellows from her place. None of them care about the town. They're just out for each others' blood. Slide said his men have sent for reinforcements."

Coffey turned around. "He told you that?"

"He did. They're out of control. His gang, her gang, the whole bunch of them."

The chief sat at his desk. He looked as if he might throw up onto it.

"The town needs help, Chief. More than you can give it. It'll take a whole bunch of state police or maybe even the Army. I wouldn't settle for National Guard. By the time they got mobilized there wouldn't be any town left. At any rate, it's time somebody put in a call to the state capitol and asked for help. If nobody else will, I'll do it myself. But it would look better if the call came from you."

I felt a little sorry for him. It was all on his face, the way he glanced around the office. The good life as Merle Coffey had known it was slipping away, and there wasn't much he could do about it. All he could do was think of next best things. Give a thought to the citizens, even. He shook his head and flipped a key on his call box. He asked somebody to get him the governor's office. I waited until the call went through and he was beginning to describe the jam folks were in before I left.

Downstairs I found another phone booth and dialed the Truck Stop to give Ma the bad news. She swore for a while, then settled down enough to say she'd been talking with somebody just minutes ago in Chief Coffey's office who was trying to arrange a truce.

"And now you're telling me that even Coffey can't arrange it?"

"That's what I'm telling you."

"Christ Almighty! Well what do I do now, Bragg? Turn tail and run or stick around here and take a chance on getting some more of the girls hurt?"

"I'd stick, for now at least. A lot of what Slide said was just talking through his hat. What he would like to do and what he can do aren't quite the same. The two gangs of thugs chasing around town are more interested in themselves right now than they are in you and Slide. And Merle Coffey is doing the unthinkable. He phoned the governor's office for help. I would guess some people will arrive by tonight and start getting things calmed down again. Have you got any straight truckers around there now?"

"What do you mean by straight?"

"Guys just interested in the cheap drinks and pretty legs. Not connected with your shed operation."

"Quite a few of them, as a matter of fact. They're sort of fascinated by what's going on."

"Good. A lot of those guys carry handguns to ward off hijackers. Ask some of them to keep guard on your place. Don't bother with the warehouses across the way. Let the ones who've been into that operation look out for themselves."

"Okay, Bragg. And I guess for as long as Joe and Sam are here they'd help out too."

"They haven't left yet? That's interesting. Could you get the Colonel on the phone for me?"

"Sure. He's downstairs. I'll get him."

While I waited I thought of another phone call to make. The Colonel came on to the line.

"Yeah?"

"Bragg here. How much longer do you think you'll be in town?"

"I don't know. The jerk who contracted for this load is still running around town like it was the Fourth of July. I don't transfer goods until I get paid. Period."

"You figure your plane is safe?"

"I don't figure anything. I phoned down and had them roll it into the hangar and told them to stay out of sight with a lot of guns at hand. With a little luck, anybody interested will think we flew out. Why do you ask?"

"I figure before the day's over I'd maybe like a plane ride. Yours is the closest one around."

"It'll be around until I get paid. Then it's up, up and away."

"Ma probably told you about how it went last night."

"She did."

"About the young psychotic called Soft Kenny."

"Yeah."

"He and his partner are on the way to San Francisco. I think maybe they have a date with the little girl I told you about."

He thought about it some.

"I can't promise anything, Bragg. I guess maybe I owe you a favor for this morning, but you know how it is around this crazy town. I just can't promise."

"Okay, don't promise. Just keep thinking about that little girl and Soft Kenny. You're a big boy, Colonel. And you have three able men plus a girl who knows how to handle a pistol well enough to give me pause. I need a couple hours. Maybe a little more."

"What for?"

"I need answers. I've been here almost twenty-four hours, but I've been sidetracked by all the activities around town."

"There's a lot in town to keep you off balance," he agreed.

"I'm going to concentrate on my own work now. If I knew you'd be here another couple of hours it would help my concentration."

"All right. Call it six o'clock. Let me hear from you by then, either here or at the field."

I took down the number of his phone in the hangar and thanked him a couple of times.

The next call was to my office in San Francisco. I'd queried a lot of people my first day on the case, about Barker and Moon and Sand Valley. Maybe one of them had turned up something by then. But it turned out there only had been one call, and that just ten minutes earlier. Only it wasn't from one of the people in San Francisco I'd talked to on Sunday. It had been from Mrs. Foster. She left word that I should go back out to Sand Valley Hospital when I had the opportunity. She said Mr. Morton, the banker I'd taken out there, wanted to talk to me. She'd said he had some information for me.

SEVENTEEN

The first thing I did at the hospital was to congratulate Mrs. Foster for having had the presence of mind to reach me through my office in San Francisco.

"It's not all that sensational, young man. Being around doctors you learn about offices and answering services and the people who use them."

I was directed to a private room on the second floor. A nurse went in to see if Morton were conscious. He was. The nurse cautioned me to keep my visit short, and left us.

Morton had a little of his color back, but he was far from well. The head of his bed was elevated slightly. Without his glasses, the pale patches of skin around his eyes made his face look run-down, ready for replacement. The wounded arm rested limply alongside him. He smiled up weakly at me.

"I was afraid you wouldn't get here in time. They want to give me something more to knock me out again. I told them to wait a little while. To try getting in touch with you. Young Cathy Carson stopped in to say hello when she came in to work. She's the one who told me you aren't in the poster business after all."

"That's right, Mr. Morton. But I didn't want to alarm anybody about my real reason for being here."

"It doesn't matter, Bragg. They also tell me you're the one who scraped me up and brought me in here. Maybe saved my life, even."

"I won't be around for long. A local cop named Michaels helped. You might remember that."

"I will. Thanks."

"They said I couldn't stay for long, Mr. Morton. What did you want to see me about?"

"Are things still going to hell around town?"

"It's worse. Two warring factions are out there, one brought in by Carl Slide, the other from out at the Truck Stop. They're out of control. Merle Coffey has called the governor's office for help. I think there'll be some changes around town."

Morton took a shallow breath and shook his head. "I was afraid of that. I was afraid of that lying there on the pavement after I'd been shot. It wasn't really so bad, you know, being shot. I felt sort of numb is all, and it would have been all right except for Mrs. Morse, one of the ladies trapped in the doorway with me. She kept wailing about how I'd been shot and was bleeding to death and all. That's what unsettled me. She had me half convinced I was dying, and I was too weak to ask her to pipe down."

His voice played out in a little rasp, and his eyes drifted to the water glass with a plastic straw in it on the stand beside him.

"Should you?" I asked.

"Please. It's all right."

I held the water so he could have some. He nodded his thanks and his head sank back to the pillow.

"Funny," he continued, "how the questions you had asked me in my office earlier came back to me while I was lying there. Law and order sort of stuff. One thing leading to another. I remember how I'd bragged to you about keeping outside elements out of Sand Valley. I guess we haven't done that after all."

"It doesn't look that way."

There was a rustle behind me. I turned. A nurse gave me a warning frown and went away.

"They won't give me much more time, Mr. Morton."

"All right. I guess you're here on some kind of job, Mr. Bragg. I know a lot of things about this town, both good and bad. I can even suspect the sort of thing that might attract a private investigator.

I think you saved my life today. I'm of a mind to help you in return, if I can. Do you want to tell me about your job, or just ask some random questions."

"I'll ask, it'll save time. Do you know Carl Slide well?"

"Quite well, in a business way. He's a director of the bank."

"Now that is something. Mr. Morton, I have a very strong suspicion that there is something a lot more questionable than girls and gambling that Mr. Slide is dabbling in. Could you offer any suggestions?"

He didn't answer right away. His jaws worked slowly in a random pattern and he stared at the foot of the bed. "Well, Mr. Bragg, you have a way of getting to the heart of things." He raised up on his good elbow with some difficulty. "Close that door over there."

I closed it.

"This is my suggestion. I couldn't prove it right now, of my own knowledge, but I know it in my heart. And an investigation of the bank's activities and holdings might prove it. I have had a routine of processing enough transactions to know that something like this is taking place."

"Like what, Mr. Morton?"

"Mr. Slide has ambitions to move on to bigger things, Mr. Bragg. Like the action in Las Vegas."

"I've heard that."

"He has come close two or three times, I believe, and after the last unsuccessful attempt I believe he made certain arrangements with certain parties, to ensure his success the next time he might try. As you might be aware, there have been government investigators concentrating again on Las Vegas in recent months. They suspect that it has become an important center of financial activity to organized crime. And I'm not talking about the fleecing that goes on out on the casino floors, Mr. Bragg. I'm speaking of the laundry that operates elsewhere."

And then I knew what caused Carl Slide's stomach muscles to go slack when he thought about outside probers. "Stolen securities?"

"Absolutely, Mr. Bragg. Absolutely. There have been millions of dollars worth of securities stolen in this country that haven't surfaced. They haven't surfaced because they become valuable again without exposing the holders by being posted as securities for loans. Some of them make their way to Europe, but not all of them by any means. You can bury them for forty years by posting them for loans." He was growing weaker, and lay back down on the bed.

"You think Slide has been doing that at the bank here in town?"

"I am certain of it. There is a quirk or two in this state's banking laws that would make it easier here than in lots of other places. As I said…a thorough investigation…"

He closed his eyes and swallowed a couple of times.

"Mr. Morton, are you up to one more question?"

He nodded, with his eyes closed.

"Did you know a former policeman here named John Caine?"

His eyes blinked open. "Funny you should have heard about him. Yes, I knew him. And I think he suspected what Slide was doing. He made inquiries. I talked to him briefly. He was a little oblique in his approach. I didn't know what he was getting at. Didn't suspect it myself just then. It wasn't until later."

"I understand Caine was suspected in turn of accepting some kind of payoff money. I heard he had a special bank account! Could it have been at your bank?"

"Yes, but I'm a little hazy about that. I don't remember who opened it, in Caine's name. He might not even have known about it. But I do remember the man who made deposits to it twice a month regularly, in cash. He caught my attention on several occasions, and I asked around to see what he was doing. A rough-looking fellow."

"Do you remember his name?"

"No, I can't think of it now. He was a big fellow. Dressed colorfully. I believe he was some sort of henchman for another unsavory character who used to live here. Fellow named Barker. He owned the Truck Stop before Ma Leary took over."

"Would you remember if they called the big fellow who made the deposits Moon?"

He smiled weakly. "Yes, that was it. Funny name. Fearsome fellow with a funny name. Moon. That was it."

The door behind me opened and nurse Cathy Carson stalked into the room with a hypodermic needle in her hand. She pushed me aside and shot something into Morton's good arm.

"You ought to be ashamed of yourself," she told me. "When I heard you were still in here talking to poor Mr. Morton I almost fixed one of these things for you," she said, waving the needle under my nose. She ushered me out of the room and followed.

"You look cute in white. Does that mean you're chaste?"

"I don't flirt while I'm on duty. Why did you have to stay with him for so long?"

"There were things I wanted to know and that he wanted to tell me."

"What sort of things?"

"All sorts. How is it going down in emergency receiving?"

"It's quieting, somewhat. We've taken in ten or our local citizens and two policemen for gunshot wounds."

"How about the outsiders shooting at one another?"

"We've had the bodies of five strangers brought in. No wounded. They must be looking after their own."

"Not too bad for all the gunfire going on."

"I hope it ends soon. We're not used to this much activity."

"I think it will. Outside law enforcement people have been sent for. Can you spare a couple more minutes?"

"For what?"

"Anything more you can tell me about the day Burt Slide was shot. You said the ex-cop, John Caine, brought him in. Burt was unconscious. Caine had been drinking. Caine witnessed the shooting and said Burt started it. What else can you remember? What else did Caine say?"

She thought for a moment. "After they wheeled Burt Slide into surgery, Mr. Caine sat in a corner of the lobby. He looked very distraught. I went over to try comforting him. He said a funny thing. He said it was his fault."

"The shooting?"

"I guess so. He said the girl, Theresa Moore, had phoned him and warned there was apt to be trouble when Mass let out. He tried to get there in time to stop it, but was too late."

"So Caine knew Theresa Moore too."

"Oh, yes. She got into some minor scrape a few years back. Mr. Caine sort of took her on as his own responsibility. His wife was still alive then. They let the girl live with them for a few months."

"When was all of this?"

"Quite a long time ago. I don't remember if I was even out of high school then."

"You don't look as if it could have been all that long ago."

"Now you're flirting again, Mr. Bragg."

"What else is a guy to do around here?"

I followed her back down to the reception area. Her crisp white uniform didn't detract at all from her appearance. I wondered why it was I had to run into her just then in my life. Back in San Francisco was slender, impish Bobbie, who wanted to make me feel boy-girl silly. And I think she could somehow manage that. And here was nurse Cathy Carson with her dark, wise eyes, efficient, smart and playful. I'd always been a lousy juggler when it came to women. I hunched my shoulders, figuring I was setting myself up for some hilarious trouble, but thinking it might be worth it.

Cathy walked over to a desk at a nursing station to speak with the people there, then came back and walked outside with me.

"It looks as if the good guys are going to win," she said. "None of the gunshot victims are in danger any longer."

"That's good news. Maybe you could take some time off, then."

"Maybe."

"You could even consider coming up to San Francisco and letting me show you around, maybe."

"I'm a very independent woman, Mr. Bragg. I can consider almost anything. It would all depend."

"What on?"

"Different things. You really are serious about this, aren't you?"

"I think I am."

"What sort of hospital insurance do you have?"

It made me blink, but the face with the wise eyes wasn't giving any clues as to why she had asked. "I don't have any."

"Why not?"

"I'm healthy as a horse. It's expensive. I don't have a boss to share the cost of the premiums. And I don't plan on getting hurt."

She gave me a womanly little snort. "You may not plan on it, brother, but it looks to me as if it's already happened one time not long ago. What is it you're doing here in Sand Valley?"

"I'm trying to find out who's been threatening the lives of people in San Francisco. Somebody from around here, I suspect. The most recently threatened person is a little girl. That's Theresa Moore's child. Whoever threatened her had earlier threatened a big lout named Moon. He's the man who shot Burt Slide. Moon was murdered this last Monday. I came down here to try to put an end to it. Why do you want to know?"

"I have to have an idea about how far you might go in some directions. I'll be candid with you, Mr. Peter Bragg. I would not, ordinarily, consider tripping off someplace to spend a few days with somebody I've known for such a brief time. But there is something unique about you. I think it might really be fun. And I've always wanted to explore the area around San Francisco. But I'm rather of two minds about it. I'm a little worried that having even a brief encounter with you could eventually do bad things to a girl's head. At least this girl's head."

"Why is that?"

"The sort of work you do. I was very close one time to a boy who lived here in Sand Valley. He climbed on a jet plane one day, just like in the song, and flew to Vietnam. He didn't come back. I don't think I ever fully recovered from that. I wouldn't want to experience anything the least bit like that again. Not ever."

"I could understand your feeling that way about a regular cop, maybe. But it's not the same for a private investigator. We get to pick and choose the risks we take."

"And what sort of risks do you pick and choose?"

"It depends."

"What if you think a little girl's life is at stake?"

I shrugged. "I might take a little bigger one than normally."

She leaned back against the front of the building, her arms folded across her tidy chest. All she said was, "Yes, Peter, I think we've hit on it."

"Look, Cathy, I'm not suggesting a profound and disturbing relationship. I can't handle those things any longer. I just thought we could spend a pleasant few days together. A little time in the sun at Stinson Beach. Lingering cocktail hours. Some cha-cha-cha in the Venetian Room at the Fairmont. Cable car rides, the view from Telegraph Hill. A ferry boat ride on the Bay. A climb up Mt. Tamalpais. Maybe a little time in each other's arms."

"I'm telling you up front, Peter. I'd just be a little bit afraid of making love with a person who two hours later might be lying in a cold metal bin in the coroner's office."

"I wouldn't work while you were in town."

"But sometimes things from the past have a way of looping into your life again when you least expect them. From clear out of the ballpark, as you men might say. It happens to me. It must happen to you as well."

"Sure it does. But if you're not careful you can slip in the shower and brain yourself too. I try to be that careful, all the time."

"I hope so, Peter. Really. But I'll have to think about it some more. Try to give me a call before you leave town, huh?"

"Sure." I watched her go back inside, took a deep breath and headed for my car. Someday, I knew, it was going to happen. Someday, right in the middle of a job I was doing for some troubled sap, I was going to say to hell with it and go out and get a normal job again, just like other people. Someday. But for right then I had to take one of those little risks Cathy Carson had been asking about.

EIGHTEEN

I parked a block away from the Sky Lodge and hiked around to the loading dock for my normally furtive entrance. I was beginning to feel like the guy who filled prophylactic machines in the men's room. The place was back in business, more or less. The casino was patched up and operating. A temporary plywood front had been put up in place of the glass in the lobby. Some large characters with bulges in their armpits were sitting around keeping an eye on things. There were new security measures in force. Guards blocked all the stairways leading upstairs to the mezzanine. I didn't have much choice. I used a house phone to call Slide's office. I think my brashness was beginning to intrigue him.

"I assume you're calling from about a hundred miles down the road, Bragg."

"No, Slide, I'm right here in the house again. I have to talk to you one more time. By my reckoning, I have another few minutes before your guys are supposed to hang me out to dry."

"That's right, but it doesn't mean we have anything to talk about."

"I think we do. I hear tell you run a laundromat for some people in Las Vegas."

What could he do besides sit and suck air through his teeth for a while?

"All right, you bastard, come on up."

I was intercepted in the hallway and relieved of both the handguns I'd been dumb enough to carry. Then they led me down to Slide's office. Three mugs occupied all the extra chairs in the room. Nobody stood up to offer me one of them. I nodded to Slide and sat on one corner of his desk.

"Dumb," I told him.

"What?"

I indicated the room with a wave of my hand. "I should think you would have moved your command post. You're lucky you weren't in when the bully boys swept through this morning. They must know this is where you hang your hat, from what they did to the poor cat. If they come back..."

Slide stared at the ceiling and took a deep breath. He told one of his aides to check at the downstairs desk to see what was available. The messenger got up and left. I sat in his chair.

"Just so you know where we stand," Slide told me, "I hate your fucking guts. But you are smart, I'll give you that. Want these guys to leave?"

I leaned forward with elbows on my knees. "Frankly, Carl, I don't care whether they do or not. Because I don't think any longer that my business touches on theirs—meaning yours. That laundromat I mentioned on the phone, I'm not here about that."

"How did you get on to that, by the way?"

"You know better than to ask. Carl, you're classic. You're just like Armando. Heavy-handed, blunt and suspicious. And I'm not any more interested in seeing you again than you are in seeing me. The only thing I'm interested in is how to make the world just a little more secure for a little girl in San Francisco. And for that reason, I had to come back and talk to you one more time about your brother Burt, and a girl named Theresa."

Slide did something with his eyebrows that prompted the other two gents in the room to get up and leave.

"Let's get it over with," he told me.

"I've heard some rumors. That maybe a story about Theresa Moore having a husband in the Army who got wasted in Nam was just that. A story. I heard some gossip that maybe the baby girl was Burt's."

A faint color spread across Slide's cheeks and reached for his throat. Other than that he didn't react.

"If that were true," I continued, "maybe you would have an urge to help me in my job even more. Because I never lied to you about what my job here is. It's to keep that girl from harm. And if she really was your brother's daughter, that would make you her uncle."

"But I'm not," he said quietly. "I would be her uncle if I were Armando's brother, not Burt's."

I sat back in my chair. It didn't make sense for Armando not to have told me that. "You're saying Armando is the child's natural father, not just her stepfather?"

"That's exactly what I'm saying. It's why my brother is dead. Why I couldn't do anything about him being dead. It's just one of those—tragedies, you know, like they make those tearjerk soap operas out of. Only it really happened."

"Will you tell me about it?"

"There's not much to tell. The Sunday morning it happened, I was here in the office working. My brother and Armando both had been chasing after this Theresa Moore. I couldn't understand it, myself, but you know how it is with girls. Some attract certain guys. She attracted those two. She had for years. I was glad when she left town. Burt met another girl and married her, but it didn't last. When Theresa Moore came back to town with the little girl, I prayed that Burt wouldn't get mixed up with her again. Aside from that one conflict, Armando and I managed to do our own thing without getting in each other's way. But within a week of Theresa Moore being back in town it was like old times. It went on that way for several months, then that Sunday morning Burt stormed in here like a madman.

"He'd just been out to see Theresa. By then she was pretty thick with Armando, and wasn't seeing much of Burt. Armando was brought up in the church, though, and he still went to Mass on Sundays. So it was a good time for my brother to stop in and visit Theresa. This Sunday she told Burt he'd have to stop seeing her. She told him she and Armando planned to get married. Burt tried talking her out of it. That's when she let him have it right between the eyes. She told him the baby girl was Armando's child."

He hunched around in his chair some before continuing. "He stormed in here, Burt did, half crazy. He told me what Theresa had told him, got a pistol out of the safe and steamed on out. I tried to stop him, but he was not stoppable that morning. I went after him, but it was all over by the time I got to the church. Moon went everywhere Barker went, so of course he was at the church too. Mass was letting out when Burt had got there and made his dumb play. People who saw it say Burt got off a couple of shots in Armando's direction. They say Moon even yelled at him to stop shooting, but Burt ignored him. It goes to show how you shouldn't get into the shooting business when you're so upset. Burt was pretty good with a gun, most times. Anyhow, Moon finally shot him. Just once. And there wasn't anything I could do, you know? I'd lost my brother, but who could I blame? Theresa, maybe. But before long it became common knowledge that she wasn't going to live much longer. So that was that. There wasn't anyone I could hate, even. It's hard, when your brother dies that way, and you can't have someone to hate."

"You don't hate the little girl, do you?"

"Of course not."

"Then level with me. Is she really the reason why Lou and Soft Kenny went to San Francisco? And who hired them?"

He sat staring at me, weighing things. It took a while, but as he regained his composure and his face once more took on its perpetually enduring granite quality, I knew I'd lost.

"I don't know," he told me. He got up and walked over to the door and held it open for me. I asked for my firearms back. He said he'd mail them to me.

Walking back to the car I heard a new outburst of gunfire. It sounded as if it were coming from the direction of Doc Carrington's newspaper office. I wondered what sort of job he would do in the next issue of the *Sand Valley Piper*, describing the events of the day. Maybe somebody in Washington would write an editorial deploring the mess in Sand Valley: "The Wild West Lives."

But brooding over reprehensible journalism wasn't helping my own problems any. In fact the longer I spent in Sand Valley the more unreal it seemed, compared with its links to San Francisco. Armando was a ham hock, but he seemed sort of comic and real. A different sort from the evil realities of Sand Valley that day. And the little girl hardly seemed a product of the town or of Armando either. It was hard to bridge the psychic distance. Part of the problem of course was that it didn't add up in orderly fashion. Not that I was apt to let that bother me. I'd had jobs in which I hadn't understood what it'd been all about even after doing the work and getting my pay. But it wouldn't work out that way this time. I'd have to figure out the link between the violence of Sand Valley and Armando and Beverly Jean and Moon's death.

I leaned against the side of my car, staring down deserted streets and listening to distant gun battles. I had forgotten to ask Slide if he intended still to leave in force the orders for my own scalp. Probably he did, I decided. He still wanted me out of town and he didn't like me.

I thought about Cathy Carson. Copper legs and a white beach with blue water. An expensive hotel room with air conditioning and tall rum drinks and piped in music. I thought about Beverly Jean and her grown-up ways and the wall and fence around the Mission Academy for Girls, and Lou and Soft Kenny. I'd been impressed when I'd seen the security arrangements at the Academy. But then I hadn't been thinking about guys like Lou and Soft Kenny. I hoped Bobbie and the girl were well away from there.

By now the phone booth in front of the drug store had been shot up some more, making it inoperable. I drove around looking for another. There was just one more ghost in this town I could think to go chasing after. When I finally found another phone I called the hospital and asked for Cathy. When she got on the line I asked her if the ex-cop, John Caine, had any relatives left in town. She said no. I asked where Caine used to live. She knew approximately, but didn't know the house number. So next I called the police station again. Coffey was out of the building, but after I briefly explained my business, the desk officer looked up Caine's old address for me. I thanked him and headed out that way. There's an astonishing quality I'd learned about old houses. Sometimes they can tell you things. The sort of things that have gone on inside them. Things to make you smile, or things to make you shiver. I was hoping that John Caine's old house would have a story for me.

NINETEEN

My ID got me through police roadblocks and into the town's residential area. I found the address I'd been given was in an older part of town. The homes all looked as if they'd been built between the two World Wars. They were high-ceilinged and two-storied for the most part. Frame construction with overlapping board siding and some filigree around the edges as if someone from there had driven through the older sections of Alameda and San Francisco and Oakland and tried to put down some of it in this desert town. The old Caine home was a boxy place that needed a coat of paint and some yard work. I parked across the street and went over and up the front walk, stepping over a tricycle and toy dump truck. The door was open and inside a television set was competing with children's voices. The doorbell didn't work and it took a while rapping on the open door to get some attention. The smell of food steamed down the hallway and into the late afternoon air.

A slight, dark-complexioned man with a thin black mustache and a napkin in his hand came to the door. I apologized for interrupting his dinner.

"I'm looking for information about a man who used to live here. His name was John Caine. Did you know him?"

"No, sir, I have never heard that name before," he told me with a faintly Latin accent. "We bought this home through the real estate. We did not know the people who lived here before us."

A small head peered around the far end of the hallway, from where the man had come. It must have been the kitchen. Up front, off to one side, was a room with scuffed, overstuffed furniture. A picture of the Madonna hung on one wall and votive candles were on a mantle. I had thought it would help if I could prowl through the place, but there were new forces at work there now. Maybe the old house would have forgotten much of what I wanted to know. I thanked the man and went back down the walk.

There was a vacant lot to one side of the house. A home, closed up and dark, was on the other. I crossed the street to my car, but didn't climb in right away. I had parked in front of another big old house, but this one was well tended, and the lawn was green and trim. Of more interest was the old fellow standing just inside a little picket gate, drawing on a pipe and watching me. I crossed to him.

"Excuse me, sir, I wonder if you could help me. Have you lived here long?"

"Long enough. You selling aluminum siding?"

I grinned. "No."

"Painted shutters? Air conditioners? Insurance or encyclopedias?"

"I'm not selling anything. In fact, I'd be more likely to buy, if I could find what I was looking for."

He gave me a good once-over. He was a man past seventy, erect and alert, wearing a New York Mets baseball cap. The hand clasping the pipe was large and freckled.

"I thought the police were keeping strangers out of here," he said finally. "What is it you'd buy?"

"Information." I took out one of my cards and gave it to him. He held it up in the fading daylight and studied it.

"You have anything a little more official-looking than this?"

I showed him the photostat of my license.

"This for real?"

"As real as they make them."

He handed it back. "You carry a gun?"

"I was carrying two of them until a little bit ago."

"What happened a little bit ago?"

"Somebody took them away from me." I opened my jacket and showed him the empty holsters.

That got to him. He had a good laugh over it, swung open the gate and invited me in. He led me over to a cluster of lawn furniture. He sat in a canvas chair and I settled on the edge of a bench he might have pinched from a park somewhere.

"Bragg, huh? My name's Nolan. Tom Nolan. What sort of information are you after?"

"I'm looking for somebody who might have known John Caine. I was told he used to live across the street from you. Did you know him?"

"Yes, I knew him."

"Good. I'm curious about him. What sort of man he was."

Tom Nolan studied me awhile, then knocked the cold ashes from his pipe. "Why don't you first of all tell me about the job you're on."

"That would take quite a bit of time."

"Splendid. I have plenty of that these days."

"You don't look it."

"What does that mean?"

"I mean you look to be pretty active and alert for such an old fart. I figured you must keep busy doing things."

He liked that and blessed me with another grin. "Well, I don't have my head as stimulated as much of the time as I'd like. And that's what any information I might have is going to cost you. Don't need your money, but I'd be interested in your story."

He meant it, so I told him as quickly as I could what my problems were, why I'd come to Sand Valley, about Beverly Jean and Moon and Armando. I didn't go into all the gang fighting downtown. I figured he probably knew as much about that as I did. Tom Nolan listened attentively. When I'd finished he remained still, as if marshaling a few thoughts of his own.

"That's some story," he said finally. "But I'm afraid I don't know anything much that could help you."

"What about Caine's leaving the police force? The chief says he was on the take."

"The chief is a crook. I wouldn't believe anything he says."

"But there was a bank account. And there were regular deposits made into it."

"I don't know why that was. It was John's bank account, but he told me he hadn't used it for years. I believed him. He said somebody was trying to frame him, to keep him from doing his job. He was on to something big, and he was trying to find ways to prove it to the state attorney general's office. He kept trying to do that even after they forced him out of his job."

"I've heard that. But what made him quit digging?"

Nolan took a gusty sigh. "Maybe he just got tired of it all."

"That doesn't make sense. A man lives in a place for as long as John Caine did doesn't act that way. If he was a good cop, the way some people seem to think, he got wind of something he felt threatened his town. I mean, I know cops, Mr. Nolan."

"Well, he started drinking, John did." The old man shook his head and patted around his pockets for a tobacco pouch. "A terrible waste."

He found the pouch and began stoking another pipe. "He'd be drunk by midday, and he'd just stay that way. After..." His voice broke, and he cleared it. "After he killed himself they found empty bottles under his bed. He either lay there and drank them during the day, or he woke up and drank from them at night. Have you ever seen a man destroy himself that way, Mr. Bragg?"

"I've seen some after they'd gotten that way. I never spent any time around them while they were doing it."

"It is a tragic, tragic thing."

"How long was it before he died that he started drinking that way?"

"It was several months, at least."

"Less than a year?"

"I would say so. Not more than that."

"That's surprising. Most of the heavy drinkers I've encountered have been that way for years. Something must have made him do it that suddenly. Something pretty big."

Nolan wasn't ready to tell me what it might have been, if he even knew. He stalled around diddling with his pipe then struck a match getting it going just the way he wanted. It was just slightly maddening. I was running out of time. There was a generation between us, and I had to cross it in a hurry.

"I guess you must be retired, Mr. Nolan."

"Yes, sir."

"What did you do before?"

"Did a lot of things. Was a cowboy up in Montana when I was just a youngster. Drifted around a lot. Fought in a war. You don't want to hear about all that."

"But it's a part of my technique."

"What technique?"

I pursed my lips a minute, then shrugged. "Okay, you're an intelligent man. I'll tell you about it. You see, Mr. Nolan, I don't think you're being as frank with me as I'd like. So I was going to work around to which job you'd liked the most of all the things you'd done. Then I was going to compare that to John Caine and his job, being a cop. He sounds as if he was a good one. He must have liked his work. Something turned him into a quitter. The people who run the town didn't do that, because he kept on acting like a cop even after he was bumped off the force. It was something else. Something that made him drop his investigation of what was happening to his town, and hit him so hard that he had to turn to heavy drinking to keep his mind off it, or at least to dull it enough so it didn't hurt so much. I'm trying to find out what that was, because it might be tied to whoever is now threatening my client and the little girl. I think you could tell me what it was, Mr. Nolan. If you just understood how important it might be."

I had gotten him thinking about it. He stared off across the street to where the television and kid's voices and the smell of food came out an open door.

"You're another intelligent man, Mr. Bragg. Yes, I could tell you what it was that hit John Caine like a mule's kick, but there isn't any way it could be connected to your problems, I don't think. It was just a tragic, personal thing. I think I'm the only living person John ever told about it. And I've never told another soul."

"I'm not here to get information I can spread around, Mr. Nolan. I never do that unless it's mighty important that I do. About the worst thing you could tell me was that John Caine killed somebody in circumstances other than in the line of duty. But brutal as it is, murder is an understandable crime, in some instances."

"No," he said so quietly I could hardly hear him. "It wasn't a killing. Quite the opposite." He took the pipe out of his mouth and wrapped both hands around it, staring at the glowing tobacco as if he might find something there that he'd lost. "You see, it's something that had happened quite a few years earlier, only John didn't know it then.

"You say that you've heard rumors that the little girl, Theresa Moore's daughter, was Burt Slide's. And you say that Carl Slide told you it was Armando Barker's. Well, that's all baloney. John Caine fathered that child."

I leaned forward with a tingling at the base of my neck.

"John had known Theresa Moore for many years. He and his wife took her in for a period. It wasn't then, but later. Things happen to a man sometimes, you know. He's afraid he's on the verge of losing something, then somebody comes along who shows him it isn't so, and he sort of loses control of his senses. John's wife was a pretty sick woman the last years of her life. It wasn't a happy time. And I guess Theresa just happened to lighten the misery for John. She never told him she was pregnant. She just went away and had the child and came back later with the story about the soldier husband. The little girl must have been six or seven then. Theresa still didn't tell John it was his child for another year or so.

"She told him after he'd been kicked off the police force. I don't know if she really loved this Barker fellow, but she knew then she didn't have much longer to live, and I guess this Barker promised to take good care of the child after she was gone. To bring her up proper and all. Well, here was John Caine snooping into all the dirty business starting to go on around here, down-town and out at the Truck Stop, and maybe some people might have gone to jail over all that. Barker was one of them. So Theresa told John the child was his. And she told him she was going to die. And she told him that Barker was going to look after the little girl. John wanted to take the child himself, but Theresa didn't want that. She wanted the girl brought up somewhere else besides in Sand Valley. And of course, John Caine would never leave here."

He groped in his pocket for a stick match and relit his pipe. "And so John just sort of fell apart inside. He lost interest in eve-rything and he began drinking. Within a year, both Theresa and John were dead."

Tom Nolan took out his pipe and just stared at me. The telling of it seemed to have angered him. "Well, now you know. Does it make you feel any better?"

"I won't feel any better until I know the threat to John Caine's little girl is gone. Does Armando know it's John Caine's child?"

"I'm sure he does not. They had all left town by the time John told me. And he said I was the only one he'd told."

"Why would Theresa tell Burt Slide the girl was Armando's?"

"Because she'd cast her lot with Barker and wanted Burt Slide out of her life. It was all of it for the little girl. Of course she had no idea Burt would go off half crazy like he did when she told him that. Burt swore to her he was going to kill Barker. So Theresa called John and told him what she'd done. John raced down to the church to try stopping the shooting, but it was too late."

"Why do you suppose he told you all this, Mr. Nolan?"

"Because I guess we were about as good friends as men can be. I went through some terrible times with him after he began hitting the bottle. I sat up with him, more than once, trying to talk him out of what he was doing to himself. I guess my words caused him enough grief or shame or whatever, that one night he just broke down and told me why he was doing the things he was. I haven't even told my wife about that night, Mr. Bragg. And Mary and I have been married for fifty-three years."

"I guess that does make you and John Caine some kind of friends."

"You bet it does. Good enough friends so I didn't even show the police a note John left me when he killed himself."

"A suicide note?"

"I guess you could call it that. But it was a personal message for me. Nothing more. It was his parting token of friendship."

"Do you still have it?"

"I do not. I destroyed it the day that terrible thing happened."

"But you remember what it said."

"I do. And I'll repeat myself. It was a personal message for me alone."

"What did it say, Mr. Nolan?"

"Damn it all, Bragg. Nothing good can come of it. That's why I never told anyone about it. It's like picking at a grave, what you're doing."

"Tom, I guess you thought John Caine was a pretty good cop."

"You're darn right I did."

"I do too, Tom. From what I've heard, I think he was one damn fine cop. Smart at his work. And I'll tell you something else. In my own way, I think I'm a pretty good cop myself. And if I were John Caine, and my little girl was in any sort of danger, I'd want a pretty good cop to know anything Tom Nolan could tell him."

We looked at each other steadily. Tom Nolan came from the old days, and he did things the old ways. He figured if he could look at a man hard enough, and the man looked back the right way, then it was somebody you could trust. It had never worked for me. People I would have trusted my mother's left leg to had lied right to my face and sent me off to trouble. But then, maybe that was some flaw in me. Maybe if you had whatever Tom Nolan had inside of him, it would work for you.

"All right," he said. "It was a brief note. It said: 'I can no longer stand the scorn in her eyes—Good-bye, old friend. My time is now a part of yesterday.' "

Tom Nolan pulled out a handkerchief and bruised his nose with it. I gave him a moment to compose himself, but it was hard to do, because I had one more question to ask him, and probably it was the most important one I had asked in the two days since I'd hit Sand Valley. He finally put away the handkerchief and turned back to me.

"Tom, who was John Caine writing about? The scorn in whose eyes?"

"Why his daughter of course. The grown daughter he and his wife had."

TWENTY

It was one of those things Cathy Carson had been talking about, looping in from clear outside of the ballpark. After a while I closed my mouth. Tom Nolan saw how it affected me and screwed up his face in thought.

"I hadn't thought about her in some while. You didn't know about her?"

"I guess somebody did mention a daughter this morning, but that seems like about six months ago. What can you tell me about her?"

"Not too much. Her name was Debbie. She grew up quiet and alone. Off by herself most of the time. After she finished high school she went off to college, up in Colorado somewhere I believe. Never saw much of her after that. Her ma was gone by then. She spent her summer vacations working in some other part of the country, I guess. I think in a year's time John would hear from her twice, maybe. A note at Christmas; a card on his birthday. I think that bothered him too, that they weren't closer."

"His note mentioned the scorn in her eyes. When did she see him last?"

"She came through town during the holidays. Christmas or New Year's. Only stayed a day or so. Can't blame her, really, John being in the terrible shape that he was. I'm sure she was disgusted at what had happened to him. But I've never felt that really was what made John kill himself. I think he was just trying to make one last excuse to me. I think it was the way his whole life had come unglued."

"Was she at the funeral?"

"No, sir. Nobody knew how to get hold of her. It wasn't until the next summer she found out about it. She tried phoning him. Found out the number had been disconnected. Then she called my wife. It was Mary's unpleasant task to tell her about it. She came back then for about a month. Haven't heard from her since."

"You don't know where she is?"

"Haven't the least idea."

"What did she do while she was here?"

"Did I guess whatever needed doing with John's affairs. I had a couple of talks with her during that time. If you can call them that. I did most of the talking. She asked almost as many questions as you do."

"About what?"

"Her father. And the things that had gone on around here since she'd been off to school. And I wasn't the only one she spoke to. I hear she was asking a lot of folks questions."

"Like who?"

"People at the bank. She might even have gotten the money from that bank account. I don't think John ever touched it."

"This could be important, Tom. I need to know everything you can remember about your conversations with her."

"Oh, gosh." He leaned back and rubbed the back of his neck. "I told her about the snooping around her dad had been doing. The things around town that were becoming more blatant."

"At Slide's casino?"

"Yes, but at the Truck Stop too. I know John was on to some racketeering elements coming through there. Barker had some pretty tough friends. And they kept coming back even after Barker moved away. And I told Debbie about the bank account that got John kicked off the police force, but how John kept digging away on his own. And I told her how one day he just gave up and started drinking. I told her that I wished she had been here when that started. It might have helped John. She didn't like my talking that way, naturally enough. She was more interested in the bank account—who put money into it and so forth. I couldn't tell her, so I guess that's when she questioned people at the bank. Then she came back here later and asked about the men working for Barker, and their girlfriends. I didn't know that much about them, to tell the truth."

"Did she ask you about a man they called Moon?"

"Oh, yes."

"Would you know if Moon had a girlfriend?"

"Yes, but I can't tell you any more about her than I told Debbie. And if she hadn't asked about them just last year I probably wouldn't have remembered at all. It was something John mentioned during one of his drunken times. Didn't make a great deal of sense. But he did mention Moon and that fellow's girl. Don't know her name. I just know she was someone who worked out at the Truck Stop. The next day or so, Debbie left town again. No good-byes, nothing. She just left. I haven't heard a word from her since."

"You didn't tell her about Theresa Moore's child?"

"No, I did not."

"I don't suppose you have a photo of Debbie around the house."

"No, we quit taking pictures some time ago, Mary and me. Old folks like to look at them, not take them."

"Can you describe Debbie for me?"

"Not as well as you'd like, probably. She was a bit tall for a girl, perhaps. Hard to say. I was always sitting down the few times she came by to ask questions after she'd grown up. She wasn't fat. Pretty plain looking."

"Did she wear glasses?"

"I don't think so."

"What color was her hair?"

"Sort of mousey. I don't see all that well. Why do you ask, Bragg? You think she's into mischief up in San Francisco now?"

"It might be that way, Mr. Nolan."

I thanked him as profoundly as I knew how and left him the way I'd first seen him, standing at the front gate.

The police manning the roadblocks at the edge of the residential section warned me about going back through town. They said things seemed to have flared up again. The governor apparently had come to the same conclusion I did. It would take too long to mobilize the National Guard if the town was to be saved. He'd conferred with officials in Washington and they were sending in Army troops. But they weren't here yet.

I thanked them for the information and continued on down through town. I would have thought that by then the warring parties would have gotten tired and holed up to lick their wounds. I found it wasn't that way at all. I witnessed a few more high-speed chases through intersections in the distance. I drove over to Nevada Street and started out to the Truck Stop, but before I got out of the town proper I was overtaken by one of those chases. I heard the sharp crack of gunfire. In the rearview mirror I saw a truck coming up behind me. I braked into the curb and hunkered down low in the seat. The truck went by with a roar. It was followed seconds later by the whine of a car engine and more sounds like firecrackers.

When I sat back up there were a couple of holes in the windshield. The gunfire caravan went around a corner two blocks away. I figured to get out of there before they came around again. I drove about ten bumpy feet before pulling into the curb again. I got out and looked over the car. Both front tires were flat.

I stood in the middle of the street and felt like shouting at the sky. I'd lost my guns and now my rented car. A dry breeze began to stir the evening air. It blew a speck of sand or dust into one eye. So much for wanting to holler at the gods. I went looking for a telephone, but I was in a stretch of service stations and auto parts stores and what outside phones I found were either shot up or out of order. Some of the newcomers to town must have harbored deep resentments against the phone company. I estimated it to be between one and two miles out to the Truck Stop. I transferred my wallet to my hip pocket then took off my jacket and rolled it up under one arm and started jogging. It was not the way I wanted to travel out to the Truck Stop, but nobody I'd care to thumb a ride with was apt to be coming my way.

Nearly a mile down the way I passed the smoldering hulk of a truck. It looked as if it had been hit by cannon fire. Nobody was around and I kept on humping down the road. It was getting dark enough now so that as I approached the road leading into the Truck Stop I could make out a glow against the sky. By the time I got to the rutted section of road and the little shack beside it, I was walking, with my tongue hanging down to my belt and my shirt soaked and clinging to my damp body. There wasn't anyone in the shack, which was fine by me.

The flames were coming from the service facilities at the Truck Stop. The warehouses and maybe some fuel tanks had gone up. The bar and casino building, and the barracks-like structure nearby seemed undamaged. Trucks were parked in an arc between them and the road. I didn't see the Colonel's camper around. That depressed me. I did not want to have to jog all the way up to San Francisco. A guy stepped out from behind one of the trucks and came over to check me out. I showed him my ID and he recognized me from earlier.

"Okay, Bragg, go on ahead."

I wheezed something appropriate and stumbled over to the main building. Inside I tossed my coat over a chair and stood at the bar, taking deep breaths. I pointed at the beer tap. The people working there were dressed a little more fully than they'd been the night before, as if they wanted to be ready if they had to run off into the woods along the river or something. The girl behind the bar was wearing slacks and a blouse. She filled a beer mug and put it on the bar. I finally sat on a bar stool and just sagged there for a time. Business was slow. The place looked like an old bus station where the buses didn't stop any longer. In addition to the bartender and a waitress, I only saw two other girls who worked there. One sat at a table by herself playing solitaire. The other was in the next room dealing blackjack to a couple of drivers. The girl behind the bar must have called Ma to let her know I was there. She came through the casino and joined me.

"You look like you been run over."

"Just running." I finally got enough of my wind back to try the beer. It tasted sour to me. I didn't drink much of it. "Front tires of my car were shot out back at the edge of town. Where's the Colonel?"

"He and his people left for the airfield about a half hour ago."

"Ma, I need to know something. I understand that Armando's pal, Moon, used to go with one of the girls who worked here. Who was it?"

"Oh shucks, that gorilla liked all the girls."

"Don't stall, Ma. I been kicked around enough in this town. I don't have any patience left. Who was it?"

She looked at me with a dignity that lasted about five seconds. She'd lost status, such as it had been, and she knew it. "I guess he did feel sort of special over one of the girls. She was behind the bar here last night. Harmony. She was just another body for rent around here in those days. I sort of promoted her to bartender to make her feel better after Armando and Moon left town."

"Where's Harmony now?"

"At her place. An old house trailer set back in the trees near the river."

"Can I use the phone?"

She snapped her fingers and the girl behind the bar brought one up and put it beside my beer. I took another sip then shoved it away. "Can I trade that in on an Early Times over ice?"

The girl poured it while I dialed the number Saunders had given me for the hangar. It rang for a while, but the Colonel finally answered.

"Yeah?"

"This is Bragg. Can I still hitch a ride?"

"If you hustle ass over here. I got what I came for. We're all headed up that way now. Plan a little celebration over in Sausalito."

"The Banana Inn?"

"Hey, you're a smart man."

"It's my town. How about another thirty to forty-five minutes? I'm at Ma's now. I have one more thing to do, then I'll be ready to leave."

"It depends. If things stay quiet around here, okay. Otherwise we blow."

"The little girl..."

"Forget it, Bragg. You told me all about the little girl. But all God's chill'un got trouble. I hear the Army's on its way. The fastest way for those khaki asses to get here would be by helicopter, and they'd probably use my field to land in. There is no way I intend to be around when they arrive. So that's it, Bragg. You have until the Army arrives. That first blade I hear in the night sky—we are gone."

"So be it."

"Wish it were otherwise. Good luck."

"Yeah, the same."

I hung up and gulped the Early Times. "I have to visit Harmony," I told Ma.

She looked at me with a crooked smile. "Aren't you going to ask me how things are around here?"

"I can see how things are around here. A little slow."

I left her sitting at the bar and went out and around back. A wide path led through the grove of trees, past cabins with occasional lights inside, toward the sound of the Grey River. At the river was an old, rust-colored house trailer, not looking a day over ninety years old. There were lights on inside and a radio was playing low. The door was wide open and I called Harmony's name.

"Pete? I'm over here."

I turned. She was sitting at a picnic table near the bank of the river, but she got up in a hurry and crossed to me, wearing some warmer clothes than she'd had on the last time I saw her. She put her arms around me and squeezed.

"My golly, doesn't this show you how wrong a girl can be? I figured when you left this afternoon you'd walked out of my life for good. But you came back. My God, Pete, you don't know how happy I am that you came back."

I didn't know how to say what had to be said. She took my hand and led me over to the table. "Come on over and sit with me for a while. I find it relaxing, sitting here looking at the old Grey go by. It's a good thing to do when things go the way they been going around here."

I sat beside her. We put our elbows on the table and chins on our hands. The moon, low and pale in the sky, was trying to sprinkle a little silver on the water, but it was fighting a losing battle with the lights shining through the open door of Harmony's trailer behind us. But then I guess different people see different things in the Grey Rivers of their lives. And I learned what Harmony saw.

"You know, Pete, the Grey here starts out as just a little stream up high in the Sanduskis. It's just beautiful there. I discovered this meadow. You have to backpack about a half day to get in to it. There's these big old pine trees all round it, and the old Grey here laughing through the middle of it. And the stars, Pete. My God, the stars look like they're ready to brush the top of your hat. Would you like me to show it to you sometime?"

"It sounds great, Harmony. I would like to see it. When I have a little more time."

I felt her stiffen beside me. "What's that mean, Pete?"

I sighed audibly. "It means there are people getting killed, Harmony. Somebody I'm working for might be next, unless I can stop it. And I have to get back to San Francisco tonight, to try to stop it."

A little flutter crossed her mouth. She turned away and looked out over the Grey River. "Pow," she said softly. "Right between the eyes."

She was still a moment, then wiped her nose and turned back to me. "Goddamn it, you are a real bastard, fella. Why did you come back? Just why? I went through this once today already, when you left this afternoon. I said to myself, shoot, why should I let it bother me? He's just another fellow travelin' through with his flattery and all. Shucks, the sort of life I've had, I shouldn't let a little something like that bother me."

She wiped her nose again. "But it did bother me, Pete. And then you came back again. What for? A little quickie before you hit the road? I heard you calling me over at the trailer there and my little heart just went *zing* right up to the stars there. I said to myself, Harmony, honey, you finally got yourself one who isn't so bad after all. So I just let it all hang out and told you about my secret meadow and..."

"Now, Harmony, stop it." I got up so I could step back and shout some. "You're blowing up this whole thing way out of proportion. You haven't any right to get all squishy over me. Why, hell, a couple of pats on your fanny is as close as we've been. I mean, you're just upset over things that have been happening. Don't you think I'm upset too? I've been beat up and threatened and lied to. I just had my car shot out from under me back in town like it was an old horse, and had to run what seemed like about twenty miles to get out here and say good-bye to you. But Harmony, I have a job to do. I have to save a little girl back in San Francisco who just happened to have been spawned in this hell-hole, but who hasn't done a thing to hurt anyone in her life. And that's what I'm going to do and that's why I have to go back to San Francisco tonight."

She took a breath and nodded her head a half-dozen times. "Okay, but don't try messing up my brain by telling me you came all the way out here just to say good-bye, Lucky."

"Oh, now I'm just another country John, am I? Harmony, I swear..."

She gave me a look that brought a chill to the air. I sat back down on a corner of the table. "Well, there is maybe one or two things I wanted to ask you."

"That's better," she told me. She took a cigarette from a pack on the table and lit it while I was groping for the lighter I don't carry any longer.

"Harmony, I hear you were friends with a fellow named Moon, who worked for Armando Barker."

"Yes," she said flatly. "He was my boyfriend. People used to wonder about it, him being so big and mean-looking. But he was sweet to me. Treated me real well."

"Do you know where he is now?"

"In San Francisco, with Mr. Barker, so far as I know. He said he'd come back for me some day. It's been a couple years now. I shouldn't have believed him any more than I shoulda believed you."

I got up and paced around some. There wasn't a single reason I could think of to tell her Moon was dead. Or how he died. "Now something else, Harmony, and this is important. Do you know whether Moon ever happened to work both sides of the street around here? By that I mean, do you know if he ever did any jobs for Carl Slide?"

"I don't think so. He was a pretty loyal fellow in his way. I'm sure Mr. Barker is the only one he worked for here."

All the plugging along was beginning to pay off. I felt now I had a pretty good idea what it was all about, and could almost understand the cold fury of an ex-cop's daughter who believed the things Debbie Caine must have. Barker almost deserved whatever he got. I didn't feel any sympathy for him any longer. Just for the little girl who had to get in the middle of things.

"Thank you, Harmony. I guess that tells me what I wanted to know. There is one more thing, but I couldn't expect you to know about that."

"Might as well ask, Lucky, as long as you're here."

"There was a girl who used to live in town here. About your own age, I would guess. She was in town last summer, asking questions about Moon and Armando."

"You mean Debbie Caine?"

"Yes, but how did you know?"

"We both grew up here. We were never close, but we knew each other. I hadn't seen her in years. She came out here to the Truck Stop last summer, like you said. When Ma found out who she was, she made her leave. But I was in town a day or so later and ran into her. We talked awhile. That was about all."

"What did you talk about?"

"Nothing much. But I remember she did ask where Moon was. So I told her."

"What did she look like?"

"Nothing to make you turn your head. She was about my size, but didn't know how to do anything to her hair or face, or didn't care to. Doubt if she'd be your type. Why are you interested in her?"

"I think she's the root of my problem. She found out Moon had been depositing sizeable sums into an old savings account he had while he was still a cop. She figured out her dad had been set up by Armando for the bribe charges that got him tossed off the force. She figures that's what turned him into a lush, and ultimately, a suicide. She's now in the process of taking a little revenge."

Something about the night air had changed. And then I saw the winking green and red lights in the sky out over the desert beyond the Grey and heard the unmistakeable flop-flop-flop of helicopter engines. I bent to kiss the top of Harmony's head.

"And now I got a plane to catch, honey."

"But that's wrong."

"I know. I wish I could stay around and become really good friends, but…"

"No, I mean about the bank account."

The flopping in the sky grew louder.

"What do you know about the bank account, Harmony?"

"Well—" She took a drag off her cigarette. It went into her lungs wrong and she gagged, then started a fit of coughing. I whacked her back a couple of times. The helicopters had switched on searchlights. Their beams crisscrossed the desert floor ahead of them. They were making a beeline for the Colonel's airport.

"Come on, Harmony, what is it?"

She took a wheezing breath and coughed some more. I sprinted across to the trailer and clambered inside. I was surprised at how neat she kept it. I filled a glass with water, held one hand across the top of the glass to keep it from slopping and ran back out to where Harmony sat, doubled over and gasping. She took the water thankfully and sipped it, then took a deep breath.

"Whew, thanks. I sure have to quit inhaling like that."

"Harmony, the bank account!"

The noise of the overhead copters was beginning to make it hard to carry on a conversation.

"Moon didn't make the deposits for Armando!" she hollered.

"That's why I asked you if he ever worked for Slide!" I shouted back.

"But he didn't do it for Mr. Slide neither. He did it for me!"

I sat back down on the table as the helicopters slapped past and on over toward the airport.

Harmony's face was lined with thought. "Come to think of it, maybe he was working for Slide in a way, only he didn't know it at the time. Because I guess it turns out I was working for Slide in a way."

"Maybe you'd better tell me about it, Harmony."

"Well, it was to keep the Mafia out, you know?"

"Yeah, I've heard everyone around town was working on that one."

"That's what Slide said. He asked me up to his office there one time. He knew I was Moon's girl. He said he'd had his eye on me, you know, and maybe sometime I could come work at his place, if I ever broke up with Moon. He said I might meet some really rich old boy there that I'd never have a chance to meet here at the Stop and all. But in the meantime he said I could do a favor for the town in general. You know, helping to keep out the Mafia and all."

"Sure."

"He said Debbie's daddy was working undercover to keep out any fellows who might be connected with the Mafia. He said it was sort of a hush-hush operation that Mr. Caine was doing for a bunch of the local businessmen. But he said it took money. For him to pay informers and all. That's what the money in the bank account was for."

"But how did Moon end up making the deposits?"

"Mr. Slide said that's the way you had to do things when fighting the Mafia. He said you had to be as devious as they are. He said the money had to pass through several hands, so it couldn't be traced back if the Mafia ever caught on to what was going on. He said that was how the CIA did things."

She looked at me, trying to get some idea if maybe she'd done something dumb.

"It's okay, Harmony. That's how the CIA does things."

She nodded, a bit relieved. "Anyhow, he asked me to have Moon make the deposits, only I wasn't to tell Moon where the money came from or what it was for. Actually, Moon didn't have to do anything but go into the bank and hand an envelope to one of the tellers. I guess there was a deposit slip already made out inside the envelope. I went in with him once when I was in town shopping. It wasn't anything all that wrong, was it?"

"It's all right, Harmony. The important thing is what Caine's daughter thought. You've been a big help."

"I hope so. I'd sure hate to see Debbie get into any more trouble. That sure is one star-crossed family."

"How do you mean?"

"Well, you heard about Mr. Caine, didn't you? Taking his own life and all?"

"Yes, I heard."

"Then Debbie herself, of course."

"What about Debbie herself?"

"Oh, it was a long time ago. When she was a kid. But it must have left a scar. Sure would have with me."

Somebody dropped a trapdoor in the bottom of my stomach. I guess my face showed it.

"What's wrong, Lucky?"

"What was it that happened to Debbie Caine when she was a kid?"

"She got raped. Several times over. One day on her way home from school. It was a dreadful thing."

I was up and running again, along the path back to the Truck Stop. I was almost there when the Colonel's Beechcraft flew overhead and out into the bleak desert night.

TWENTY-ONE

Back in the truck stop I tried to phone Armando. There was no answer in San Francisco. Maybe he'd broken his crutches and his trick knee kept him away from the telephone. Maybe he was lying in the middle of his polar bear rugs with a bullet through his ear. Maybe he was on his way to Hawaii. Maybe I was the dumbest, most gullible private detective ever duly licensed by the state of California.

I asked for another Early Times over ice and put through a call to the Mission Academy for Girls in San Rafael. Bobbie—at least the girl I knew as Bobbie—had picked up Beverly Jean a couple of hours earlier. I hung up and called Bobbie's apartment. I didn't expect her to be there. But I had to try. I had to let her know the little girl's life she might be fooling with was her own half sister.

Nobody answered. I hung up. Ma Leary came back into the bar. Business was picking up and she looked around approvingly. The truckers were taking turns standing watch outside. Those not on guard were bringing the bar and casino back to life. She saw me and came over.

"What's wrong with you?" she asked. "You look as if someone just kicked you where your legs part company."

I drank from the drink. "I always look this way when I realize how riddled with dumb my brain is. How regular is the air service out of Spring Meadows?"

"I don't think there's any more tonight, if that's what you mean. But they have some guys who'll fly charter out of there. I'll get you the phone book."

I phoned around and made arrangements for a flight down to Phoenix. It was about the same distance to Salt Lake City, and Salt Lake was closer to San Francisco, but I figured Phoenix was the bigger city and, hopefully, might have more flights out. I asked Ma if she had a handgun I could borrow. She went away and I dialed the hospital and asked for Cathy Carson. She had left for the day. I called her at home. She was there.

"I'm about to leave town," I told her. "You said to call. You could even help me leave town, if you're of a mind to."

"How is that?"

"I've blundered badly. The little girl I told you about?"

"Yes?"

"I've practically handed her on a platter to the person I think is behind all this ugliness. I have to get back to San Francisco in a hurry. I've arranged a charter flight out of Spring Meadows. I could use a fast ride there. My own car isn't working."

"What happened to your car?" She didn't try to keep the suspicion out of her voice.

"It just broke down on me. You never know with some of these rental outfits. How about it?"

"I want to hear more about your car. But all right. Where should I pick you up?"

"I'm at the Truck Stop. I'll meet you on the road out front."

"Fifteen minutes," she told me.

Ma came back down with a .32 caliber pistol. It wasn't as big as I would have liked, but it was a sight better than just me and my mighty fists, if I encountered Lou and Soft Kenny. Ma promised to have my car picked up, repaired and returned to Spring Meadows when things quieted down. I tried to leave some money with her, but she still was grateful for the night before and refused it. Then she led me out to a garage behind the barracks building and backed out a brand new Cadillac to give me a ride out to the road. There was a lot of traffic moving along it now. Busses from town had gone out to the airfield to transport the Army troops who had flown in. There probably were more Army units with their own transportation coming over the Sanduskis.

I got out and thanked Ma for her help. "And tell your girls to get a good night's sleep."

"What for? I don't even know if I'll be in business tomorrow."

"With all those soldier boys in town? Don't worry, you'll be in business. The officers will drift into the Sky Lodge and the ranks will find their way out here."

"I'll have to raise my prices some, losing out on what the shed operation paid me."

"That's okay. Nobody expects a cut-rate whorehouse these days."

She turned the car and drove off with a wave of her hand. Five minutes later Cathy Carson picked me up in her red Ford. She was still in her nurses' uniform. I climbed in beside her and we roared off toward the freeway.

"I should have asked you to throw some things in a bag," I told her. "In case I could talk you into flying up there with me. I could actually use your help. That's until I clean up the mess I've made of things. Then we could play."

"How could I help?"

"Did you know Debbie Caine? John Caine's daughter?"

"Not intimately."

"But you could recognize her?"

"Maybe. Girls can do lots of things to change their appearance."

"I'd like you to try anyhow."

"You think she's in San Francisco?"

"I know she is."

"And you'd want me to identify her, if I could."

"That's right."

She thought about it some. It was a nice car she had, and she recognized the urgency of the situation. We were doing almost 80 miles an hour up the Lodi grade.

"If you promise to try very hard not to get either one of us killed," she said, "I'll do it."

"I promise. I'll even buy you some new duds when we hit town."

"You needn't bother. I keep a bag filled with basic outfits in case I'm called out of town in an emergency. I put it in the car trunk after you called."

"How did you know I was going to ask you to come to San Francisco with me?"

"I just thought you might. I hadn't made up my mind to do it, but I thought I'd be ready. You did surprise me by telling me I could help out in some way. I guess that made the difference."

I studied her in the soft glow of the dashboard lights. They made her look even more as if she played in a pixy band than she did in the daylight. She noticed me watching and gave me a brief smile.

"I hope," I told her, "that the plane we're catching in Spring Meadows is big enough so we can sit together in back and neck all the way to Phoenix."

"I'm not exactly sex starved, Mr. Bragg. That isn't why I'm making the trip. I made some fast phone calls after I heard from you, making arrangements for other girls to fill in for me in the event you should ask me to leave town and I should decide to do it. I called in every favor owed me over the past four years. We'd just better, Mr. Bragg, have a swell time in San Francisco."

As it turned out, we couldn't have necked all the way to Phoenix even if she'd been agreeable. There was turbulence, and the pilot I'd hired was determined to find the middle of it and stay there. It was like flying in an old-fashioned cocktail shaker. At the Phoenix airport we wobbled over to the commercial counters and a half hour later were on a Western Airlines flight to San Francisco.

At San Francisco International I tried again to phone Armando. This time somebody answered the phone. At least they lifted the receiver, but they didn't say anything.

"Hello, this is Peter Bragg. Who is this?"

Whoever it was hung up. I did not like the implications of that. On the day I left town I'd been lucky and been able to park in the garage just behind the passenger terminals, instead of three miles down the road where you then had to catch a jitney bus back. We got my car and I took off for Armando's place in the city. Roaring up the Bayshore Freeway I told Cathy where we were going.

"I want you to wait here in the car until I make sure things are under control inside the house."

"What is it that might not be under control?"

"How should I know?" I left traffic behind.

San Francisco had a freeway revolt of sorts several years ago. It prevented the crosstown construction of any more concrete ribbons. The Bayshore ran north-south up to the Bay Bridge. Off this were fingers curving around the edges of the downtown area into the city proper. I took the one that emptied into Franklin Street. About eight minutes later we were parking in front of Armando Barker's Pacific Heights home. I left Cathy and went up the walk to listen at the front door for a minute. Things sounded quiet inside. Lights were on. I rang the bell and waited.

Bobbie was the one who answered the door. We were surprised to see each other. For half a heartbeat she might have been the same lonely kid who had started to leave my place in Sausalito one night but came back. For that half a heartbeat I think we felt the same way, and she made a move as if to reach out to me, but my brain warned me to keep my shoes flat on the pavement or I might end up a dead man, and the moment passed.

"You're back much sooner than I expected," she told me.

"And later than I should have been. Where's Beverly Jean?"

"In a safe place." She was staring past me to the street. "Who's with you?"

"A new acquaintance." I turned and signaled for Cathy to join us. Bobbie went back inside. Cathy and I followed a moment later. Armando was in the playroom, slumped in a chair with one foot propped up on a cushion atop a hassock. He looked as if he were tired of holding up his head. A pair of crutches were on the floor beside him, and there was an empty glass on the stand next to his chair. He looked as if he'd been drinking. He didn't break out into any grin when he saw me.

"Some dick you turned out to be," he said slowly.

"You wouldn't know until you heard how I spent the day. How's your knee?"

"Glorious."

"You're both acting kind of funny," I said. "What's going on?"

Armando started to raise his head, but then it slumped again, as if to explain things demanded too much of him. Cathy Carson gave me a tug on my sleeve.

"What is it?"

She nodded across the room to where Bobbie was fixing herself a drink at the bar.

"That's the girl you were asking about," she told me. "She's done a lot to her appearance, but that's John Caine's daughter."

Bobbie glanced up. She continued swirling amber liquid around ice in her glass with a tight little smile on her face. "You know, Armando, he really isn't a bad detective at all. In fact, he's almost too good. I thought it would take him at least several more days to learn that."

"Has she told you she was John Caine's daughter?" I asked Armando.

He sat a little more erect and wagged his head. Bobbie came out from behind the bar and crossed to where Cathy and I stood.

"I don't know you, do I?" she asked Cathy. "But you must be from Sand Valley."

"I am."

"Huh," said Bobbie. "Small world." She turned toward Armando. "Would you care for a drink, love?"

He gurgled something unintelligible.

"There is something very wrong here," Cathy said quietly.

I took out the .32 Ma Leary had given me. "Bobbie, go sit down over there while we talk about things."

"In a minute." She went over to lean down near Armando. "Armando, do you remember last Sunday, when Peter first came to the house here and you reached out with your hand and pinched me? And all the other times you've done that?"

He stared at her blankly.

"Well," she said, straightening, "that wasn't a nice thing to do at all."

Before I realized what she had in mind she kicked Armando sharply on his trick knee. I lunged for her arm and threw her none too gently into a nearby chair.

"Where's Beverly Jean?" I asked her.

Bobbie shrugged. "I have friends looking after her."

"Where?"

"I don't really know."

"In San Francisco?"

"I doubt it. We just talked to her a bit ago. Didn't we, Armando?"

Armando didn't say anything. He sat glassy-eyed in the chair.

"How about telling me what's going on?" I asked him. He didn't reply. "You know who John Caine was, don't you?"

He managed something that sounded like yes.

"He committed suicide about a year and a half ago. His daughter here didn't find out about it until six months later. She went back to Sand Valley then and asked questions around town. From what she learned, she decided you and Moon were responsible."

Something approaching a frown crossed Armando's brow.

"It wasn't only that," Bobbie said quietly. "My father was in the middle of killing himself long before then. The last time I saw him. With his drinking." She looked up at me. "You don't know what that was like, Pete. To return home and find your father a hopeless drunk. He couldn't even carry on a rational conversation. He made me sick to my stomach."

"So you packed up and ran. Six months later you found out he'd killed himself and, I suspect, felt a little guilt."

"Never mind what I felt."

I crossed to Armando. "You probably heard about the bank account John Caine had. The one that eventually got him bounced off the force. What you didn't know was that your man Moon was making regular cash deposits to that account. He didn't realize that's what he was doing. And when Bobbie began asking around town following her father's death, she heard about Moon making the deposits. And since Moon worked for you, she assumed you were the one behind it. To get her father kicked off the police force. And she thought that because he'd lost his job is why he started drinking, and in the end killed himself. That's why she took it upon herself to kill you and Moon. She found out you were in San Francisco from one of Moon's old girlfriends working at the Truck Stop."

Armando didn't say anything, but just stared dully across at Bobbie.

"Then she came to San Francisco, probably watched your operation until she had you figured out, then came on the scene and performed in a manner she knew would interest you. She's good at that. She suckered me in the same way."

Bobbie looked at me briefly, then turned away.

"She worked up a really good hate for you, Armando. She shot at you from the street above the Chop House, but she purposely missed. And she sent the sympathy cards. She wanted you to sweat for a while. When you hired me, she had to do some fast improvising. On Monday, when the whole household takes the day off, she made arrangements to meet Moon at the Pimsler Hotel."

Armando raised his head.

"Sure," I told him. "She had him in her pocket as well. It just occurred to me how much she looks like one of Moon's old girlfriends. He must have been daffy over her. So she tells the poor sap to rent a room at the Pimsler, so that no landladies or anyone will see them together and snitch to you sometime. What she really wanted was for him to die in a manner nobody would suspect a girl of pulling off. She must have gotten him out in the hallway to look at the view down in the lobby while she was describing the swell time they were going to have back in the room. Then the ice pick in his neck and heave-ho over the railing. That would have been the hardest part with a man Moon's size, but a girl could do it with a little thought and dedication, and she seems to have had both."

"That's not true, about Moon," Bobbie told me. "Not all of it."

"Maybe not. I'm not even worried about Moon. He'd done enough things in his life to have deserved that a long time ago. But I am worried about Beverly Jean. I want to know what you did to her."

"I'll bet you do. I forgot to thank you for that."

"What does she mean?" Cathy asked.

"I was the smart guy who suggested to Armando that he send Bobbie to take her out of a private school she was in."

Armando made a snorting sound.

"That was before I became so interested in John Caine's daughter."

"You really did do an amazing job," Bobbie told me. "My father would have admired you."

"I don't think he would have admired what you've done. What happened to Beverly Jean?"

"Relax, Pete. She'll be all right, as soon as Armando does me a favor."

"What do you want him to do?"

"Die," she said simply.

"That would be a mistake," I told her. "Same as killing Moon was a mistake."

She glanced up sharply. "I don't believe that business about Moon not knowing what he was doing, putting money in the savings account in Dad's name."

"It's true, Bobbie. I know because I'm better at this sort of thing than you are. If you'd spent a little longer talking to Harmony you might have stumbled onto the truth. Moon was banking that money as a favor to Harmony. He didn't know what it was going for. And Harmony didn't know the real purpose of it, either."

"What was its purpose?"

"Just what you suspected. To set up your dad so he'd be tossed off the force and out of everybody's hair. But it was a little more elaborate than it appeared. Armando wasn't the man behind it. Carl Slide was."

Bobbie stood up. "I don't believe that."

"Don't take my word for it. Call the Truck Stop in Sand Valley and have Ma get Harmony herself to the phone. Slide gave her the money and said it was for a secret fund for your dad to use to keep organized crime out of Sand Valley. She was dumb enough to believe it, and she swallowed another story Slide told her in order to get Moon to make the deposits. Slide did it that way so if something went wrong everybody would believe just what you did, that Armando was behind it. But he wasn't, and believe me, maybe John Caine didn't approve of some of the action Armando was letting into the Truck Stop, but it was stuff Slide was starting to pull that he really was interested in."

Bobbie's face had taken on a stark expression. Cathy crossed to Armando. His head was slumped to one side.

"Something's wrong with this man."

"What did you do to him, Bobbie?"

"Oh, Jesus, Pete, I had no idea…"

"What's wrong with him?"

"Just before you got here I made him drink a bottle of vodka. The whole thing, in about one swallow. Along with a few pills I had handy. I told him that was the only way he could save Beverly Jean's life. I wanted him to die the same way my father was dying the last time I saw him."

"Get him on his feet," Cathy told me. "Where's the kitchen in this funhouse?"

Bobbie pointed to a far doorway.

"But he's got a bad knee," I reminded Cathy.

"I don't care if he's missing a leg. If you want to save him, get him up and moving."

I went over and tugged at Armando's arm. He was limp.

"Get me some ice," I told Bobbie.

She brought some from the refrigerator behind the bar. I took a handful and held it to the back of Armando's thick neck. There were a few things I'd learned during the spell I'd worked at the No Name. How to get a passed-out drunk up and moving when two o'clock closing rolled around was one of them. Armando stirred and raised one hand toward the uncomfortable cold I was pressing against his neck.

"Come on, pal," I told him, just like in the old days. "You gotta upsy-daisy."

Bobbie got on his other side and between us we got him onto his feet. He didn't protest from pain in his knee. I guess he couldn't feel it any longer.

"Walk, Armando. Walk!"

We moved around the room some. He didn't contribute too much. Cathy came back in with a jar of soapy water and headed for the hallway. "Bring him along," she said. "We're going to have to give him a lot of room to vomit in."

We dragged Armando to the front door and outside onto the lawn. Cathy held up the jar to his mouth.

"Drink this, Mr. Barker."

He didn't drink.

"Hold his head back," Cathy told me.

I held back his head. Cathy forced open his mouth with her fingers and poured in some of the stuff. Armando gagged and tried to brush her away.

"You have to drink this, Mr. Barker," she told him. "If you don't drink this and void your stomach, you're going to die."

He still resisted.

"But he wants to die," Bobbie cried. "He thinks it's the only way he can save Beverly Jean."

"Come on, Armando," I roared in his ear. "Open up!"

Maybe he didn't have enough left to resist further. We got the soapy water into his mouth and over us and some nearby geraniums as well. He swallowed, and a moment later he gave a violent retch and doubled over to relieve himself on the ground and my shoes and down his own pants. It was really enjoyable.

"Keep him at it," Cathy told me. "When he seems done, get him back inside and wrap some blankets around him. I'll call an ambulance."

"He's throwing up all over me," I complained.

Cathy paused in the doorway. "Would you rather help me give him a coffee enema?"

She went on inside while Bobbie and I tended to Armando.

"It would really take a devious mind to get at Armando this way," I told her.

She looked at me across the sick man's hanging head. "I'm not as smart as you might think. It was Slide's idea. He came up with it after I convinced him I wanted Armando dead. He told me to let him know when I was ready to do it. He said he'd sent up a couple of men. I phoned last night. The men arrived today. I met them after I got Beverly Jean out of the Academy. They went somewhere with her. I told her we were arranging a surprise party for Armando."

"I guess you were, at that."

Bobbie's face was grimly set. She was blinking back tears. "Don't look at me like that, Pete. I'm not an evil person."

"Too bad you can't tell that to Moon."

"That was an accident."

"Sure it was. Guys go around poking ice picks into their own neck and pitch over high railings every day."

"It wasn't his neck, it was more toward his shoulder. Honest, Pete, I knew what I was doing. It wouldn't have harmed him that much. Only it went wrong."

Her face was all twisted up now, and by this time she was crying. It was one of those moments I treasure in the business I'd decided to be in—a man beside me throwing up on my shoes and next to him a hysterical woman.

"If you're going to have me believe that, you'll have to stop bawling long enough to tell me about it."

"Would you even want to hear about it?" she sniffed.

"If it's the truth, I would."

She choked and sniffed some more. "I wanted it to be like the night I shot at Armando. Not to really hurt anyone. I did tell Moon we could spend the night at the Pimsler. He had already checked in. I showed up with a little overnight bag. When he came to the door I raved about the view of the lobby from the railing. In the bag I had the ice pick from Sand Valley and a sort of improvised billy club I'd read was supposed to work—some wet sand in a stocking. My plan was to wallop him one on the head, then jab him with the ice pick where I knew it wouldn't do anything but give him a sore shoulder for a couple of days. Then I'd leave and tell him later he was attacked by a stranger who came down the hall. I was going to tell him the man hit and stabbed him, then I tried to throw him over the railing, but that I'd fought him off, and after the stranger had run off that I'd done the same, not wanting Armando ever to find out we'd been together. It was a really good plan. It just didn't work."

"What went wrong?"

"I walloped him, all right, but instead of crashing to the floor like he was supposed to, the big ox just looked up at the ceiling, as if something had fallen on him. I couldn't believe it. I hit him hard enough to lay up a normal human being for a week. Then he started to buckle, just a little, and I poked him with the ice pick. I was shaken badly enough so it wasn't exactly where I meant to stick it, but it wouldn't have killed him. But when he folded up he grabbed the railing and was sort of half hanging over it. I figured that was okay and ran back to grab the bag I'd just left inside the room doorway. When I turned around again the big lummox was still trying to pull himself back to consciousness, only in the process he was working himself farther over the rail.

"I almost wet myself. He was half there and half gone. I ran over and tried to pull him up by his coat tails. That's when he tried to rear up and swing at me. One foot slipped out from under him…And he was gone."

It was just possible. Moon was that big, that headstrong and that dumb. "What did you do next?"

"Are you kidding? I closed the door to the room and got out of there like a streak. I went home and changed and then drove over to Sausalito. I'd had that part planned too. I was going to tell you about the mysterious attack on Moon. I figured you would have believed me if I was willing to tell you I had planned to spend the night with him."

"You're right. I would have."

"But it turned out I didn't have to tell anybody anything. In fact, it was such a screwy death I guess even the news services picked up the story. Slide heard about it on the radio. He figured I'd done it deliberately. It convinced him I was serious about wanting Armando done in. The next time I phoned him he offered to send the two men to help."

"I should have known he was lying to me all along. About the two men. What was the arrangement?"

"Slide told me to phone him when I had things set up. I did. He knows where the men took Beverly Jean. Then he phoned the two men, wherever they are, and they phoned here. They convinced Armando they'd kill Beverly Jean if he didn't do exactly what I told him to."

"Do you know the names of the two men?"

"One of them is Kenny."

"Yeah, they could convince him."

Armando hung between us. He seemed emptied and exhausted. We struggled back over toward the front door. He was heavy and Bobbie lost her grip on him. I set him down in the doorway.

"Don't worry, Pete," Bobbie told me. "They won't really hurt her. I made Slide promise that."

"My God, Bobbie, what sort of people do you think these are that you're dealing with? Of course they would. In fact the one called Kenny enjoys hurting people. And he's got something kinky going with girls. I've seen him work."

"Oh, Christ," she murmured. She looked up in a moment, trying to blink back fresh tears. "It really wasn't such a bad plan, though. If only I'd had the right man."

"But there is no right man, Bobbie."

"There's the bank account, and Carl Slide."

I knew then that I was going to tell her. It was the only thing that might get her off this vengeance trip. Besides, my well of humanity was running dry. I had only the vaguest outline of a plan to save Beverly Jean from whatever sickness Soft Kenny might have in store for her. The plan, while vague, promised a measure of discomfort for myself.

"The bank account isn't what started your dad drinking that way, Bobbie. He kept up his investigation even after they fired him."

"What did, then?"

"Something a little closer to home. You must have known Beverly Jean's mother, Theresa Moore."

"Yes."

"When Theresa Moore learned she only had a little time left, she decided to marry Armando, and she told your dad about it. She told him that Armando had promised to look after her for whatever time she had left. And that he'd look after her daughter as well. That's what started your dad's drinking. It was a pitiful effort to make things more bearable. Because Beverly Jean's father wasn't some soldier boy who was killed in Vietnam, as Theresa told everyone. And it wasn't Burt Slide, as some people suspected. It was your own father, Bobbie. He told that to just one person. Old Tom Nolan who lived across the street. And Nolan told me."

Bobbie stared at me with a terrible look on her face. She knew I was telling her the truth. And then she screamed, and the sound of it made an eerie harmony with the approaching siren.

TWENTY-TWO

They got Armando trundled inside of the ambulance. Cathy talked briefly to one of the attendants, and then the thing shrieked off into the night the way it had come. We went back inside the house. In the main living room, Bobbie was just turning away from the phone on the bar. Her face was falling apart again.

"What's wrong?"

"I just talked to Slide. I told him it was all over, and asked him to call the men who have Beverly Jean and tell them to let her go. He said he would call them, but that it might be a while before they freed her. He said it was a part of the deal. Because of the risk involved. He said he'd promised to let Kenny—play with her some."

"My God," said Cathy.

"Where are they holding her?"

"He wouldn't tell me."

"Where is Slide? At the lodge?"

"No, he's at home."

I crossed to the telephone. If I had been in Sand Valley then, I could make Slide tell me where Lou, Kenny and the girl were. I am not a vain man. What I could do, others could do. I put through a call to the Sand Valley police. Merle Coffey was still in his office. I asked how things were going.

"The Army's got things back under control. I think we've broken the back of this thing."

"That's good news. How does your own situation look?"

"Not particularly good. I have to fly up to the capitol tomorrow morning."

"Maybe I can brighten things some for you. I have some information about Carl Slide and the bank. You should talk to one of the vice presidents, a man named Morton. He's in the hospital. He's one of the people who were shot today. He probably could give you some information that might make you look pretty good."

"Are you going to just dangle it like a chunk of meat in front of a dog, or are you going to tell me what it is?"

"I'll tell you, but in return I need a favor done. The sort of favor you would have to do with the door closed, without a lot of witnesses standing around."

"Tell me about it."

I told him about Slide, the girl and Lou and Soft Kenny. I particularly told him about Soft Kenny. Most cops have this thing about people who go around hurting children. Merle Coffey was no different.

"I just want to know where they're at. Slide knows, but he won't tell."

"I'll see that he tells me."

"I need it fast. He's at home."

"I'll drive out there right away. Tell me about this other thing."

I told Coffey what Morton suspected about stolen securities. Coffey agreed it would make an interesting story when he went up to the state capitol in the morning. I gave him my home telephone number and asked him to call me there after he'd visited Slide. He said he would.

When I turned from the phone I found I was the only one still in the room. I went up the hall. Cathy was at the front door. "Where's Bobbie?"

"She just ran out. Drove off in a Porsche."

I went back and turned off lights and closed up the house. On the way over to Sausalito I told Cathy how things stood.

"So I can't take the time to check you into the Pimsler right now. You can crash at my place for the night. I'll be out working."

She murmured something about the sort of holiday she'd always wanted to spend in San Francisco.

She found my apartment "quaint." She fiddled around with the television set while I went into the bathroom for a fast shower and changed into some clothes Armando hadn't been getting sick all over. When I came back out Cathy had changed from her hospital whites into a pair of Levis and a black turtleneck top. She had a nice figure. I started to tell her about it when Merle Coffey phoned.

"I got what you wanted."

"Good."

"I hope so. It wasn't easy. He's in the hospital now having his jaw wired back together. At least Lou and Kenny are pretty close to you. They're holed up in a place belonging to Lou's brother in the Oakland hills. The address is 1247 Hatten Avenue. The brother and his wife are out of town. I've already called the Oakland police and told them roughly what was going on. I figured the faster we got somebody up there the better, and they'd probably get there quicker than you could."

"I appreciate that, Chief. Good luck on tomorrow."

"I'm not so worried now. I think a talk with Morton will make quite a difference."

I still had the .32 automatic Ma Leary had given me, but I wanted a little more whop than that would give. I unlocked the bottom drawer of my desk and got out the first handgun I'd ever bought, back before I even knew I'd be going into this sort of business. It was an old .38 caliber Colt Army revolver, the basic 1892 model that had been modified two years later. It was an old veteran of the Spanish–American War and the Philippine Insurrection, but I kept it cleaned and oiled and it worked just fine.

Cathy asked to go with me. "I could help. If the little girl is hurt."

"You're right enough about that. She might need a woman. But only on the condition that you do exactly what I tell you. I don't want to have to worry about the both of you."

It was nearly midnight. I went north, curved around by San Quentin and sped across the Richmond–San Rafael bridge. The house we found was in a remote section up near one of the regional parks behind Oakland. It was a large, two-story frame structure with slope-roofed dormers caging upstairs windows. There was a late model Cadillac with Nevada plates parked at the curb in front. Across the street were a couple of Oakland police cars. One was empty. Inside the other an officer was talking on the radio. Another cop lounged against the side with his arms folded. I parked a ways in front of the Cadillac and went over to the officer leaning against the patrol car. I showed him my ID and explained my interest.

"What's happening?"

"Not much. We went to the door and a guy answered. Dark complexion, thirty-five years old, five feet ten or eleven."

"His name's Lou."

"He wouldn't tell us that. He wouldn't tell us anything. He said we must have gotten a crank call. He said there was no little girl there. People downtown are trying to find a judge who'll give us a search warrant on the basis of the phone call from Sand Valley. It's not easy. But at least we figure if there is a little girl in there, they won't do anything to her while we're camping on their doorstep. We have another man around back to see that nobody leaves that way. Things have been very quiet."

"When did you get here?"

"About twenty minutes ago."

"I'd like to look around the place. What's the name of your man in back?"

"Spence. Tell him Carter said it was okay."

"Thanks." I circled the house. On one side was a paved driveway leading back to a closed and padlocked garage. On the other was a narrow strip of lawn and a hedge. Window shades were drawn shut throughout the house. There were lights on downstairs and in one room on the second floor.

Spence was keeping watch from alongside the garage. The back of the house was dark. I explained things and asked what he'd seen so far.

"I came back here before Carter and Bullock went to the front door. Carter came back a couple minutes later to tell me they'd been denied entrance. A little after that someone peered out from that window up there," he said, pointing. "So they know we're around the neighborhood."

"Have you heard anything from inside?"

"Nothing."

I went back around to the front and crossed the street to the officer named Carter. "Any luck on the warrant?"

"Not yet."

"Okay. Let me tell you what I think. I think the girl is in there, and while you're right about their not doing anything to her while you're here, there's no way of telling what might have gone on before you arrived. One of the men inside is very psychotic about girls. So whatever might have gone on, I think we ought to get her out of there as soon as possible. The young woman waiting in my car over there is a nurse."

"Sounds fine with me, but legally..."

"Legally, if you hear a loud ruckus and gunfire and stuff going on inside, you have a right to investigate, right?"

"I think it's a judgment call we could make."

"Okay. Then I'll ask Spence to join you here. That way he won't be a witness to any illegal entry. I have a big, noisy revolver in my car. I'll go through the back door. They probably have the girl upstairs. I'll make a lot of noise and you guys can come through the front."

"It sounds a little chancy. For you."

"I know, but I think time is important."

"Okay, but I'll create a diversion. Make it easier for you to slip inside."

"How?"

"I'll get the guy to move his car. I'll tell him there is an ordinance banning overnight street parking, and that he'll have to move the Caddy or we'll have it towed in."

"What if the two guys just come out, lock up and drive away?"

"We'll follow and see somehow that they drive right back."

"Okay. I'll wait until I hear the car moving."

I went over to get the Army Colt.

"What is it?" Cathy asked.

"No big deal. I'm just going to make some noises to give the cops an excuse to move in. Just wait here. It'll be all over soon."

I went back around behind the house and told Spence what was happening. He looked at me as if I might be a little bit loopy, but went on around to the street. I crept up onto the back porch. The door had a glass pane in it. There was activity around at the front of the house. Somebody was cursing about having to move a car. The door slammed. A few seconds later the Caddy engine started and there was some squealing of rubber on pavement and the car came up the driveway. I wrapped my coat around the gun barrel and poked it through the glass pane.

It made a nice hole. I reached in and undid the latch and went inside quietly. I was in the kitchen. A swinging door from the kitchen led to a carpeted hallway that ran to the front of the house. I walked down it half on tiptoes. At the end of the hallway was the front door and a stairway going up. Off to one side, in the front room, Soft Kenny was peeking out at the edge of the curtain. I held my breath and started up the stairs very quietly. From the upper landing I went to the room at the back with light coming from beneath the door, listened a moment and went on in.

Beverly Jean was sitting on the edge of a bed with her eyes about the size of silver dollars. Her hands and ankles were bound and there was a gag across her mouth. She wore only her under-panties and she was shivering. I made a shushing noise with one finger in front of my lips, took out a pocket knife and cut the cords. She was starting to shake.

"Take it easy, honey," I whispered. "You're going to be all right. I'm the man who came to visit you last Sunday, remember?"

She nodded vigorously. I worked on her as gently as I could. "Did they hurt you?"

She shook her head no. I removed the gag and winced. Lipstick was smudged across her mouth.

"I had to kiss one of them a lot," she said quietly. "He's kind of strange."

"I know. Now listen, I want you to be a big, brave girl, and go sit outside on the roof for a few minutes. That way you won't be hurt. There are policemen outside, and they'll come help us soon."

I grabbed a blanket off the bed and wrapped it around her. She still was shaking, but there was no helping that. I raised the window. It had a broken sash cord and wouldn't stay up by itself. I held it as high as it would go and put one leg outside. There wasn't going to be room for Beverly Jean to come through while I was there, so I climbed all the way out onto the roof. My grasp slipped and the window crashed down. I signaled quickly for Beverly Jean to raise it again. She got it started and once I could get my hand under its edge I jerked it back up, held it there and helped the girl out and up onto the top of the dormer.

"Now just sit there," I told her. "Somebody will get you in a few minutes."

I went back through the window, turned out the light and opened the door. Lou and Soft Kenny had heard the window fall. They were coming up the stairs. They both had guns out. I shot into the stairs in front of them. It made enough noise to lift the roof. I ducked back into the bedroom and tried to find the lock. The door didn't have one. I heard cops pounding on the front door. The bed wasn't big enough to crawl under. I decided the safest place would be out on the roof with Beverly Jean. I raised the window and had one leg and my head through when Lou and Kenny came crashing through the door and began shooting. I shot back and tried to roll out the window, but it dropped and caught one knee. I felt searing streaks on my legs, but just kept on rolling, only when I hit the roof my legs wouldn't work right for me any longer. I heard the girl scream above me as I just kept rolling. Then I hit the ground and nothing mattered anymore.

TWENTY-THREE

I came to in my Sausalito apartment. I was in the front room, on the sofa bed somebody had made up. It was daylight outside. My thighs hurt. And my butt. The back of my head felt as if someone had whacked it with a baseball bat. Small pillows were propped beneath my calves and thick bandages swathed my upper legs. Somebody had been burning incense. There was a small mound of white ash in a dish on the countertop between me and the kitchen. Somebody had been into my stash of grass. That also was on the counter.

Cathy Carson came out of the bathroom, brushing her hair. "Hello, there," she said. "Welcome back."

She looked great, in tan slacks and matching shirt with a black scarf around her throat.

"What day is it?"

"Thursday. All the heroics were last night. You were lucky you didn't land on your head."

"It feels like I did."

"At least it wasn't the first part of you to hit the ground. There's just a slight concussion. At first everybody thought you had a bad fracture, but then it occurred to me you were probably just tired. You put in a pretty sensational day yesterday."

"How's Beverly Jean?"

"She's okay."

Cathy had set up a card table beside the sofa bed, and now began carrying stuff to it from the kitchen. There was a filled ice bucket, then she brought in bottles from my liquor cabinet.

"The girl's still a little frightened. I don't think she quite knows what was going on with that Kenny person. By the time she's old enough to realize things, maybe the sharp edges of it will have blurred."

"How many times was I shot?"

"Four. You were very lucky. No chipped bones or damaged arteries. They got you once where you sit down and the rest hit your thighs. They must have been aiming for your you-know-what."

"I think it was just the way I exposed trying to get out the window. Did I hit them?"

"You slightly wounded the one called Lou. You tore up the stomach of the other one pretty badly. They're not sure yet how he'll do. Not that it matters. One of the Oakland officers phoned here a while ago to let you know a fingerprint check showed those two were wanted in four different states for various nasty things. They're very happy to have them in custody."

"Any other calls?"

"Several." As she talked, she did more fussing around. She brought over the phone with the long extension cord from the counter, transferred the makings for funny cigarettes to within my reach and supplied me with sandwich makings. She had annointed herself with a scent that would charm anybody.

"Mr. Barker called. He's been released from the hospital, and is properly appreciative. He said for you to send him a bill."

I snorted. "He needn't worry. Boy, will I send him a bill."

"And about an hour ago Merle Coffey phoned. He said it looks as if he'll keep his job. He also said that Bobbie was seen in Sand Valley this morning. She was at the Sky Lodge looking for Carl Slide. When Slide heard about that he got up from his hospital bed and left town. And the state banking commissioner has ordered a temporary closure of the bank while some things are looked into there. You really made some waves."

I grunted and started to swing out of bed. The pain nearly paralyzed me. I fell back.

"What was that all about?" Cathy asked.

"I want to get up."

"No way. Not for a few days. Why do you think I'm setting you up like this? I even bought you a bedpan. It's on the floor beside you. Even when you're able to get up you'll probably have to use crutches for a while and walk with your legs spread like a cowboy who's spent too long on the trail. The only reason they let me ambulance you home from the hospital was because I'm a registered nurse and I told them I would pamper you for a few days. You can't move much and you won't be conceiving any babies for a while."

"That's not fair."

"You're telling me? 'Come with me to San Francisco,' he said. 'For some sun at Stinson beach. Lingering cocktail hours. A little cha-cha-cha in the Venetian Room.' "

"Maybe I'll heal fast. Especially if you pamper me."

"I'm not going to pamper anybody. I came to San Francisco to have a good time, and by God, I'm going to have a good time."

She went back to the kitchen, picked up my car keys from the table and dropped them into her purse. "I'll be using your car while I'm here."

"I guess you will. Have a swell time."

"I intend to. I'll check in on you tomorrow or the next day."

"You're not even coming home at night?"

"Of course not. I'm going to check into the Pimsler. Have a good rest."

She went out the door and a minute later I heard my car start and she drove off. I lay there for a while feeling sorry for myself. Then I poured me some bourbon, and then some more, and then I called down to the No Name and asked if there were any chess or gin rummy players around. There weren't right then, but a little later on a couple of local guys named Milton and Scrubbs came by and we played cards and got a little drunk into the evening, and after they left I watched some television then turned out the light and went back to sleep.

I don't know what time it was, in the middle of the night, I guess. I never fully woke up. But I had a phone call from Bobbie. She wanted to know what had happened after she left. I told her. I also told her I'd heard that she'd been seen in Sand Valley, and was asking about Slide.

"Yes, but I gave that up, finally. It's not worth it anymore. I'm all burned out inside."

"That's kind of good. I wouldn't want you to do anything that could be pinned on you. Where are you now?"

"Los Angeles. I'm going down to Mexico for a while. To lie on the beach and think about things. Do you hate me, Pete?"

"No, Bobbie, I don't hate you. You made a fool of me, but I guess you figured you had your reasons."

"I was very bitter over what happened to my father. I guess it made me a little irrational."

"Irrational. Yeah, I guess that's a good way to describe it."

"But I've put that behind me now. When I think what could have happened to Beverly Jean..."

"If you really feel that way, Bobbie, there might be hope for you yet."

"I think so too. The reason I had to call, Pete—the things I told you, I wasn't really fooling that much. I mean, I used you some, but I felt something pretty real for you too. I'd like to try it again some day. When enough time has gone by. When I'm more sure of myself, and know I won't hurt either one of us."

I lay there in the dark with a lot of turmoil going through my head.

"What do you think, Pete? Could you give a kind of lonely kid a second chance?"

"I don't know, Bobbie. I honestly don't know."

"Well think about it some, huh? Because someday, I'd really like to be your girl."

She was crying when she hung up. I put down the receiver and shoved the phone away from me. I lay back and though some about a girl with long legs who moved in a way that reminded me of a young colt. And after a while I slipped back into what I guess you could call a troubled sleep.

SPECIAL PREVIEW

Here is the opening scene
from

THE MISSING AND THE DEAD

Second book in the Bragg series.

THE MISSING AND THE DEAD

For the first time in his life he had to figure out what he was going to do with a body. He didn't have much time for it, either. And it had to be very nearly foolproof if he wanted to preserve his identity and, perhaps, his wife's sanity. She had said that to him the last time they'd had to pack up and dash off, leaving no trace, assuming new roles.

"One more move and I'll lose my mind."

No hysterics. His wife wasn't that way. In fact, she had been the one to hold him together during the rockier times of his long career. She was firm and strong. She understated things. If she told him she was afraid of going to pieces, so be it. And it had been their last slapdash move. Into retirement for John Roper—his most recent identity—and the Hobo, the name by which he was known in certain police and prison circles. Retirement also for the reclusive painter, Pavel, who conjured portraits of his victims to curb the blinding headaches. Good-bye, all. Retirement time. Ta-ta. They traveled abroad for the better part of the year. In style and comfort. God knows he'd earned it over the years, along with enough money to do it.

He opened the hood to his Land Rover and stood staring bleakly at the engine. His mind was on other things. Nearly thirty years. God Almighty, that was a long time to have gotten away with it all. Not a serious miscue, either. Not one mistaken victim. Never an arrest. Probably stalked at one time or another by more lawmen than anyone in the history of crime and punishment.

His wife, poor girl, who could blame her? Moving here and there and then off someplace else. The new identities. A career of role-playing, that's what it had been; long before the term had become jargon. The ever more clever and involved arrangements for solicitation and payoff, all those codes and maps, the letter drops and midnight phone calls…

It was intricate mental work. He felt sure that was what led to the headaches. Anybody burns out after a while. An outsider, he knew, would suspect some form of guilt or remorse for his victims, but such was not the case. He and his wife used to talk those things through, long into the night. His work was no more demeaning than that of the heroic young warrior. And certainly more noble than that of the vivisectionist with his tortured animals. He never consciously hurt anybody. Something quick and sure, for the most part, a rap on the head followed by a needleful of arsenic. Quick and very nearly painless.

And there were, he knew with utter certainty, a lot of miserable bastards out there whom he'd gotten rid of. Not that he ever let such judgments influence his work. But it was a fact and he knew it, and knew as well that many of the police who pursued him would equally have clapped him on the back for having helped purge some of the world's scum.

But back then, as the Hobo, he hadn't thought about such things. And as the name suggested, he was a moral tramp in those matters. If the price was right, if he could set it up to guarantee execution and escape, he would do it, be the victim saint or scamp. He couldn't let those things gnaw at him.

There of course had been those who paid society's price for the work that the Hobo did. Among the hundreds who had hired him over the years, there had been plenty whose boasting, stupidity, drunkenness or conscience had led to their own arrest or confession. But none of them ever knew enough about the Hobo to identify or describe him, which was only fitting. The Hobo was but a smoking gun. Let the twisted or jealous or hate-filled or greedy minds that conceived the act in the first place pay the price of it.

Pavel, a different, creative side of his nature, had emerged late in his career, after the onset of the crippling headaches. One of his victims, a young man in Oklahoma, had realized at the last moment what was about to befall him, and had exhibited a stark, terror-filled expression. It had been unsettling, to say the least. Back home he told his wife about it. And in one of those quantum leaps the mind is capable of, she had urged him to try to capture the expression on canvas. He'd been doubtful at first. He'd never been more than a half-hearted painter at best. It was a challenging discipline and he'd seldom used it for anything except relaxation.

But he'd tried it. He'd painted the young man's face, as best he could recall it, and the headaches had receded to little more than an annoyance.

He had thought about that some in the years since. Wondering if somehow that portrait business was what had very nearly unraveled his identity and led to his capture in Southern California. But he couldn't think of how it might have, any more than had a dozen other facets of the aging process. His work, though, had taken a ragged turn there. He knew that, now. He should have stuck with sap and needle, rather than get into the decapitation business. It was messy and awful, and dangerous. But to curb the headaches he'd found it was very nearly the only manner of impending death that could evoke the stark fear he could later reconstruct on canvas, and through whatever chemical workings of the brain, banish the headaches. He didn't even like to think about that late period.

He liked to dwell more in the present. He and his wife had talked and thought about the roles they would assume in retirement. They had decided to return to California. It was a large enough place so there could be little fear of having events in one end of the state connected up with those in the other. And his wife always had wanted a garden. To watch the growing cycle through the seasons. That pleased her, and they'd never been able to do that before. He on the other hand was able just to kick around and feel the soil and tramp the hills and read voraciously and putter at the palette, as his wife put it.

He might have known it was too good to last. In recent days there had been a disturbing sequence of events. Call it chance or whimsy or whatever, Fate was showing him her heels. First had been that surprising showcase of the Pavel portraits in San Francisco. He'd had to take quick steps there.

And now, there was the detective. The very man who down south years before had tripped him up, forcing his retirement. And just minutes ago he had been in the heart of town, asking his questions. He was the man who had made the connection between John Roper and the Hobo and Pavel. What in God's name could have brought him to Barracks Cove?

No matter. He was there, that was the thing to be addressed. Fortunately his wife had recognized him and helped steer the man out to their home. He would be arriving soon, and he would have to be killed. No question about that. That's why the Land Rover's hood was raised and he pretended to be fussing with the engine. At his side, on the fender, was a dirty rag. The detective would drive up, get out of his car and address him. He in turn would look up, turn and take up the dirty rag to wipe his hands and to grasp the pistol concealed within it and then blow out the man's brains, just like that. No time for nonsense. Not even a hello. No sir.

Then there would be the body. He'd never had to conceal a body during his years in the business. But he had to this time and he had to be very good about it. His wife had told him. She couldn't move again. She just couldn't bring herself to do that again.

He had a half-baked plan. That was his strong suit, of course, the mental work of planning these things. It had pulled him through time and again. It was the surprises he hated.

And then, just as he heard the sound of a car's engine approaching up the old road leading to their home, another, absolutely sickening thought occurred to him. He was a sitting duck, now. He still had enough confidence in his nerves and skills to kill, but this time he couldn't fade away after.

And suppose, just suppose, there was another. Oh, God, what if there was somebody else who could make the same connections the approaching detective had? What might he look like? Who would he be? Dear God. Who?

ABOUT THE AUTHOR

JACK LYNCH modeled many aspects of Peter Bragg after himself. He graduated with a BA in journalism from the University of Washington and reported for several Seattle-area newspapers, and later for others in Iowa and Kansas. He ended up in San Francisco, where he briefly worked for a brokerage house and as a bartender in Sausalito, before joining the reporting staff of the *San Francisco Chronicle*. He left the newspaper after many years to write the eight Bragg novels, earning one Edgar and two Shamus nominations and a loyal following of future crime writers. He died in 2008 at age seventy-eight.

Printed in Great Britain
by Amazon

34594381R00133